The
DINOSAUR'S EGG

The DINOSAUR'S EGG

EDMUND CANDLER

COACHWHIP PUBLICATIONS
Greenville, Ohio

To Rosalind Hichens

The Dinosaur's Egg, by Edmund Candler
© 2023 Coachwhip Publications edition

First published 1925
Edmund Candler, 1874-1926
CoachwhipBooks.com

ISBN 1-61646-545-X
ISBN-13 978-1-61646-545-2

I

UNCLE BLISS

Uncle Bliss was an hour late. Naturally it was an hour of conjecture. None of us had ever seen him except Angela, and Angela was not very good at answering questions. She could be extremely vivid, though, when she was not being catechised.

All we had extracted from her so far was that he was that he was "rather an out-of-door sort of person." And "hairy." We had to be content with that for the physical picture. To the children at least it was full of suggestion.

"Out-of-door and hairy!" Irene repeated. "Mummy, how exciting! Is he like an animal?"

"No, dear. Not in the least."

"Is he tame?" Val asked. "I mean, is he like a tame animal?"

Angela, who was absorbed in her knitting, did not answer at first. "Four light, three dark, two light.—Tame, did you say? No, I certainly should not call him tame. That does not at all describe him."

At this Irene danced with excitement. "Mummy! How lovely! A wild animal! Is he like a bear?"

"I told you, dear, he is not like an animal. You mustn't be so quick at jumping to conclusions, and you must remember to be very polite to Uncle Bliss and not to stare at him."

This, of course, only confirmed Irene's belief in Uncle Bliss' resemblance to an animal. "Anyhow," she concluded, "if he is not like an animal, he doesn't sound like a real person who lives anywhere."

Val here confided to Irene in an undertone that he had heard Mummy tell Daddy that Uncle Bliss was rolling. "I expect that he walks like the bear at the Zoo," he added.

Irene in her superior wisdom enlightened him. "Rolling means rich," she said. "Rolls-Royce and all that. Mummy said he would come in a Rolls-Royce."

"But who is he like?" Irene persisted. "He must be like somebody."

Angela looked at her, and seemed to be searching her memory. "No," she said, "I don't think he is like anybody."

I had been rather bored with the idea of entertaining Uncle Bliss all the afternoon, but I was beginning to be infected by the children's curiosity. Irene was right. When you come to think of it, everybody is interesting until you know them. In five minutes there would be a new person in the room, different from anybody I had seen before. An empty place at a table in a hotel or restaurant raises a profoundly interesting problem if one has a curious mind. Presently some one will come in and sit down at it. A new face. If after the millions of faces one has seen it is possible to conjure one more variety out of the same old recipe—a round or oval cranium with six apertures in it, seven if one counts the nostrils as two. And the face is only the beginning of the enigma. There will be a new voice allied with it, a new manner, new movements of the head and shoulders, a new way of looking at people and considering things, a new way of hanging a hat on a peg. The simplest problem in individuality is as mysterious as the higher mathematics.

I had often heard of Uncle Bliss, but I had never tried to picture him before. Not consciously. Now I had a vision of the stage Anglo-Indian Colonel in the empty chair with a sola topi on his knee. I suppose because I had heard that he had travelled a great deal in tropical countries and collected things—rather indiscriminately, so far as I could gather. One or two of his white elephants had come to us at Homersfield. Uncle Bliss, by the way, was nobody's uncle, not even a relation. Our only claim to kinship was that he happened to be Irene's god-father; even how that came about I had forgotten.

"I have only seen him twice," Angela continued, "and he was different each time."

Now if she remembered that he was different, she must remember what he was like—in one of these encounters, if not in both. I knew Angela could give us more details if she chose. But she was like that. It was a kind of obstinacy. When challenged, her mind became too indolent for precision. Still "different each time" was a clue. Uncle Bliss was a man of moods as well as being "an out-of-door sort of person" and "hairy."

Irene's picture of the bear seemed quite plausible.

"Of course, lunch was spoilt an hour ago," Angela complained; "but if people only think of themselves—"

"He has probably had a puncture," I suggested.

We had agreed to give Uncle Bliss another five minutes, when I looked out of the window and saw him in the garden.

How silently that Rolls-Royce had come up! Not a sound of the engine or wheels on the gravel, or the motor-horn we had been listening for. Where was the car, by the way? And what the devil was he doing poking about in the garden? Why didn't he come up to the door and ring? I was so intrigued by his movements that I forgot to compare the concrete Uncle Bliss with my mental inventory.

Irene's quick eyes detected my astonishment. She flew to the window. "Mummy!" she cried, "quick! He's here. In the garden. Why doesn't he come in?"

Angela carefully put aside her knitting and joined us at the window. Her movements never express surprise, but there was just an inflection of it in her voice. "Well, I never!" she said.

Uncle Bliss was botanising in the rock garden as if he had the whole day in front of him instead of being nearly an hour late. Irene was the first to notice his bicycle leaning against the catalpa.

"You had better go out and bring him in," Angela suggested. I obeyed.

Uncle Bliss was, so absorbed that he did not hear my steps on the gravel. "Oh, how do you do?" he said when I greeted him. "Clayton, of course. I see you've got the Pyrenean androsace."

Was it? I did not know. The garden was Angela's affair. "Come in," I said, "and have some lunch. We had almost given you up. Had a puncture?"

Uncle Bliss ignored the suggestion. "Your androsace is starved for soil," he said, "and it wants more shade. Did you say lunch was ready?"

I explained to him that it was past two.

"Your clocks are all wrong," he retorted pleasantly. "However, I am quite ready for lunch, rather peckish, in fact. I thought you were in the Sudan," he observed, as he wheeled his bicycle farther into the shade.

"I ought to be," I said, "but the Medical Board turned me down. I've got to go up and be vetted again in October."

To this Uncle Bliss made no reply. He seemed to have lost the context.

As I escorted him in across the lawn, I could see the children at the window—their eyes stretched to Oes, no doubt—fidgeting with excitement. Angela, of course, was not spying. She would be knitting quietly in the recesses of the drawing-room, as if Uncle Bliss' invasions were a daily event. I thought of our hour of conjecture. Here was the new variety of *Homo sapiens*. Quite a distinct species. With the children's gaze upon me I felt rather like a showman. Or a bear-leader, shall I say? Irene had got it in two guesses. Val, too, had reason to be satisfied with Uncle Bliss' roll. Our guest did not exactly lurch or shamble, but there was something in the movement of his shoulders, a kind of alternate rhythm, which one might, without exaggeration, describe as a roll. He was as completely unself-conscious as an animal, or, one might say, unconscious of others of his own species. Awkwardness and unself-consciousness. There again you have the bear.

And he spoke with a bear-like gruffness, though not ungenially. I could see that the children were afraid he was going to kiss them, or hug them, which would have been more in character and, perhaps, not so unpleasant, as his hairiness was of the bristling variety. He shook hands with us all in turn, but did not seem to notice any of us much. "Are you fond of games?" he said to Val. "Yes, that's right." And to Irene, "You like games, don't you? Yes, that's right. We shall see." And here he tapped his pocket. At this cryptic utterance and gesture the children's eyes became glued on Uncle Bliss' pockets, which were bulging. The character of those bulges was now more interesting than the character of Uncle Bliss. One more instance of the secular triumph of matter over mind.

Uncle Bliss was so heavily encumbered that I was surprised he did not unload in the hall. But no. The dining-room door was open, displaying an array of agreeable objects on the sideboard, and he visibly gravitated towards it, carrying us with him. A quite unconscious manoeuvre, I believe, but irresistible. Uncle Bliss had what you might call a dynamic way with him; I was going to say magnetic, but it was propulsion rather than attraction. He waved aside Angela's suggestion that he might like to wash his hands before lunch. He was hungry, he explained; but it did not seem to enter his head that we might be hungry too, and that he had kept us waiting an hour.

So he sat down, hot and hungry just as he was, talking incessantly, mostly about the androsace. Some one had sent it to Angela from Simla, but Uncle Bliss insisted that it was an exclusively Pyrenean variety. If it had been found at Simla, some one had planted it there. "You probably mixed the seeds," he said. "After lunch I will dig it up for you, and show you how it ought to be planted."

Angela smiled gratefully, though I knew that if Uncle Bliss, or any one else, laid a finger on her androsace, it could only be by an act of violence.

"We thought you must have had a puncture," she said with studied irrelevance. "But you came by train, didn't you?"

"Yes, and bicycled from the station. I thought I saw you there. In fact, I saw two or three people who might have been you."

Whatever social gifts Uncle Bliss might possess, tact was not one of them. Three of us were estranged by this remark to the point of committing assault and battery upon his person. Irene and Val blushed crimson. As if there were anybody in the world in the least like Mummy!

"Women all wear the same clothes nowadays," growled the bear. "Makes them all look alike."

Again I could have kicked him. I know no woman who dresses with such subtle distinction as Angela. She was wearing a light gossamer dress which hung straight from her shoulders, and revealed a new grace of outline whenever she moved. It was the most perfect garment for a hot June day, of a shade of green you only see in dragon-flies. It made you feel cool to look at her. If she had been a dragon-fly, Uncle Bliss would have noticed her; or if she had been an aboriginal bushwoman, he could have told you what she was wearing. Anthropology was another of his hobbies.

Uncle Bliss, Angela's antithesis in the category of *Homo sapiens,* looked far from cool. Drops of perspiration stood on his forehead and nose, and no doubt irrigated the scrubland that stretched upwards from his beard on each side of his face to meet his close-cropped hair. Nevertheless he rejected our iced claret cup. "No," he said, "thank you. I will have some whisky. My own, if you don't mind. I always make a point of bringing it with me." This was very polite for Uncle Bliss. He might have added, "You never know what you will get in other peoples' houses." Luckily we had the necessary siphon.

Irene and Val had been unnaturally quiet, but they had forgotten Angela's injunction not to stare. I watched their eyes open wide as the whisky gurgled and bubbled from Uncle Bliss' flask into his glass. The extraction of this huge vessel from his pocket, by the way, removed one of the most promising bulges. There had been talk about gifts, and in the discussion I had overheard before lunch anticipation was heightened by Irene's definition of "rolling." The bicycle, I believe, was the first disappointment. And the whisky flask must have left a big hole in the prospective inventory.

I was afraid the children were going to be disillusioned. However, Uncle Bliss played up in his own way before very long. We had been trying to get him to tell us about the Clapperhouse at Renton Parva, that "desirable country mansion" with its thousand-acre park. Old Slingsby, the M.F.H., used to live there, but he hunted no more, and the kennels were empty. Uncle Bliss was buying the estate as a repository for his collections. Or so we concluded. He collected everything, dead or alive, from giraffes to bibelots, but for many years he had had nowhere to put them. The museums and zoological gardens of England and France

were packed with his "loans." We heard of him occasionally, and very rarely from him, in Papua, Nigeria, or Brazil,
and gathered that this home-coming was a surrender to the
tyranny of objects.

Naturally we wanted to hear his first impressions of the
Clapperhouse, and what he intended to make of it. Would
he keep okapi or racehorses in the stables? And how was
he going to stock the lake? Did he fish? Angela did not
remember. We gave him more than one opening, but Uncle Bliss was a difficult person to deflect in conversation;
impossible, one might say, unless one were fortified by
callosities equal to his own. It was Val in the end, insinuating strategist, who sapped a way into his defences. Two
or three times I had seen his lips move, and caught a thin
voice about as audible as a cicada in the roar of Niagara.
"Uncle Bliss! Uncle Bliss!" I saw Irene nudge him derisively, as much as to say, "You little idiot, what's the good!"
Val, however, persisted, biding his time. There were occasional intervals of seconds, in which Uncle Bliss, his glass
to his lips, recharging the battery, became vulnerable, so
to speak, defenceless and inarticulate. In one of these Val's
thin shaft went unerringly home.

"Uncle Bliss, would you like to see our museum?"

Uncle Bliss put down his glass, and surveyed his vis-à-
vis attentively.

"I should very much like to see your museum," he said.
"What have you got in it?"

Val, encouraged, launched on his inventory. "A caddis
worm, a purple emperor, an envelope with forty-five postmarks on it, a lava green lizard, a flying-fish's fin, coral
from Aden, a wooden shoe made by a lunatic at Colney
Hatch—"

"That's very interesting," Uncle Bliss interrupted. "I
have got a wooden shoe too, also made by a lunatic, only
he was an African."

Our visitor had become very attentive all of a sudden, and even courteous. He listened patiently to the rest of the catalogue.

"I think that's all," Val concluded. "What have you got in your museum, Uncle Bliss?"

"I've got a hippopotamus. Stuffed, mind you. I am going to have a live one, though."

"A live one!"

"Yes, in my zoological gardens."

Irene gave a cry of delight, and Val turned a little pale. Uncle Bliss was bringing out his big battalions. This was the end of manoeuvres, but it was also the crown of adventure. It did not matter in the least that he had become a camp-follower in the rival army. A real live Zoo only a few miles away, and private too, belonging to a kind of relation! It was almost as good as having a Zoo of one's own.

Of course, it was all still in the air, but the animals were coming, and the children were invited to come and see them whenever they liked. It was quite possible that they might arrive by the same train as the giraffe.

Uncle Bliss beamed encouragement. Whether it was the discovery of kindred spirits, an audience really worth talking to, or merely the mellowing effects of the flask, I cannot say, but for the rest of the meal he was a different person. Conversation became triangular, between him and the children. And he did not talk down to them, but answered all their questions sensibly, as if they had been grown-up people. Was there going to be a lion? Certainly a lioness and cubs. And this opened up the question of accommodation. Where was he going to put the animals? Uncle Bliss invited suggestions. There were the stables. He was not going to have a horse on the estate. That would give him twenty loose-boxes. Then there was the coach-house and the garage. No need of a motor when you can bicycle. And the kennels. He was not going to

have any dogs either. He hated dogs. "What shall we have
in the kennels?" he asked Irene. "No jackals, or hyenas, or
wolves, mind you. They make too much noise." Irene was
for armadillos, Val for sloths or skunks.

"Have you ever smelt one?" Uncle Bliss roared.

"Ant-eaters?"

"Where are the ants coming from?"

"Turtles?"

No. The turtles would be in the lake. The lake was to
be artificially heated for crocodiles. The beavers would
live at the other end—behind a partition, of course, and
the penguins would live with the beavers and seals. They
would have to build an icehouse for the King Penguin, or
he would be too hot to bow. No snakes. At Irene's request
it was decreed that the serpent should be banned in this
Eden.

So Uncle Bliss could be tame after all. He was feed-
ing out of Irene's hand. Between them they stocked their
zoological gardens. It was like the first chapter of Genesis
come true. "Let there be ant-eaters and armadillos. Let
there be sloths and beavers." And if there were no ant-eaters or armadillos, or sloths or beavers, they were convinced
that there soon would be, which came to the same thing.
Either way they tasted the joys of creation.

I reminded Uncle Bliss that he could always build when
he had used up all the stabling. But here I ran up against
one of his strange economical kinks. "Not a penny on
mortar or bricks," he snapped. "Sheds, perhaps." He had
designed a wooden hut for the pygmy. He began to tell us
about it, but almost choked at the reminiscence. The part
of his face which was not hairy became a deeper purple.
"Pestilential fellow!" he muttered. "Botulist! Saprophyte!"
Of course, we all thought he was anathematising the pygmy.

"What did he do, Uncle Bliss?" Irene asked in an awed
whisper.

"What did he do! The pestilential fellow"—here Uncle Bliss named an eminent and highly respectable Colonial Governor—"had the impudence to refuse to let me take the pygmy home with me."

Happily Uncle Bliss was a good churchman, and could be violent without profanity. I never heard him use a swear word, though his wrath was terrible. He had given two sacks of salt and ivory to the value of twenty guineas for this pygmy, and, of course, he never got any of it back again.

"Did the pygmy want to come?" Val asked him.

Uncle Bliss retorted with another question. "Would you rather live in the Clapperhouse or the Ituri forest, young man?"

But Val was too shy or tactful to answer this poser, which involved either an untruth or discourtesy.

"If I were a pygmy," Angela said, "I think I should prefer to live in the Ituri forest."

But Uncle Bliss was not listening. Obviously his pygmy had not been consulted. He told us quite shamelessly that he had bought the little man from an Arab chief, one of the Wangwana—"a real live little Bambute, the best I have ever seen, 3 ft. 9 in., very hairy; his face and body were covered with down." Here Irene and Val tried hard not to look at each other, and Uncle Bliss went on to tell them how the Arab chief called the pygmies out of the forest with blasts on his sitalunga horn, and what wonderful trackers they were, slipping through the bushes like ferrets, and how they dug up roots and climbed trees for honey, and the bees never stung them; and how they used poisoned arrows and could with one shot bring down a monkey from the top of the tallest tree, and how their women carried babies on their backs no bigger than small rabbits. I think it never occurred to him that his pygmy might not like to come home with him to the Clapperhouse and live on

Narbonne honey, preserved ginger, and cultivated roots,
and Southdown mutton instead of monkey. Uncle Bliss
would have been very kind to him, I am sure, only he
would have expected him to like the same things as himself. He was a little lacking in sympathetic imagination.

On the whole, the dramatic figure in the story was the
superman who could say yea or nay to Uncle Bliss. Anyhow, I gathered that this was the children's view. We all
had an immense respect for that Colonial Governor.

It was nearly three before we finished lunch, and the
children were allowed to stay for coffee. Happily the
androsace was forgotten. With the example of the Colonial Governor in my mind, I feared the effect of Angela's
firmness.

The children were borne off with Uncle Bliss to the
schoolroom, and I could hear his boom vibrating through
the house for the next hour or so, a distant menace like
hailstones against a window-pane when one is snug inside.
I had been afraid that he was going to be on my hands
all the afternoon, but my offices as host were not requisitioned until tea-time. Uncle Bliss was a great success so
far as the children were concerned.

At tea I noticed that he was still bulging. His trousers
were very tight and his coat was very loose, but they both
bulged, the trousers with calves, and the coat with—parcels, I was going to say. This was our impression. When
we had discounted the whisky flask, restored to the right-
hand breast pocket, there still remained three other protu-
berances equally bulky. It could not be said of Uncle Bliss,
as of the needy, that the linings of his pockets touched.

In the middle of tea he slowly extracted from an inner pocket—a sort of poacher's sack which might easily
have concealed a brace of pheasants—a large oblong box
wrapped in brown paper. To make room for it on the table
he laid his cup and saucer—Angela's precious Spode—on

the floor. "Now," he cried, "who plays fish-ponds? There's room for three."

"Oh, Uncle Bliss!" cried the children, and there they stuck, which I thought was rather tactful of them. A too definite "Thank you" might have been premature. All Uncle Bliss had said was, "Who plays fish-ponds?"

He laid the gadgets with the small-eyed rings on the table, and distributed the rods. The children drew up their chairs. For nearly an hour they played emulously. Uncle Bliss was absorbed. We admired the steadiness of his huge brawny hand, the colour of a ripe medlar. His red eyes gleamed like a hunter's. His steaming cup lay unheeded on the floor, perilously near his heels, until it ceased to steam. "Your tea is cold," Angela reminded him; "wouldn't you like some more!" "Thank you, I would," said Uncle Bliss, and Angela poured him out another, but this, too, remained neglected by his heels with the half-eaten slice of cherry cake in the saucer. At first they played all against all. Uncle Bliss beat Irene and Val every time. Their hands trembled with excitement, but his were so steady that his hook seemed to slip into the rings one after another as if attracted by them. "I'll take you both on," he said, and he beat them again, nine to three.

Now, what is he going to do, I wondered? I was as full of speculation as the children. In fact, during the few hours of our acquaintance I had arrived at a sort of theory about Uncle Bliss. Angela and I discussed him in the garden while they were clearing away the tea things. "I don't mind betting," I said, "that he hangs on to the fish-ponds."

Angela by subtler premisses had arrived at the same conclusion. She said, "If he thinks they are expecting them, he probably will."

We returned to the drawing-room just in time to see the last fish swinging on Uncle Bliss' hook. "There, now!"

he said, and very methodically gathered up the fish and rods, packed them in the box, and absentmindedly put the box back into his pocket as if to balance the whisky flask. "You like fish-ponds!" was all he said to the children.

But even then I was not sure. It might be a bit of play-acting. Cross-grained, provocative Uncle Bliss probably had as much up his sleeve as in his pockets. I half-expected some dramatic avuncular dénouement. In the hall, perhaps, when the bicycle was at the door, he would give himself over to the children to be rifled like a bran-pie.

But Uncle Bliss was not like that. Punctually at six o'clock he said he must go or he would miss his train. He hoped he would see us all at the Clapperhouse soon, when "things were more ship-shape," told Irene that he would send her a postcard when the lioness and cubs came, mounted his bicycle, and disappeared, mysteriously bulging, down the drive. What the other bulges were we never knew.

"It just shows," Angela said.

II

THE PYGMY

Fish-ponds became a catchword in the family after that. It meant something one looked forward to, but which didn't come off, castles in Spain, chickens counted before they were hatched, the general cussedness of things, and the way they had of conspiring against the Claytons in particular. Angela was convinced that every Clayton and Booth—her family and mine—were born under an unlucky star. To begin with, none of them had any money. I, of course, blew a countervailing wind of optimism, more out of contrariness than conviction, Angela believed, though I flattered myself that it was principle. It was somebody's business to preserve the illusions.

This being so, I agreed with Val that Uncle Bliss must have brought the fish-ponds as a present, and then put them into his pocket and forgotten all about them.

"I thought he only put them in his pocket to tease us," Irene said.

"When he gets home he will find them," Val said, "then he will send them to us. Won't he?"

"No," said Angela. "He will go on forgetting them."

Angela was Spartan in her truthfulness. Small shins were meant to be barked. Ointment might be applied; that was a different matter. But nobody would be any the happier in the long-run for pretending not to see the traps and gins the disciplinary spirit strewed in our path. The general aim of nature was punitive. Even inanimate things were accomplices in the conspiracy. Angela thought it a great shame, but it was best to face it; then you wouldn't be disappointed. "Of course, if you *will* run across the croquet lawn in the dark—" she said to the children, and there she stopped. Her implication was, "Why, then, the hoops will take their chance."

Angela's theory of education was more instinctive and implicit than reasoned. Still she was tolerably consistent in her application of it. "I don't want the children to think of Uncle Bliss as a sort of walking Christmas tree," she explained on this occasion.

Nobody, as a matter of fact, could have fitted in better with her educative scheme. Uncle Bliss trampled on illusions like the proverbial bull in the china shop, only out of the débris and fracas new ones were born, like motes in a sunbeam, the more iridescent for the dust that was kicked up. But this was as it should be, since the fun is all in the chase, as the copy-books tell us, not in the prize. If it was excitement the children were after, and not merely objects, they were seldom disappointed.

For a week or more of breakfasts after Uncle Bliss' visit the children investigated the sideboard—to the neglect of their parents—in the short passage between the dining-room door and the table. "No parcels, Mummy!" "Not even a postcard?" Naturally, and as it seemed in support of Angela's philosophy of inhibition, there were no parcels. Those fish-ponds never materialised. And there was no postcard for Irene to tell her that the lioness and cubs had come.

For the next fortnight we heard nothing of Uncle Bliss. Then Angela wrote and asked him to come to lunch to meet her friend, Miss Marjorie Ismay, the African traveller, who was staying with our neighbours, the Sellingers.

She had covered a good deal of his ground on the Uganda border. But Uncle Bliss apparently was not interested in other travellers, least of all in women travellers. He replied laconically, "Thank you, I will come if it is wet," which meant, I suppose, that if it was fine he would find something better to do. He was an out-of-door sort of person, Angela reminded me tolerantly. Happily it was fine and he did not come. We had already posted the letter when we learnt from the Sellingers that Miss Marjorie Ismay was engaged to Sir Claude Critchley—that "pestilential fellow, botulist, and saprophyte,"—Uncle Bliss' Colonial Governor.

"Shall we write and put him off?" I suggested to Angela.

"No," she said; "it's quite safe. He won't come. Besides, I rather wish he would. It would be good for him."

"And what about Marjorie?"

"Oh, she can take care of herself. Uncle Bliss would amuse her."

"Suppose he gets on to the Critchleys."

"It doesn't matter what you say to Marjorie."

I was surprised at this, for Angela is generally rather a cautious person. Perhaps she thought the risk of drawing-room collisions negligible to a woman who had been tracking big game for the last six months. One can't expect African travellers to behave like other people. They have their own social laws. Uncle Bliss certainly had. The children were in luck; two lion-hunters at Homersfield in a fortnight. And my own curiosity was whetted. One might take it for granted that Marjorie would be another very distinct variety of *Homo sapiens* with the humours differently mixed, quite unlike any woman I had met.

Marjorie, like Uncle Bliss, seemed to evade definition. That she was an out-of-door sort of person went without saying.

"Can't you describe her?" I asked Angela. "What is she like? Good-looking?"

"Yes, I think you will admire her."

"Tall and strong? Not brawny, I hope." I was rather afraid of a feminine edition of Uncle Bliss.

But Angela refused to be catechised, and went on arranging the flowers, absorbed in some colour pattern. The children had brought in an armful of marsh plants from the river. Tall spires of loosestrife rose out of a foam of meadowsweet and sheep's parsley. "Too much white," I heard. "I wish you would get some foxgloves for the Najaf jar." Then absent-mindedly, and apparently without relevance to my catechism, she observed, "Marjorie is a corker."

Marjorie was now definitely labelled.

"But what exactly is a corker?"

"I wish you would get me some foxgloves. Very long stalks. The row behind the rockery."

I told Angela that I would get her the foxgloves when she explained what she meant by a corker.

"Oh, don't you know? Mrs. Brown is a corker, and Lady Potter, and—" Angela mentioned eight or nine women of our acquaintance who fell into the category. Two of them were bridge maniacs, one an M.F.H., another an ardent feminist, and the list included our washerwoman and the village postmistress. Truly a formidable regiment of women, though far from homogeneous!

"Rather a comprehensive list," I objected. "All your corkers are different. Yet there is something—"

"Yes," said Angela, "and Marjorie has got it."

"Free and opinionative? Rams her views down your throat?"

"Yes and no." Angela was becoming indefinite again. "More no than yes."

"Not like Uncle Bliss, I hope. If so, I'm off to town on Wednesday morning."

"Not in the least. Marjorie has a sense of humour."

A corker, then, is not necessarily disagreeable, I concluded, and felt more comfortable in my mind. When I
came to think of it, even Mrs. Brown and Lady Potter had
their good points. Besides, Angela liked Marjorie, or used
to like her years before when they met in Brittany, and if
Angela passed her that ought to be enough.

Anyhow, she was not like Uncle Bliss. Does there exist
such a thing as a male corker? Angela thought not. The
word presumes a quality which is too general in the over-
bearing sex. Corkerdom is something specific.

But there was one admirable distinction which Marjorie and Uncle Bliss possessed in common. Neither of
them wrote books. Marjorie was not interviewed or photo-
graphed. She didn't advertise. And one might say the same
about Uncle Bliss. So long as the world fed him and his
collections, he didn't care a rap what it thought of him.
Yet it appeared Uncle Bliss was news. He was "up," as
they say in Fleet Street. He had achieved notoriety. Neither Angela nor I knew anything about this until Marjorie
told us. Naturally I would not know, as I had been in the
Sudan for years; and though Angela continued to take in
'The Times'—for the agony column and the articles about
gardening, as she said—the last thing she was interested
in was news.

Angela was right about Marjorie. She was thoroughly
able to take care of herself. A very upright, brown, buoy-
ant person; about thirty-five I should say, but she looked
younger. Corkerdom was honoured by her inclusion in the
order. She was not the hard and masculine young woman
I had expected. Her eyes were sensitive and sympathetic
like Angela's—brown like hers, with more challenge in
them, but less subtlety. The most memorable thing about
her was her laugh. She stood carelessly in the centre of the
hearthrug with her hands in the side-pockets of her jersey,

looking like a born huntress. If you had seen her in the
centre of a group in a photograph—and you may be sure
she would be in the centre—you would have looked on
the ground for some slain beast at her feet. Not that there
was anything self-conscious or triumphant in her poise,
only somehow the picture would be incomplete without
the trophy. A rhino, for instance. Or the Colonial Governor. That awe-inspiring martinet, impregnable misogy-
nist, and subjugator of Uncle Bliss, if we are to believe the
Sellingers, had fallen flat before her.

When she heard that we had in all innocence asked
Uncle Bliss—Claude's *bête noir*—to meet her, and that the
only reason he was not present in the room was that it did
not happen to be a wet day, she laughed for quite three
minutes. I would much rather hear Marjorie's laugh than
most women's singing. It was a delicious bubbling gurgle,
long drawn out with little catches in it, like a crow pheasant. Apparently it was the one thing she couldn't subdue.

"He was coming if it was wet, was he? Pygmy Bliss.
Claude will enjoy that."

Pygmy Bliss. So that was what they called him in Uganda. It was interesting to hear the official side of the story.
Miss Ismay was surprised at our ignorance. "Didn't you
hear about the questions in the House? Claude was in a
tearing rage about it. The Indian immigration question
was giving him a lot of trouble at the time, and a native
paper in Bombay got hold of the story, and made polit-
ical capital out of it, 'The Truth about the Slave Trade,'
'Kidnapping Africans,' 'British Hypocrisy Exposed,' 'Our
Moral Right to Govern,' and all that. You see, we have to
keep the Indians out, or the colony would be swamped.
One of Claude's catchwords was, 'Africa for the Africans.'
The Bombay journalist had his teeth into that like a ter-
rier. This was how Government showed their tender care
for the African; but the British were quite ready to fatten

him up, export, and exhibit him when it was profitable. They didn't care how starved he was in his own home. The Hindu went on to air his Latin, 'Civis Romanus sum,' and said the pygmy in his cage was better off than the famine-stricken denizens of the Black Continent, ground down by taxes. Yet these torch-bearers of civilization refused to admit the cultured Indian into their colony."

I suggested that the Bombay journalist ought to transfer his talents to London. The leading Radical organ would jump at him.

"Some of them are quite educated," Marjorie said. "I saw one on the boat at Mombasa reading Comte in the original. By the way, have you read, or can you read, Rabindranath Tagore?"

Angela admitted that she could not.

"The Indians held a meeting at Mombasa to congratulate the awarders of the Nobel prize when Tagore got it, and they passed nine resolutions. You see, they hang together. They held another meeting about Bliss. You can imagine all this didn't improve Claude's temper. The Colonial Secretary was heckled. As for Claude, he was painted as a sort of Barnum carrying on a secret traffic in pygmies. The Radical papers hinted that he received a big commission. Bliss, who was presumably his accomplice, was the agent for half a dozen circuses and music halls in the United States. It would have been quite funny if one had not been so close to it all.

"Claude is a dear, of course, but I shouldn't like to be one of his staff. It was sometimes most uncomfortable at meals. His two secretaries turned pale at the outside of a cable. I remember little Hodson, the A.D.C., being sent out in the middle of tiffin to cipher one, and coming back looking as if he expected to be whipped. Whitehall wanted to know why Claude didn't put an end to the scandal. The India Office called for an inquiry; the National Congress

was coming on in a week, and the roof would fall in unless
Government could give the story a categorical denial. The
Colonial Secretary wanted to know a lot of things. Where
was Bliss? What steps had the Governor taken to repatriate
the pygmy? Bliss all the while was very much in the air; we
knew no more of his whereabouts than the Colonial Secretary—only that he was coming through from the Congo.
The first we heard of him was the pygmy story which came
from Bombay. The natives get hold of things in the most
extraordinary way—a sort of psychic wireless.

You remember the Benin massacre—it was all over Africa the next day. This particular bit of gossip was communicated by an Indian agitator, who got it from a medicine
man in Nairobi."

Marjorie described the excitement at Government
House and in the Club when Pygmy Bliss was reported
as having "blown in" somewhere on the shores of Lake
Albert. There was a pro-Bliss party among the planters,
chiefly because the Indians had made so much fuss about
it. Government was always giving in to them, the planters
said, truckling to a pack of Radicals and Trades Unionists.
"Those were the very words. I am quoting. 'It isn't safe to
hammer a black man now. Why can't Critchley keep his
end up? That fellow Bliss seems to be a bit of a sportsman.
Why shouldn't he take a pygmy home with him if he wants
to? Cause of science, you know. Fatten the little beggar up
too. They tell me his pygmy put on six pounds after he had
had him a week, and he didn't weigh much more than that
when he caught him.'"

Marjorie bubbled again like water going out of a bath,
or whisky out of Uncle Bliss' flask. "Fatten him up," she
repeated. She was probably thinking of the Bombay journalist and his ironic sensibility.

"But the funniest part of it was the arrest. I have forgotten the boy's name. He was long and lanky, like two

bamboos in Mah Jong, and looked as if you could have wound him round a chair. Wore an eyeglass. Blushed up to the roots of his hair when you spoke to him, and was in the habit of addressing everybody above the age of twenty-four with a propitiatory 'sir.' We called him Cuthbert for short. Claude had to send him; there was nobody else in the district. His orders were to arrange for the repatriation of the pygmy and to arrest Bliss if he showed any resistance. Confronted with the slave-dealer he was much too frightened to mention the purpose of his visit. He admitted this afterwards to Hodson, the A.D.C. What he would have done if he had found Bliss and the pygmy together, or how he would have set about separating them, heaven only knows. Most probably he would have fainted.

"He found Bliss in a tearing rage, but when he learnt the cause of it, he was so relieved that for once in his life he became articulate. 'Bad luck, sir. Bad luck!' Cuthbert's consolatory address to Pygmy Bliss was much quoted in the Nairobi Club. His condolences, or condiments as the n•••• called them who left his black-edged card on Claude at Government House, were accepted as official. But could anything have been luckier! The pygmy had saved his—Cuthbert's—face, and Claude's, and the Colonial Secretary's, and the Government of India's by the simple expedient of bolting. The whole story was officially denied. You see, there was not a scrap of evidence.

"Bliss dined with Cuthbert; he had run out of whisky, and Cuthbert had plenty. This seemed to put him in a better temper. But at dinner there was another explosion. Bliss' European servant came in all of a tremble to announce that the ungrateful pygmy had bolted with his master's aneroid and Zeiss glasses. This is where the poetic justice comes in. Bliss, of course, didn't see it. He was apoplectic with rage. To Cuthbert's amazement he began anathematising Government, and said he was going to put

in a claim for damage (*a*) for the recovery of the glasses
and aneroid; (*b*) for the price of the pygmy paid to the Arab.
Even the deferential Cuthbert was dumfounded at this.
He had the temerity to inquire, 'On what grounds, sir?'

"'On what grounds?' On every conceivable ground."
Bliss, it seems, had roped in a subordinate Government
official to look after the pygmy, and the man had let him
escape. Escape, mind you! Those were Bliss' own words.
Cuthbert suggested that he should put in his claim to the
Belgian Government; both the pygmy and the Arab were
Belgian subjects. Bliss fell on him like a ton of bricks.
Cuthbert, one can believe, was apologetic, but his propitiatory 'Bad luck. Bad luck, sir!' didn't throw much oil
on the waters. However, he thought of another and more
effective element. 'You are out of whisky, sir,' he suggested diplomatically. 'Let me leave half a dozen bottles with
you—see you through to Kisumu.' Claude says the boy
may have a career before him yet as a pacifist. It was only
when he got outside that he remembered he had omitted to mention the official object of his visit. Evidently
if there were any small disagreement ahead between Bliss
and his chief it would be Bliss who entered the list as the
aggrieved party.

"This was the mood in which Pygmy Bliss burst upon
an astonished Uganda. It took him a long time to tumble
to it that Government had *their* grievance against *him,* and
when he did discover it I believe he thought the official
attitude in connection with the pygmy retaliatory."

"He would," said Angela. "He wanted the pygmy badly."

Angela has a very simple way of putting things. She
meant that Uncle Bliss had a non-conducting side to him
which was ethically invulnerable.

Marjorie recognised the oracular wisdom of the remark.
"Kisumu put it down to sun," she said. "I am glad I was
not there. The meeting between him and Claude was what

you might call choleric. He accused Claude of abducting the pygmy. Claude swears that he kept his temper. It was then that he told Bliss that he had sent Cuthbert to arrest him, and he added that if he did not behave himself he would have him sent out of the country. He had only to sign a paper to have him deported. Bliss fairly danced with rage. Claude is rather vague about his language. He says he swore for five minutes on end without a single damn. 'A volume of strange scientific oaths,' is his expression, whatever that means. He called Claude an anthropoid, and had the audacity to threaten legal proceedings. They were both standing, Claude with his hand on a chair ready to pick it up and brain him. The club yarn is that Bliss told the Governor that if he had had an inkling of what Cuthbert was sent for he would have tied him up in a knot, carried him over the frontier, sold him to the Arab, and bought another pygmy. Claude does not confirm this story. He only laughed when I asked him if it was true, and said that Pygmy Bliss would have been considerably out of pocket by the transaction."

There is something very infectious about Marjorie's laugh. We had forgotten the children until they joined in. Bubble, gurgle; bubble, gurgle; bubble, gurgle, squeak, squeak. Of course, they had been listening. How much had they taken in?

"Oughtn't Uncle Bliss to have taken the pygmy, Mummy?" Irene asked.

"Uncle Bliss?" Marjorie's mock-frightened gasp of horror and incredulity was a sort of new edition of her laugh.

I hastened to reassure her. "Oh, don't mind Uncle Bliss. He is not popular in the family. Besides, he is nobody's uncle."

"He is my godfather," Irene explained loyally.

"I am afraid he is impossible," Angela observed, "even as a godfather. I don't think we ought to ask him here again."

"Oh, Mummy!" The children's loyalty was shocked. They protested. The warmth of the alliance was unmistakable.

"You are really fond of Uncle Bliss?" Marjorie asked them.

"Yes, frightfully."

For the moment the slave-dealer's prestige was re-established.

"And he is going to have a Zoo," Irene informed Marjorie.

"And he has got a museum with a stuffed hippopotamus," Val added. "Have you got a museum?"

Marjorie had skins and horns and a collection of butterflies.

Val told her about his purple emperor. Would she like to see their museum? In five minutes the children had collected another African hunter. Some of her horns, she told them, belonged to beasts she had shot, but the one she valued most was an antelope horn into which a witch-doctor had put his shadow. It seems that when you have put your shadow into a horn you can do anything with it. It gave this witch-doctor great power over his enemies, and made him so strong that he became a king.

"Could it bring a purple emperor down from a tree?" Val asked.

"Yes, but it must be your own shadow, otherwise it is no good. The witch-doctor died, so it was no good to him or to any one else in the tribe. In fact, they were rather afraid of it. They thought it brought them ill-luck. That is why they gave it to me. It was just after an earthquake."

Marjorie smiled at this recollection.

"Everybody was very frightened, but nobody was a penny the worse. They had no roofs to fall on them, you see. Can you guess why the god who lives under the earth and shakes it is a woman?"

The children gave it up.

"Because she makes a lot of fuss and does nothing. That was what Chimbashi told me. Not very polite of him, was it?"

Irene asked for more Chimbashi.

"Who made the spots on the moon?" Marjorie asked her. "The sun?"

"Quite right. You've guessed it in one. The sun and moon had a beer quarrel, and the sun threw mud at the moon. It stuck. 'How should the moon wash it off?' Chimbashi asked, having no hands."

Marjorie entertained us with folk-tales and riddles through lunch. The children's appetite was insatiable. Marjorie said it made her feel like the clown at the circus. "One more riddle, then. Why did the early Christian martyrs frequent the A.B.C.? Give it up? Because they preferred it to lions. No, Chimbashi did not tell me that. I made it up."

After lunch she was carried off like Uncle Bliss to see the museum. She was greatly impressed by the purple emperor and the lunatic's wooden shoe, and she was so enraptured by the caddis worm, or the house of sticks and pebbles and bits it had built of shell, that the children gave it her; there were plenty of duplicates in the stream at the bottom of the garden. And in exchange she promised them a Goliath beetle, the biggest beetle in the world, which goes planing down the wind like a sea-gull or an aeroplane. And a deadleaf insect; with folded wings, you couldn't tell it from a crumpled-up leaf; and a blue bird-winged butterfly, and an enormous African papilio. And when she could lay her hands on it she would send them the antelope's horn with the chief's shadow in it. She believed it was in a case at her agent's, but she had not seen it since the day it was presented to her.

The children escorted her back from the schoolroom, one on each side, with a show of idolatrous proprietorship

which made me doubtful of Uncle Bliss' continued ascendancy. Direct action of some kind was needed on the part
of the slave-dealer if he meant to maintain his prestige. I
almost wished it had been wet in the morning. It would
have been interesting to see him and Marjorie together. In
the middle of lunch the rain came down in torrents, and
went on until after tea. Angela was saying that it was a
mere fluke, a meteorological caprice, that he was not with
us, when all of a sudden he bore down on us on his bicycle
like an unexpected eclipse.

We all met in the drive. Marjorie was walking home,
and we were seeing her to the gate. Uncle Bliss dismount-
ed and shook hands quite heartily.

"I am sorry you could not come to lunch," Angela said.

"I am glad you are sorry," was his retort.

What did he mean by that? He prized Angela's disappointment, I suppose. It was a very positive statement,
and obviously sincere. Uncle Bliss sometimes came out
with things which made you suspect that he was human
underneath.

Angela introduced them. Uncle Bliss fixed our guest
with his impersonal stare.

"Who?" he said.

Angela repeated Marjorie's name. Uncle Bliss examined
her perfunctorily, as if she had been some exhibit in a
dealer's collection, and he not in a purchasing vein.

Marjorie's survey of Uncle Bliss, on the contrary, was
interested, I was going to say responsive, but there was
nothing to respond to. Anyhow, she included him in her
scheme of things. She looked at him keenly, even expec-
tantly, the friendly challenging look of the woman who is
habitually pleasant, but quite ready for a skirmish.

Uncle Bliss, however, was not in an oncoming mood. He
only said, "Been in Africa. Eh? You like Africa? That's right."

Marjorie laughed her crow pheasant laugh which touches a sympathetic nerve in most vertebrae.

Uncle Bliss looked at her again; this time a little more curiously. "Funny country, Africa," he said. Whether it was funny because Marjorie laughed at it, or because it had produced that peculiar laugh in Marjorie, he did not explain, but turned to Angela and demanded abruptly, "Where are the children?"

And that was all that passed between these mighty hunters. Uncle Bliss had his stock of formulas for these encounters. They served as *chevaux-de-frise* to his unassailable self-preoccupation, creating a solitude all round him. There was little variety in them, only he had a way of talking to children as if they were grown-ups—in which case the defences were sometimes carried,—and to grown-ups as if they were children. The funny part of it was that Marjorie had shot just as many lions as he—I believe more,—and she had stood up to charging buffaloes, and was going to help to govern Africa.

"Did you tell him anything about her?" I asked Angela, when he had disappeared with the children.

Angela had told him a great deal, and suggested that they might like to compare notes, but he wouldn't listen. She couldn't get it through to him. He was too full of the Clapperhouse. It was only when she told him that Marjorie was engaged to Sir Claude Critchley that he seemed to realise whom she was talking about. The name sank in, took him out of himself, and, of course, back into himself, but with something that connected him tangibly with his surroundings.

"Critchley, did you say? Engaged? Do you mean to say that she is going to marry him?"

Angela told him that they were going to be married at Kisumu in the autumn.

Uncle Bliss dug his pointed stick into the gravel. "Poor girl, poor girl!" he said. Then after a pause and further savage prodding of the gravel, as if he had got the point into Critchley's abdomen, "Well, well, let's hope she will make him sorry for it."

III
THE BREBIS

The children had taken Uncle Bliss to the stream at the bottom of the garden to hunt for caddis worms, as it was necessary to replace the specimen they had given to Marjorie. We were thankful they did not bring him back to the house. That might have meant a collision with Aunt Hudson, who was coming by "the supper train," as they called it at Homersfield.

Aunt Hudson was Irene's godmother, a title which implied some sort of relationship with Uncle Bliss. Irene was always a little puzzled when we disallowed the connection. It seemed unnatural. Not content with our judgment, she once appealed to Aunt Hudson herself. "Aunt Hudson, are you Uncle Bliss' sister or wife?" Aunt Hudson was shocked at the suggestion; it brought a distressed look into her sheep's eyes. She had only seen Uncle Bliss once, on the fateful occasion of Irene's baptism, and he had behaved abominably. That one meeting seems to have left a deep impression. She could not remember anything in particular which he did or said, only she had a very definite recollection that he was "not at all a nice man." Angela's first impressions were not much more favourable when they compared notes. She agreed with Aunt Hudson that he was a rough diamond, a man who called a spade a spade, but she rather liked his naturalness. "He is sincere," she said.

Aunt Hudson admitted his sincerity. Angela, probably because she felt that she had not done quite the best thing
for Irene in the choice of godfathers, sought for other
grounds of approval. Uncle Bliss was a good churchman—
that is to say, he went to church, and though his language
was peculiar, to say the least of it, it could not be said
that he was profane. These were points which she thought
ought to have given him a good start in Aunt Hudson's
estimation. Nevertheless Aunt Hudson told Angela when
they came back from the church that he was the only person she did not like. I think this is the unkindest thing I
ever heard said about Uncle Bliss.

Aunt Hudson's official assistance at the christening was
natural, but it was a long time before I understood why she
had been bracketed with Uncle Bliss as jointly responsible
for Irene's spiritual welfare. Or if I ever knew the reason I
had forgotten it. I was in the Sudan at the time, and Angela in her letters took Uncle Bliss for granted. Now, when
I asked her to be more explicit, she told me that he was
selected for the same reason as Cuthbert. There was nobody else. He happened to be staying in the house. Angela
lived a great deal with her uncle and aunt, the Dickensons,
during my first years in the Sudan. Old Dickenson, the
eminent zoologist, was a retired Cambridge don. Bliss
seems to have adopted him in his undergraduate days.
Dickenson connived at his keeping a bear in his rooms,
like Byron, though not "as a model of manners to the dons
of his day." The bear was called Ursa Minor; Ursa Major,
I suppose, was Bliss. It must be admitted that Bliss had
his loyalties. He would do anything for old Dickenson.
He even went to church for him on a week-day for this
christening with Angela and Aunt Hudson and the baby,
though it seems not with the best of grace. Grace, however, was never his strong point.

Irene was another of his loyalties—the only one, perhaps, now old Dickenson was dead, if we except Staff, his trusted servant and taxidermist. There may have been others, but I know nothing about them. Uncle Bliss corresponded with members of learned societies. He used to stay with some of them, but I never heard of him being asked to stay at the same house twice. He was not what you might call clubable. It was a complete mystery to me why he troubled to keep up relations with us. There was no reason why he should; he had given Irene quite a good mug. Still he had been most punctilious about it. Angela had heard from him nearly every year since the christening, and Irene was ten. These loyalties seemed to hint at something complex in a nature otherwise simple.

I asked Angela if she had any explanation.

"It is because he is conventional," she said.

"Conventional!" I repeated, a little mystified.

"Yes, conventional. Or automatic."

"What do you mean?"

"I mean that Uncle Bliss does certain things which other people do without reflection." When she had got to the end of her row she added enigmatically, "Like a goldfish in an aquarium.

For the life of me I couldn't see the point of Angela's simile. Now if she had said a pike—

"He goes round and round," she added by way of explanation.

Round and round like a goldfish in an aquarium. Angela was as obscure in her use of figures as Browning; and for the same reason—those ellipses which you were expected to jump without the ghost of an idea where you were taking off from.

Slowly I drew it out of her. She was thinking of a particular goldfish in a particular aquarium, and I suppose

she thought I was thinking of it too—that was always
Browning's error. There were six plate-glass partitions, and
the goldfish in the end one. The partitions were lifted an
inch, or so to let the fresh water run through. She watched
the goldfish nose its way underneath into the next tank. It
made the tour, visited the dace and the carp and the eel,
simply because the hatches were up, not because it was the
least interested in them. So Uncle Bliss. The hatches were
up in our case because he happened to have been called in
at Irene's christening.

The thin strain of conventionality which Angela detected in Uncle Bliss was his responsiveness to the opening
of hatches. He was drawn through them like other people.
But he was conventional on distinctly eccentric lines. He
was no more interested in the people he visited than the
goldfish in the dace, carp, or eel. A Martian would have
had more points of contact.

"There are the children," Angela reminded me.

True, there were the children. Uncle Bliss would most
certainly come again, and he would meet Aunt Hudson.

The children were still under his thrall. When they
came home they told us what had happened at the stream.
Val, of course, had fallen in, and Uncle Bliss had pulled
him out, though there was no need in two feet of water.
And they had found some *byootiful* caddis worms.

"Did you tell him what Miss Ismay is going to give you
for your museum?" Angela asked them.

Irene had told him, and explained that it was all in
exchange for a caddis worm. Val asked him if he would
like a caddis worm, too.

"Did he rise? You mustn't forget the fish-ponds." Angela was afraid the children were becoming acquisitive. "And
you mustn't ask for things."

"Oh, Mummy, we didn't."

Personally I rather admired Val's diplomacy.

Uncle Bliss, of course, didn't rise. He asked them to come to the Clapperhouse and play fish-ponds again and look at his collections, only he did not mention a day. He told them that the animals had not come yet.

Aunt Hudson arrived in time for dinner, and the children were allowed to sit up. She had had a very bad crossing, and this was enough to put one out of humour with the sea, or if not with Neptune himself, at any rate with the Newhaven-Dieppe service which surrendered its passengers so unnecessarily to his buffetings. One was impatient with things that hurt Aunt Hudson. She was the gentlest and most unprovocative of maiden aunts. Also she was a family institution. Angela and I always spoke affectionately of her as the Brebis when the children were not present. The facial resemblance was perfect; even the eyes, if you can imagine a sheep with a devotional expression; in shape and colour they were ovine.

Aunt Hudson was as sweet-tempered as ever after her buffetings, though the seasick remedy which Angela had sent her was ineffectual, and she had not slept a wink in the train.

Val was the first to inquire for her rheumatism.

"Oh, it's much better, thank you," said Aunt Hudson. Then to Angela, "How tre*men*dously considerate he always is!"

"Has it quite gone out of your knee?" Angela asked her.

Aunt Hudson assured us that she had got enough of their horrid waters in her to last six months.

"Did you like Dax, Auntie?" Irene asked her.

"Not at all, my dear. It is worse than all the other places. I couldn't bear the mud. They tell me the Romans used to bathe in the same mud in William the Conqueror's time, and they have never cleaned it out."

This conversation took place in the hall. It was characteristic of the Brebis' thoughtfulness that the presents she brought for the children were not packed away in a trunk, but in her bag. She produced them at once, a startlingly realistic religious picture for Irene, and for Val a beautiful edition of the 'Imitatio Christi,' bound in morocco cloth, "to read when you are older, Val dear."

"Oh, thank you, Aunt Huddie. How lovely!" said Irene.

"How ripping of you!" said Val.

But this was not all. She dived deeper into her bag, and extracted a large box of French bon-bons. She generally brought two kinds of presents, things which she thought the children ought to like, and things which she was quite sure they would like, and they came out in proper sequence like bread and butter and cake.

Our dear Brebis, having permitted herself to be appropriately fleeced, retired upstairs to change. Angela begged her to go straight to bed. She and Irene would bring a nice little dinner up to her room, just the things she liked. But Aunt Hudson was much too stoical to give in to fatigue.

She found herself *wonder*fully refreshed by the soup. "Real English soup!" She said nothing about French soup, but meant to imply that it was symptomatic, like other products of the country, of the national frivolity. One of Aunt Hudson's crosses was that she was compelled to go to France every year for treatment, much as she disliked the country and distrusted the people. Half her existence seemed to be spent in places beginning with Ax or Aix.

Dax was a slight variation, but she found it no better, rather worse in fact, than Ax or Aix. She drew a dismal picture of the place.

"But didn't you like any of the people at the hotel?" Angela asked her.

"There were some quite nice English people."

"And the French?"

"My dear, you know how I hate their idolatry."

Hate is a strong word for the Brebis. I do not think I have ever heard her use it in any other connection.

At Dax she had witnessed "a most idolatrous R.C. procession." There was a tall man at the head of it dressed up like a parrot, who looked as if he had come out of a circus, and a lot of innocent little mites carrying baskets of flowers in front of the image. "My dear, I don't like to think of it. What will happen to them? I couldn't get away. The crowd was so thick on the pavement that it was all I could do to avoid being carried along with them."

Aunt Hudson found herself squeezed up against a wall in front of a street altar. A priest was blessing a paralytic child. "Poor little mite! The smell of incense was *nause*ating. I went straight back to the hotel and wrote to Bellows, and told her to stop sending the washing to the convent."

Here the Brebis' lips pursed tightly, and the light of compassion almost entirely died out of her eyes. I thought of Angela's remark when I said that Aunt Hudson would not hurt a fly. "No," she said, "not a Protestant fly, but I shouldn't like to be a Roman Catholic fly on her window pane." The Brebis had one very hard streak in her nature: she was opposed, like Latimer, to pilgrimages and candles.

"My dear, you can't think how glad I am to get away from Dax. Dear Homersfield! Sunday was a dreadful day. And this year there was no English clergyman."

I asked the Brebis if there was no French Protestant church in the town.

"I think somebody told me there was," she said, "but I did not like to go to it. I hear that it is tainted." She went on to tell how she had been decoyed into a parish church to look at a picture. "R.C., you know"—this in an awed whisper. She described the inside as like a toyshop. "And so untidy. Would you believe it? They had hung a model of a ship from the ceiling. What the place wanted was a good spring cleaning."

Angela and I put our heads together to think of a place where Aunt Hudson might take her baths in a Protestant country.

In France things were going from bad to worse. "They have started bull-fights now," she told us, "like the Spanish. I don't know what we shall hear of next. There was one at Bayonne, quite close, and some English people went from the hotel. Can you imagine it? And on Sunday!"

The world was moving too quickly for the Brebis, and always on the downhill gradient. It was not only the French; the English were becoming corrupted by the irreligion and Socialism, especially in the big towns, where you couldn't tell the difference between a week-day and a Sunday. Among the nice people in the hotel at Dax there was a lady who was the intimate friend of one of the cleverest men in England. "I forgot his name, but he is quite famous, and he told her that if things went on in the way they were going, well, in two years' time there would be no telling what might happen."

Angela consoled her. "I don't think anything very dreadful is likely to happen at Homersfield," she said; and she began to talk about the garden, the melons, the vicar, the postmistress, and the old lady who kept the village shop. Lady Potter had bought the Bell at Homersfield and turned it into a dry house, and she was in process of buying the Bull at Renton, which would no doubt share the same fate. They were weeding the river, and dear old Smithers, the mole-catcher, had got a new velveteen suit.

In a few minutes Aunt Hudson seemed to have forgotten the ungodly. "Dear Homersfield!" she repeated, "dear, safe Homersfield!" She beamed on the children, and the brebis light returned to her eyes.

"And how is the museum getting on?" she asked Irene.

The children told her about Marjorie's visit, and the Goliath beetle that she was going to send them, and the papilio, and the antelope's horn with the witch-doctor's shadow in it.

"How *wonderful!*" Aunt Hudson exclaimed. "How tremendously interesting!"

"And she has shot hundreds of lions," Val boasted, like a squire of his knight.

"How extra*ordi*nary of her!"

But the Brebis was not so enthusiastic when they told her about Uncle Bliss, "the only man she didn't like"; and she was quite alarmed when she heard that she must have passed him driving up from the station.

IV

THE REBELLION OF CUCKOO LANE

In the absence of Uncle Bliss the onus of the partnership in responsibility for Irene's spiritual education naturally fell on Aunt Hudson. Angela thought this would be a very happy arrangement. The Brebis was the soul of piety, and she loved Irene. Neither Angela nor myself was equipped for the part of religious instructor. Angela, so far from having any definite notions about ultimate things, was not at all sure that we had been born into a rational universe. But this only made her the more anxious that the children should enjoy the comforts of orthodoxy. "We must give them every chance," she said. "People who believe ought to be much happier than people without religion." So when Aunt Hudson was not with us she made a point of taking the children to church every Sunday, generally to the afternoon service, I am afraid, in preference to the morning, as it was shorter, and sometimes there was no sermon.

Irene was three when Aunt Hudson began to occupy herself seriously with her religious education. One of her earliest homilies was delivered in the parish churchyard at Homersfield, a spot that has always filled me with an unreasoning depression, especially one corner of it in which a well-to-do yeoman family of the parish have got themselves too pompously buried. I have seldom seen such

monuments in a country churchyard, so heavy, ugly, and
pretentious. The Brebis was walking with Irene on the
gravel path between these enormities when she clutched
her hand and pointed at them. Here was the text for a
sermon, or perhaps she had the kinder thought of introducing a little brightness into the scene of desolation.
Anyhow, she told Irene in the gentle earnest voice, associated afterwards with collects and catechisms, that on
the Judgment Day the dead who lay buried under these
tombstones would all rise up and joyously shake off their
encumbrances at the blast of a trumpet. But Irene, after
what seemed an independent inspection of the too solid
masonry, shook her head sagely, and said, "No, them 'ont."
There was something of the uncompromising spirit of her
mother in Irene.

The Brebis might have postponed her message of religious consolation, for Irene was probably far too near the
beginnings of things to worry about the ends, which, as a
rule, do not enter into the heads of healthy young people
before the period when existence is divided into school
terms and holidays.

When the children grew older Sunday became a
black-letter day if Aunt Hudson was staying with us. There
was too much church-going, too many catechisms and collects, too many things about which one could never be
quite sure whether they might or might not be done on
Sundays. And the Brebis told them so many hard things
about God that they began to think that He was unsym-
pathetic, although she always assured them that He was
forgiving. Angela and I began to have our doubts about
the comforts of orthodoxy.

The first hint of rebellion occurred when Irene was five.
It was on the Sunday morning after the Brebis arrived for
one of her long summer visits. Angela said to the children,

"You are going to church with Aunt Hudson this evening. Daddy and I are going for a walk."

Irene's impenetrable expression during the silence that followed this announcement reminded me of Angela when she was thinking out a problem.

"Do you know, Mummy," she said, "I think I am going to keep going to church for a very great treat."

Clearly Aunt Hudson's system was all wrong. It was bad for the children, and involved us, as accomplices, in hypocrisy. The question now was how to relax this Sabbatarian discipline without hurting or humiliating the Brebis. It was very difficult. After she had gone we let them play games on Sunday. Even my thin conservatism was shocked when Mr. and Mrs. Noah, and the dove with the olive branch, and the horse without a head, and the broken-legged camel were relegated to the cupboard, deposed for new-fangled and secular diversions. I felt a sense of guilt, as if I were abetting a disloyalty. It was too like a revolution. Poor dear Aunt Hudson! In a few months she would be with us again, and what would she think if she found her lambs transformed to goats, and Homersfield given over to the profanities of a French Sunday? I felt sure she wouldn't stay with us. She would be happier in Dax, or Ax, or Aix. Angela and I talked it over, and agreed that we must warn the children. So *we* became *their* accomplices.

"You see, dear," Angela said to Irene, "it will make her unhappy; she feels like that about Sundays."

The children saw at once. They were very understanding and responsive. They said they would much rather give up games on Sunday than hurt Aunt Hudson. Only Irene, who has a way of reducing the most complex problem to its simple premisses, said, "Mummy, why doesn't Aunt Hudson like us to play games on Sunday? Is it because she is afraid we will hurt God, or that God will hurt us."

"A little of both, I think, Angela said. "But you mustn't talk about God like that."

So Aunt Hudson's arrow of instruction got home by a sort of ricochet. It came to exactly the same thing. The children gave up pleasant and prohibited occupations because they were afraid they would hurt the Brebis. And it was really better morality, as fear did not enter into the compact. Only I am afraid that they led double lives. Irene's godmother must be held responsible for the first downright deception of which the children were guilty. I should not have minded their playing truant from church if they had not pretended they were going. There were two churches frequented by the family, about equally distant from the house, Homersfield and Renton. It sometimes happened that when Aunt Hudson went to Homersfield the children would go to Renton, and *vice versa*. The temptation for evasion was great. And it became greater when Sunday followed upon Sunday and no questions were asked. "Where Satan can get a little finger in he will soon thrust his whole palm." So Nurse Stebbing used to tell them, and they were soon illustrating the truth of the adage by sliding down the primrose path which leads—not to church but to Cuckoo Lane. For a month of Sundays I am afraid they did not go to church at all.

One gets to Renton Church by a road which leads nowhere except to the church itself and to farms. In the last lap of the walk you leave the road and follow a path through two interminable beet fields, famous cover for partridges, but otherwise leaden-hued and monotonous, and unrelieved by flowers, an appropriately penitential conclusion to the path of duty. There is nothing in a corn or grass country more unattractive than a field of roots.

On the other side of the road in the opposite direction from the church—this sounds like an allegory, but it is perfectly true—a gate opens into Topland Barrow, a field of rest-harrow—the thornless kind—and scabious and harebell, and the bright blue succory. It is stony and uneven, and full of surprises, the kind of land on which the carline thistle grows. It contains a disused gravel pit, overgrown with convolvulus and viper's bugloss, the haunt of red admirals, and peacocks, and small tortoiseshells; and on one side it slopes down into a sheltered depression, a sort of combe, freaked with fairy rings, and toadstools, and round white stones, which you cannot tell at a distance from mushrooms. The children had found their only bee orchis here, and a whitethroat's and meadow-pipit's nest, which they visited until the young were hatched and flown. But this was only the approach to paradise. At the bottom of Topland Barrow is Cuckoo Lane. It is called a lane, but it is really a deep sunk ditch with polypodies growing in the roots of the hornbeams at the edges, and in places completely overarched with honeysuckle, and bryony, and wild roses. No cart has ever been down it. It is a place of concealment as impenetrable as Uncle Bliss' pygmy forest, something between a fairy bower and a pirate's den.

Here on Sunday mornings Irene, the leader of the expedition, would light a fire of dried sticks and brambles, and religiously fry kippered herrings. Then when the fire had burnt itself out they would rake the ashes together and bake potatoes. The reek of the wood smoke and the kippers and the burnt potato skins mingled with the honeysuckle and eglantine overhead, and made up a concord of sweet smells. And sweeter than bird music was the sound of the church bells. The chimes would affect them as one of Shelley's odes to liberty the adult rebel. As for the toll, I am not so sure. I fancy the dreadfully solemn clangour from the other side of the beet field, just before the door closed on the pious, must have frightened them a little. But without this mingled sense of awe and pleasure, and

possible or probable retribution, there would be no revolt;
no fun in conspiracy, truancy, piracy, or outrage upon the
proprieties of any kind.

It was the merest chance that the children were discovered. But Nemesis spared them nothing. It all came out
at lunch in circumstances of the most distressing publicity. Aunt Hudson was with us, and Lady Potter, who had
dropped in and stayed to lunch, as she sometimes did on
Sundays. I thought I noticed a suspicious smell of kippers,
not at all *convenable* with a Sunday lunch, and guests at
the table. But I did not pursue the trail. Kippers, in fact,
did not come into the evidence for the prosecution. If it
had been kippers only, our faces might have been saved;
but the particular brand of shame the children brought on
the family was the kind of thing that sticks.

All through lunch they were as good as gold with that
"speak when you are spoken to, do as you are bid" air
which commends young people to their elders. They were
not hungry. After the kippers and the potatoes—only
superficially baked, I am afraid—this was not to be wondered at. When I saw them nibbling at the roast duck, I
concluded that they were suffering from a pain in their
insides. Abstinence would be another point in their favour
with Lady Potter. She noticed them occasionally, and spoke
of them to me and Angela as "the young dears," a form of
reference which few children can abide. To Irene and Val
it was peculiarly galling, and made them feel as if they
looked soft and boneless and unpiratical, like puppies or
kittens. Extreme youth was a flaw which they would have
mended if they could, only it took such an unconscionable
long time. In the meanwhile they did not like having their
immaturity flung in their faces. Half the secret of Uncle
Bliss' ascendancy was that he talked to them as if they
were grown-up people.

My sympathies were with the children. I could see that they wanted to "get down." Lady Potter often makes me feel like that, but grown-up people can't "get down." They have to stick it out. Maturity has its inhibitions too. Lady Potter—one of Angela's corkers—was hard and stiff, encased in whalebone. She came to Homersfield because it was what they used to call "low church." I forget how the precedent was established of coming on to us for lunch. She did not often come; perhaps two or three times a year. Aunt Hudson admired her principles, but never felt quite comfortable in her society. Temperance reform was Lady Potter's ruling passion. In figure she reminded me rather incongruously of a hock bottle—a conscious and complacent erectness, which the high stiff collar she wore long after these abominations had ceased to be fashionable aggravated. There is a highbrow type of woman who just miss looking horsey. The cause Lady Potter was ridden by—or should I say "rode"?—imposed no privations, for the taste or smell of alcohol had the same effect on her as incense had on the Brebis. It made her feel sick. We had to take care that there was none visible when she was our guest. That was another reason why I disliked her visits. I had to forgo the consolation of wine at a time when I most needed fortifying.

Teetotalism as an abstract theme is a dry subject, but conversation became more interesting when Lady Potter began to talk about her cases. As she had bought the Bell at Homersfield and was buying the Bull at Renton, it was difficult to whip up interest in the drink question in either parish. However, there were one or two backsliders. We had heard just before lunch that old Moggs, one of the family of yeomen who got themselves too pompously buried, had had a stroke in church. Lady Potter spoke of the tragedy in a shocked voice, though I believe she was inwardly glad. Moggs was another dreadful example. He was known to be addicted to spirits.

"I hear he fell down when he was handing round the bag," she said.

Angela had another version. Jessie, the housemaid, said it was in the first hymn. Moggs was in the choir. The children were appealed to. "Was it in the hymn or the offertory?"

They turned a bright pink, and said they didn't know.

"Didn't you see Mr. Moggs fall down?" Aunt Hudson asked them unsuspiciously. "He was carried out of church."

"No," said Irene.

"No," said Val, confused and scarlet.

There was a dreadful pause. Then Val, that imperfect conspirator, blurted out, "We weren't there."

He need not have said a word more. There was the possible inference that they had been to the other church. True, the air was heavy with suspicion, but they were safe anyhow until the end of lunch. It was not likely that we would cross-examine them with Lady Potter there.

But Val was conscience-stricken. He wanted to get the tribunal over; or perhaps it would be more just to say that he rallied to the eternal verities.

"We didn't go to church," he announced bravely, but with a catch in his voice.

"Not to Renton, you mean," Angela interposed, in the vain hope of saving all our faces.

"No; we didn't go to church at all."

"Then what have you been doing all the morning?" I asked sternly.

"We thought we would go to Cuckoo Lane," Irene said.

"And you pretended that you had been to church?"

"We did not *say* we been," Val stammered.

Miserable evasion! The first sobs escaped from the children when its hollowness was exposed.

Thus the bomb fell on our tranquil Sunday luncheon party. I think of Lady Potter snorting like an intrusive warhorse, pawing the ground. This was the impression she gave me, though, so far as I remember, she sat rigidly in her chair, and never uttered a sound. The poor Brebis was almost in tears. "O Val! O Irene!" She bleated the children's names like a forlorn old sheep robbed of her lambs.

This was intolerable. I felt chilled and humiliated. The children were sent to their bedrooms, and told not to appear until after tea. Aunt Hudson retired to her room, too, and for the first time in life failed to attend afternoon service. Jessie, who was handing round the dessert plates, turned as crimson as Val and Irene, blushing with shame for them. She, too, was a witness of the family disgrace. I handed Lady Potter the fruit-dishes, nectarines, peaches, pears, and grapes, but she declined them all. The luscious pears and nectarines would have gone untasted if I had not begun to peel one with great presence of mind, though I could not have told you whether it was a nectarine or a peach.

After the shortest interval consistent with decency, Lady Potter ordered her carriage. As she drove away she gave me a look of frozen sympathy, almost professional in its correctness. Angela's theory is that she acquired it in her visits to homes for the inebriate.

Angela met me in the hall with a smile which exorcised depression. "Poor dears!" she said. "I feel as if there had been a blight. I wish Aunt Hudson had not set them against going to church so."

But it was Lady Potter I wanted to trample on.

"She won't come again," Angela said.

She meant to lunch on Sunday, of course. Angela's intuitions are generally accurate. In this case I am glad to say she proved a true prophet.

The children had brought dishonour on the family, and they had made Aunt Hudson cry. This was punishment enough—far worse than being sent to their rooms for the afternoon and going without tea.

I thought of them most of the afternoon, and especially at tea, on the lawn under the catalpa tree, when I could see an inch of curtain drawn aside in the two windows over the porch. How slowly the long hours would drag themselves out! They must have seen Lady Potter drive off stiff with disapproval. Then an hour later, when the chimes of the Homersfield bells broke the Sunday afternoon stillness, four eyes would be glued to the windows, waiting and watching for Aunt Hudson, to see how she bore it. Was it possible that she would walk down the drive as if nothing had happened? They would only see her back, but even backs tell you a great deal. The chimes ceased; all the bells topped ringing but one, whose rapid beat called to the loiterer to hurry, but still no Aunt Hudson. How deeply she must be hurt! Would she ever love them again? They saw Jessie carry the tea-tray across the lawn, and on the tray was a plate with a stiff folded napkin of the kind that covers hot buttered scones. Then another smaller tray, on which Aunt Hudson's tea was sent up to her with a plate of peaches. There were no peaches or scones for the little exiles and pariahs who had caused these wounds. And worse, we had forgotten to tell Jessie not to lay the children's table, and when we found it already laid a few yards from ours, with the cracked nursery sugar-basin, and the Japanese milk-jug of bright cinnamon with the crinkly, bald-pated, old man hugging its sides from the base to the handle, and other immemorial objects consecrated to this hour, as fixed in the order of their appearance as the evening star, we had not the heart to tell her to take it in.

They were not to appear until after tea. No precise hour had been mentioned, but the longed-for and dreaded moment of becoming visible was drawing near. How to comport oneself? How to preserve one's face with the consciousness of shame written on it as clearly as in the portrait of the young backslider in the moral picture-book? I am quite sure that if I live to be eighty I shall remember those shrinkings and misgivings of the return to the community after disgrace, those delicate and uncertain rites of the restoration to caste, the unspoken pledges of amendment and forgiveness on either side, and the difficulty of speaking in a natural voice as if the offence were decently buried with no stone or epitaph over its grave.

Angela and I kept looking up at the curtains drawn aside a finger's-breadth from the window-frames over the porch. At last I got up, cut two fat slices of cake, and mounted the stairs to the children's rooms. I flung their doors open.

"Hullo, Irene! Hullo, Val!"

"Hullo, Daddy!"

Soon we were all three looking out of the same window, two of us munching cake. Angela waved to us from the lawn. Jessie was carrying in the children's tea.

"We're awfully sorry," they blurted out together.

"Yes, I know," I said, "It wasn't like you. But Mummy and I aren't angry any longer. I am going down to the Witch Pool to see if there is a rise. Who'd like to come?"

Angela joined us, and we all went down to the marshes by the little alder-fringed beck which runs from the bottom of the garden to the river; into the stackyard; past the Baron and Baroness Fig-tree—it seems that some of the Brebis' scripture lessons stuck; through the field that contained the cow called Hungry, a dark-red beast which Irene used to approach with cabbage leaves, thinking that if it was hungry it must like being fed; past the mouse-coloured thatched cottages and barns, and through the last field of corn, or rather of poppies, a scarlet stain running down from the little flint church with its round tower on the hill, and coming to a sudden stop at the first green ditch. The poppies were the despair of Farmer Stubbs, but, I am afraid, the joy of all Claytons. "How are your poppies this year, Mr. Stubbs?" Val asked the vexed proprietor in all innocence. Farmer Stubbs was rather like a poppy himself from the neck upwards. At Val's question he became purpler still. "Oh, bain't he a sly one," he said. "True, they be as thick as the barley. You can run through my ca-arn, Maaster Val, but don't ee go trapayzing about in the haaye."

The hay was another matter, an assured crop, though not of the best quality on account of the abundance and variety of the flowers. But it was very good to smell. In April the meadows were golden with marsh-marigold; in May pink with ragged robin; and in June the buttercups changed the floor of the valley back to gold again. Yellow-rattle gave the hay its dominant hue after that. And now in the first week of August the last few fields unmown were like Jacob's coat. The mown crop had been lying in swathes for a week or more, and now after a day and a half's sun its fragrance, mingled with the warm, woody, almond-like smell of the meadowsweet, filled the whole valley. To make up for the uniform green where the hay had been cut, the dykes were a blaze of colour. Spires of purple loosestrife, woolly-headed mops of hemp agrimony, and the lush untidy willow-herb—the subtly-smelling kind which the children called cherry-pie—blended in pink and purple masses; and between these stout double borders there were lanes of sky-blue forget-me-not starred with arrowhead and frogbit, and pink flowering rush, and Angela's dream flower, water-violet.

The cocks were standing in the meadow by the Witch Pool, and we were drawn to the one nearest the river, and spread ourselves in the prickly grass stubble with our backs and heads in the equally prickly hay. The grass in the crop was in much the same proportion as the barley in the poppy field, but it did not smell any the less delicious for that. Half of it was clover and meadow-sweet. The children began to play a lazy family game. You bury something, and something which it reminds you of comes up.

"I buried a fruit, and two of them came up," said Irene. "What was the fruit?"

"A pear," said Val.

"You knew it," said Irene.

"I buried a fish, and a place where a bird sits came up," said Val.

"A perch," said Irene. "Your turn, Daddy."

I thought of all the things one could bury, hatchets, Sabbath-breakers, teetotallers, R.C.'s, but I could not think of anything appropriate to come up, or the things that did come up were too appropriate, and one couldn't say them. At last a teasing bumblebee provoked invention.

"I buried a beehive, and a buzzing meadow came up."

"Homersfield," said Angela.

"Hummersfield" was the happy way they pronounced the name of our village, not Homersfield, though Homer, the river, was pronounced like the poet. But no classic suggestion could make either of them more paradisiacal than it was.

"The big things pass and the little things remain." I remember that afternoon as if it were yesterday—the blight before tea, the children's restoration to caste. The "as you were" feeling, partly perhaps because of the benedictory fragrance of the hay and the river, became something more than the pretence that nothing had happened. Something *had* happened, something endearing. That must be why the little things remain, the mole that poked his white hand out of the earth, the small black whirligig insects under the alder skimming just at the edge of the shadow in the sun, Irene's name scratched in the mud with my walking-stick, the soft blue English sky streaked with

herring-bone clouds, our childish inventions in the bury-
ing game, and all the silly things we said.

Or was it the hay? Smells preserve associations as in
balm. Or the pungent reek of the ditches, an aromatic
blend of fleabane and water-mint? Or—more delicious—
the smell of the river? In the shallows where the stream is
strangled with rank umbelliferous weed, sium and œnan-
the, stacked and rotting in the sun, you have the true
distillation, the sweet August smell, pure Homer. I have
carried it away with me in the seed-pod of a yellow
water-lily and released the soul of the stream—which the
ancients tell us is the same thing as the smell—in the most
prosaic places.

And down by the mill there was another kind of smell,
a cool smell, the most local smell I know, a blend of
water-weed that has never been warmed by the sun, and
flour. A smell associated with a certain noise, soft, musi-
cal, and monotonous. Having once smelt it, though you
may become blind or deaf, if you smell it again you will
see and hear running water. There is a shelving bank just
where the water comes out of the mill. You must wade and
drop your cast under the branches of the horse-chestnut
tree on the other side. To make the dream smell perfect
the horse-chestnut must be in flower, and the leaves still
curled and crinkly, not yet spread out flat and hard in
a fan. And the cast must fall in the undecided inches,
about the span of your palm, between the backwater and
the swirl. Then, if you do not get hung up in the chestnut-tree, there will be another smell, the consummation of
all, fresh fish-scales in a landing-net.

The smell of the hay and the river began to act as a
narcotic, and the game fizzled out, as games do. I heard a
"Sshh" from Angela. A water-rat was swimming across the
Witch Pool. We became as still as lizards, and watched it
land and smooth its coat with its paws in the roots of the

gnarled, dingy, old alder the other side, where the water is black under the shadow. In the middle of the stream the submerged waterlily leaves swayed slowly with the current, curled and crinkled and covered with green slime. A water-hen slipped out of the rushes with her chicks, and explored the alleys in the weeds. We listened to the subtle river sounds, liquid splash, ripple and bubble, the diving rat or grebe, the rising fish or dipping swallow, or the sudden swirl of the jack that has been lying motionless among the arrowhead in the sun.

Soon the children disappeared to climb trees, those ancient pollard willows that bent over the Homer, with the bird-sown gooseberry-bushes and woody nightshade in their bowls. They bent so over the river that you could walk up some of them, if you balanced carefully, without using your hands; and the wood was powdery and soft and rotten underfoot, and smelt of the caterpillar of the goat-moth. Irene once found one. A day to mark with a white stone. And Val found a missel-thrush's nest the same week in a tree to which he was tying night lines for eels.

"Val! Irene!" Angela was calling them. She looked like a naiad in her pale-green dress, eternally vernal, as fresh as Irene. It was the cockchafer hour, and the light on the opal and the seed-pearl earrings she wore, as subtle as her complexion, made her look more like a river-sprite than ever.

"Here you are. What a wonder! And nobody's tumbled in." This was rather a sore point with Val. It was a habit of his to tumble in. But it didn't matter, as he and Irene could both swim like fish.

"Home, Homer, Homersfield," said Angela.

But the children implored, "Just one story."

I told them the story of the lady who lost her earring, and how Mrs. Sounder happened to call on her the very afternoon she came to live in Rose Cottage, and, hearing her say that she had lost her earring, went away and told everybody that she dropped her aitches and was slightly deaf; and how this story went the round of the neighbourhood through the wives of the postman, publican, farmer, parson, squire, until it came to the ears of the Duke himself, who, of course, naturally and rightly, would have nothing to do with such a lady, which meant that nobody else would have anything to do with her, as the Duke led the fashion, and people the Duke did not know were nobody at all. So for a long time, though she was a very kind lady and fond of seeing people, she lived alone and had no friends. Then one day the Duke gave a very grand garden-party, and invited everybody in the neighbourhood to it except the lady who had lost her earring and her reputation at the same time. Even the Home Secretary was there; and while the Home Secretary was talking to the Duke, the Public Prosecutor came up and told him that the seed-pearl earring of the lady who lived in Rose Cottage had been found.

"Seed-pearl earring!" the Duke exclaimed in astonishment. "God bless my soul! Then it was her earring she lost and not her h-hearing, and she does not drop her aitches after all."

Here the postman who brought the message remarked to the Duke, "And what a comfort it is, Your Grace, to think that the lady is not suffering from that terrible affliction, the loss of 'earing."

But nobody seemed to see his point. The Duke, as a matter of fact, was not listening. But he was a very just Duke, and the first thing he did was to order his coach-and-four and his postilions and coachman and footmen, in their powdered wigs, and to take the reins himself and drive off to Rose Cottage. In half an hour he returned with the lady who had lost and found her earring sitting by his side on the box. Of course, she became a very great lady after that. Nobody could make enough of her. Not even Mrs. Sounder.

Here, to the children's disgust, invention flagged. They cried out for the end.

"Daddy, don't say that you have forgotten the end!"

"Yes, I have forgotten the end. Either she became the Duchess, or she had *too* many friends, so many that she began to drop her aitches on purpose, because she wanted to lead a quiet life. But enough. The dogs are scattered after having their evening meal, which is the Indian way of saying that the story has come to an end."

"Perhaps she married the postman," Angela suggested, "who didn't mind the aitches, and the Duke died of unrequited love."

By this time the dew was on the grass, and the big fat slugs, Angela's abhorrence. A rudderless cockchafer kept tacking across the path in front of us, just missing her hair. The harvest moon was growing bigger and redder, and the marsh smells were increasing in potency. Soon it would be dark. It was time to be getting home.

We were passing the barn which contained the cow called Hungry—I am not sure that hers was not the nicest smell after all—when I remembered that there were still raw edges to heal. I believe that we had all four forgotten the existence of Aunt Hudson.

Dear Homersfield! Well might we echo the Brebis' benediction! The time was coming when we should look back to it as the Paradise from which we had been driven by the Angel with the flaming sword.

V

THE PTERODACTYL

The rebellion of Cuckoo Lane happened in the days of tranquility; to be exact, a year before the invasion of Uncle Bliss, after which hardly a week passed without something eventful happening. It had got about in the neighbourhood that Uncle Bliss was a sort of connection, and that he had come to the Clapperhouse to be near us. We soon wished the Clapperhouse and its tenant the other side of the county.

Lady Potter had witnessed, and no doubt advertised, the disgrace of Val and Irene, but the children's offence was a mere bagatelle compared with Uncle Bliss' flagrancy. In his case, Lady Potter was both witness and complainant. She asked him to dinner. Uncle Bliss accepted unprovisionally. He did not say, "I'll come if it is wet," which would have been more natural and excusable than his reply to Angela's invitation, seeing that it was a "dry house" he was invited to. Even our dear Archdeacon used to have a bottle of sherry concealed in his carriage when he dined with the Potters. I have no reason for supposing that Uncle Bliss knew anything about his hostess' propaganda. He would not have been interested in her fads if he did; and if any one had told him he would have replied that it was no concern of his. Was he not provided against such emergencies?

Angela is more competent than most people at solving problems of evasion, but we could not refuse the Potters three years running. Their last two dinners coincided with an annual Club dinner I had to attend in town—that coincidence could not be stretched any further. Another year we found we were unable to dine out on account of the death of a relative. The bereavement plea is an effective "non-posthumous," as the Babu said. Angela and I might have fallen to employing it again, only it occurred to us that this would be too much in the character of Nabi Baksh, khansamah. Nor was it possible at Homersfield to pretend that we were dining anywhere else. There was nothing for it but to accept and "stick it out," though, of course, if we had known that Uncle Bliss was going to be there, it would have been a case of adding another inch or two to the arm of coincidence, or drawing on our Nabi-Bakshish invention.

We found him in the drawing-room when we arrived, the centre of an attentive group. He was telling the Archdeacon about Africa. Lady Potter regarded her captive approvingly. She was a bit of a lion-hunter. "The African explorer," I heard her whisper to Mrs. Brown; "he has taken the Clapperhouse." Old Sellinger took me aside. "He's got more in him than ever came out of the parish pump," he said. "I wish Lady Potter would collect a few more like him. A connection of yours, I hear." I denied kinship.

In the centre of this group of parsons and squires Uncle Bliss looked most distinctly ultra-parochial. Yet I don't know why; there was something in his peculiar rig-out that reminded me of a robust sexton. He wore a very voluminous old-fashioned dress suit, with long, broad, flapping tails reaching almost to his heels. I could see by his creased and muddied trouser-ends that he had arrived on his bicycle. I looked anxiously for bulges. The breast pockets, if there were any, were innocent; but it was impossible to say what might be concealed in the tails. I caught Angela's eye as she concluded the same scrutiny from a more favourable angle. Her smile was most profoundly discouraging. Then Potter came up and told me I was taking in Mrs. Sellinger. I passed Angela as I crossed the room to the lady who was sentenced to be entertained by me for the next two hours. "Will he dare?" I asked her in a low voice. "They all seem to think that we brought him here," she replied. I knew what that meant. And, to quicken my apprehension, I thought I heard a metallic clink as Uncle Bliss' coattails came in contact with the back of a chair.

So far responsibility for Uncle Bliss was rather an honour. Lady Potter's guests were impressed by him. "Just returned from Darkest Africa," I overheard from the lady on my left. "A great character!" That, of course, explained a great deal: Uncle Bliss' neglect of the *convenances* and the lady he had taken in to dinner among other things, and the way he monopolised the conversation.

"His conversation is so suggestive," I heard on my left.

"Yes, most unusual."

"I call him refreshing," said Mrs. Sellinger.

"Like strong beer after the parish pump." This from old Sellinger across the table. I saw him pull himself up and look nervously at Lady Potter.

The boom of the hunter drowned all this tittle-tattle. Uncle Bliss was thinking aloud, and thinking very fast, a mingled stream of reminiscence and speculation. The Archdeacon had started it in the drawing-room. "Talking about collections," he said, "did you see the paragraph in 'The Times' this morning about the discovery of the dinosaur's egg?" It was a super-dinosaur, by the way, which had laid this egg, totally unknown to science. To everybody's amazement, Uncle Bliss announced that he had bought it, or was on the point of buying it. He was expecting a cable from New York.

It was a rapid flight from the dinosaur to the pterodactyl. In ten seconds Uncle Bliss was astride his new hobby-horse. Potter, in the sorting and segregating of his guests into incompatible couples, had the greatest difficulty in detaching him from the Archdeacon. Uncle Bliss continued his monologue as we passed through the hall to the dining-room, entirely neglectful of the lady apportioned to him. Angela was in the direct line of fire, between him and the embarrassed Archdeacon. "He was so full of his pterodactyl," she told me, "that I began to hope that he might forget his flask."

He did forget his soup, and made some of us forget ours. We were all listening to him. When the pterodactyl was under discussion nobody was likely to agitate the handle of the parish pump.

"By the way," Mrs. Sellinger asked me, "what *is* a pterodactyl?"

"To tell you the truth," I said, "I don't know. A kind of fowl, I believe." I think most of us were a little vague.

"And what is a minotaur?"

"A dinosaur, isn't it?" I corrected her tentatively. "Another kind of fowl, I suppose, or it wouldn't lay eggs."

"And which is it your cousin is going to shoot, a dinosaur or a pterodactyl?"

"My cousin?" Mrs. Sellinger was surprised when I denied the connection.

"I hear he doesn't hunt," she said.

"No, he hates horses."

"What's going to happen to the kennels?"

"I don't know," I said, "he hates dogs too, I believe he is going to turn the Clapperhouse into a menagerie." It was not my mission to popularise Uncle Bliss.

Mrs. Sellinger, though a hard rider to hounds, tolerantly passed these serious shortcomings. She passed Uncle Bliss, because he was a character.

"I should think he knows exactly what he wants," she said.

I agreed.

"And generally gets it."

"He can generally buy it."

"Do you like barley water?" she asked me inconsequently.

I missed the subtlety of the connection until I followed her eyes to the array of poisonous-looking fluids on the sideboard. I began to envy Uncle Bliss and his provision against emergencies. I am not sure that I did not admire him.

"There are occasions when money *won't* buy things," Mrs. Sellinger explained.

I confessed to a great longing for a whisky-and-soda.

"I think people can carry principles too far. Don't you?"

"I don't like being made to swallow them," I said, with my eyes on the sideboard.

"I wonder if the archdeacon will find he has forgotten his spectacles. Last year he left them in the carriage, and insisted on going to look for them himself."

"And returned fortified?"

Mrs. Sellinger smiled. Everybody had heard the story of the archidiaconal sherry except Lady Potter.

"You saw the new sign on the Bell at Homersfield? 'Alcohol is prohibited from being drunk on these premises.' The lovely part of it was the two s's."

"The major and the minor premiss," I suggested. "Our hostess' profession of faith. They forgot to subscribe it at the foot of the notice."

Potter's father was the son of a beer baronet, but the family fortunes were safely invested in an Aerated Water Company.

"Let's talk about the pterodactyl," Mrs. Sellinger said. "I feel as if we were getting cattish."

I accepted the rebuke, which, I believe, might have been applied equally well to Lady Potter's other guests. That is one of the evils of carrying principles too far.

We were all rather thankful for the diversion of the pterodactyl.

We were soon to learn that it is not a bird after all, but an amphibious monster, a sort of cross between a featherless fowl and a reptile, with smooth skin and wings and saw-like teeth in its beak as big as boars' tusks. Bliss was convinced of its continued existence. He had independent evidence, native and European.

The Archdeacon asked where the prehistoric monster might be found.

Bliss described its habitat in the unexplored morasses of the Jiundu River in Northern Rhodesia on the southern border of the Belgian Congo, a black peaty country, forest and swamp, which swallows up a network of rivers. The natives believe there is a deep hole in the middle of the swamp, a profound abyss into which these streams empty themselves. Anyhow, none of them emerge. It is here that the pterodactyl, or kongamato as they call it, has its home; but, as nobody has ever visited "the black hole of death" and returned, this part of the story may be legendary. The brute, however, happily for science, has its restless moments, generally in the rainy season, when it invades the inhabited part of the swamp, lies in wait at the fords and ferries, attacks and capsizes boats, and swallows their crew.

Everybody was listening to Uncle Bliss now.

The Archdeacon suggested that he would have difficulty in persuading his porters to follow him.

"They precede me," Uncle Bliss announced quietly. I thought of the pygmy.

Sellinger asked him what rifle he was going to use.

"It is a pity you can't catch the pterodactyl alive and bring it home with you," the Archdeacon suggested.

Uncle Bliss reflected a moment. We all reflected. The least imaginative of us was translated from our prosy dinner-table by the vision of this apocalyptic beast on show at the Clapperhouse.

"I might do that," he said, after a pause in which no one spoke. "My first idea was to fish for it. Hand lines, chains, a 14-pound hook. If one can land a sawfish of 5700 pounds—"

"What bait will you use?"

"Ah," said Uncle Bliss, "I will have to watch the haunts of the pterodactyl before I can tell you that. Fish or birds. Probably both."

I wished the children were with us.

He reflected again. "Or a decoy—Fritton fashion. Catch it flying. A few hundred yards of steel wire netting, double thickness. I shall have to take a big tank, 12 foot by 8 at least, fitting in segments for porterage."

"How about getting the tank back with the pterodactyl inside?" Sellinger suggested.

"Motor transport." Uncle Bliss was always cocksure and practical.

"But the swamps?"

"Corduroy roads. If we had to lay out two hundred miles of them, it would be worth it. And I could fix up a mono-rail, use it for timber afterwards. An investment, eh! Float a company."

It was the butler who brought him back to actualities.

"Lemonade or barley-water?" I heard.

Uncle Bliss' hand shot down to his tail-pockets under his chair as if he had received a wound in this quarter. He extracted his flask. "Thank you," he said, "I will have some whisky. My own, if you don't mind. I always make a point of bringing it with me!"

For a moment, I believe, we all looked as if we had been electrocuted, as the whisky bubbled and gurgled from Uncle Bliss' flask into his glass.

I looked at Lady Potter. She was gazing speechlessly at the vile thing in starched abhorrence. I looked at Sir Edward; his frightened gaze was fixed on Lady Potter. At last our hostess found words.

"Mr. Bliss, if that is whisky, I must ask you to abstain."

"As a matter of principle—" began Sir Edward.

Uncle Bliss looked at his glass. I was afraid he was going to raise it, but he turned to Sir Edward, and said—

"You don't like alcohol, eh?"

"No alcohol has ever been drunk in this house," Lady Potter declaimed icily.

"Funny thing, I can't eat without drinking it." He paused and added, "Doctor's orders." This was the only insincerity I have ever known Uncle Bliss guilty of. But he was in what the children called "a good shape," fired by the quest of the pterodactyl, and inclined to be conciliatory.

"But if you like, I'll drink it outside," he conceded. "Then there'll be no record broken."

He rose and crossed the room with his glass in his hand, leaving the flask on the table. One could not help being struck by his magnificent aplomb. The glass was full to the brim, and his whole soul seemed to be occupied with the problem of equilibrium. Not a drop was spilt. The butler opened the door for him. We heard him stump across the hall. Then the hall door opened. Uncle Bliss was drinking his libation on the doorstep.

The butler followed with the flask, which Lady Potter, in frozen accents appropriate to the scene, told him to remove from the table. We heard Uncle Bliss' "Eh, thank you!" in the hall, followed by a suspicious pause. In a moment he was with us again, one side of his tail pockets bulging, and the complacent look on his face of the person who has made a graceful concession.

He looked at me across the table as much as to say, "All this is very silly. But I spared them, you see." Then he returned unconcernedly to the pterodactyl.

"After dinner will you introduce me to your cousin—I mean your friend?" Mrs. Sellinger asked me. "I have not met him yet."

I thought I detected a note of added respect in her voice. Old Sellinger looked as if he were sorry he had not joined him on the doorstep. The Archdeacon continued an attentive listener. He suggested that the pterodactyl might be a descendant of the fiery flying serpent of Isaiah.

"It must be nice," Mrs. Sellinger observed, "to be so entirely independent of stratagem. Now the Archdeacon—"

"Cannot afford to be so direct in his methods," I suggested.

"I like people to be elemental," I heard on my left.

Evidently Lady Potter's guests were not all horrified. There seemed to be a pro-Bliss party at the table. "He is so natural," I heard. "A law unto himself." Explorers and leaders of expeditions had to be like that, or they would never explore or lead. "Can't you imagine him cutting a path through the heart of Africa?"

The eccentricities of such men are a distinction. Provided his assumptions were right, which, of course, they were not, one might say of Uncle Bliss that he had what Angela calls well-bred bad manners.

"Our hostess is a lion-hunter," Mrs. Sellinger observed.

"Yes, and she has bagged one to-night."

"People who hunt lions must expect to be scratched."

I was surprised at her tolerance. I think Lady Potter had something to do with it; she was the kind of woman who provokes reaction. Now if he had behaved like that to the Brebis—!

Lady Potter was no good at carrying off a situation. She stiffened, and the blue inherent in starch invaded her complexion. She had not a word to say to Uncle Bliss for the rest of the evening. Indeed, she spoke very little to any one. I thought Angela and I came in for more than our share of her frigidity.

Uncle Bliss, however, made one gallant effort to draw her into the conversation.

"You've no children?" he asked her when he had exhausted his arguments for the continued existence of the pterodactyl.

The negative movement of Lady Potter's head was eloquent of tired disgust.

"That's a pity," he remarked with the detachment of a naturalist, and began to scrutinise Sir Edward, who looked more ineffectual than ever.

Here Mrs. Sellinger turned to me and said,

"I don't think I will ask you to introduce Mr. Bliss after all. To tell you the truth, I am rather afraid of him. One can carry naturalness too far," she added.

As a matter of fact, she was not given the chance, for Uncle Bliss made his escape before any of the ladies.

"He is impossible," Angela said driving home. "And they all think he belongs to us. I do wish he would go to Africa and shoot his pterodactyl."

I told her that Mrs. Sellinger had passed him, and the woman on my left, also old Sellinger, and I believed, out of a fellow-feeling, the Archdeacon. They liked his naturalness.

Angela reminded me that this was the very thing she had said to Aunt Hudson after Irene's christening, and Aunt Hudson replied, "Yes, my dear, naturalness is a very agreeable quality, provided one has a nice nature."

I think that was the most epigrammatic remark the Brebis ever made.

VI
URSA MAJOR IN THE ASCENDANT

The children came down to breakfast without looking at the sideboard; parcels had long ago passed into the domain of "fish-ponds." We were telling the Brebis how badly Uncle Bliss had behaved at the Potters', and they listened open-mouthed, to the neglect of their porridge. "Did he bring his own flask?" Val asked. Glances of covert delight passed between him and Irene. They, too, were of the pro-Bliss party. Ghost of Cuckoo Lane, their hero had become something of a dragon-slayer!

The Brebis was horrified. "My dear, I do hope he will not come here. I don't think I could *bear* it."

"He will come all right," Angela said.

"How can we keep him out of the house?" she asked me.

"Say we are not at home?"

There was a chorus of distress from the children. Evidently Ursa Major was in the ascendant.

However, we had another constellation up our sleeves.

"Who's blind? What are those bulky packages on the sideboard?"

There was a scramble as of terriers. "Parcels! Two! From Marjorie!" A confusion of knives that would not cut, knots that refused to be untied. We knew better than to offer to help them. Irene had hers open first, Val being handicapped with the butter-knife.

Two square collector's boxes, of beautifully grained white deal, light as cardboard, smelling of camphor, cork-lined inside. The Goliath beetle almost completely filled the first, a fearsome hammer-headed insect, but exquisitely streaked about the head with chocolate and cream. I have seen smaller birds. But the papilio was bigger still, nine inches between wing-tips. And how it shone! Poor purple emperor! There was just room between the tails—which reminded me in their disproportionate length of Uncle Bliss' dress-suit—for the blue bird-winged butterfly and the dead-leaf insect.

In their excitement they quite forgot the other box. "Quick, Val! It's the antelope's horn. How clumsy! Take care, or you'll break it. I'll fetch Mummy's scissors."

Irene was off like the flash of a kingfisher to the drawing-room. But Val, with a mighty wrench, tugged the string round the end of the parcel, and slipped it off, scattering the cloth with wood shavings. He had it out before Irene returned, and held it up in triumph. It was the antelope's horn.

Irene flew to it. She and Val kept turning it round and trying to look into it at the same time, searching for the shadow. "Can you see it?"

"Yes, there it is." "Hold it still." "Look, it has gone."

Apparently it came and went like other shadows.

"Can you see it, Daddy?"

I picked it up. "Yes, the shadow's there all right. It seems to be moving."

Angela thought she could see a white shadow.

Then Aunt Hudson examined it, but could see nothing, only darkness. "It seems all shadow," she said. "I must look at it in a good light with my glasses."

Val handed it to Jessie. "Can you see a shadow inside?" he asked.

Jessie could not. It was rather a test whether one could see that shadow.

"I hope it won't get out," I said. "We don't want a witch-doctor in the house upsetting things."

"Upsetting things?" The Brebis was mystified.

"Turning the milk sour, breaking the crockery, setting the chimneys on fire, scaring the maids."

Angela suggested a cork.

"But why?" asked the bewildered Brebis.

She had not heard Marjorie's story of—Chimbashi, was it? They had forgotten the witch-doctor's name. However, the horn was Chimbashi now. The children explained how it had belonged to a wizard who, by putting his shadow into it, obtained everything he desired and became a great king.

"How tre*men*dously interesting!" said the Brebis.

It was rather interesting, when you came to think of it, this translation of Chimbashi from witch-bound Africa to quiet Homersfield, where nothing more predatory invaded our life than a rabbit in the kitchen garden.

"It gave him great power over his enemies," Val continued.

"He tortured and burnt them, and when they were dead he jumped on their corpses," added Irene.

"My dear!" protested the Brebis.

The children had been reading adventure books. Heaven knows what visions of sorcery and midnight incantations Chimbashi conjured up, alarms, ambushes, massacres, tribal revolutions, superstitious dread!

Irene concluded, "And the chief put his captives to the most hideous forms of death. Some he disemboweled while they were still living."

"My dear, please do not tell me any more. Whoever can have put these dreadful ideas into your head?"

"But it is all right now," Irene added soothingly, to allay the Brebis's fears. "The shadow can't do anything now the Chief is dead. It must be your own shadow, you know."

Angela picked it up and looked into it again. "It does smell a little of Africa," she said.

Then as she lifted her cup, the handle fell off and spilt all the coffee over her dress, the beautiful Chinese alder dress which I had given her for a birthday present. She had put it on because she was going to the Sellingers' bazaar.

"There now!" she said, "it's quite done for."

Angela blamed Jessie. Rather unfairly, I thought, but Angela was unfair sometimes when she was hurt. As a great philosopher once said, we judge human actions by the pleasure or pain they give us.

"She must have broken the handle and glued it on without saying anything about it. She ought to have told me."

"Can't you wash it?" I suggested fatuously, and received a look of pitying scorn.

It was her Chinese alder dress, a light champagne colour. It had rows of intriguing black figures cunningly distributed on the sleeves and the neck and the hem of the skirt, like bars of music or Chinese characters. They reminded me of the fruit of the alder. That was why we called it the Chinese alder. It was quite ordinary stuff, I believe, and of a rigorous simplicity. I am not a connoisseur in these things, and it was too subtly conceived to reveal any contrivance; but I gathered that its worth lay in the way it happened to hang, so that, when Angela moved, it conformed rhythmically with the movement, more like a natural thing, a part of Angela, than a man-created integument.

"It just shows," she said, as she paused at the door. Angela had a way of pronouncing this formula with a positive and knowing emphasis.

What she meant, I suppose, was that her philosophy of the waylaying malice inherent even in inanimate things was vindicated once more. This time I was inclined to agree with her that it did show. The Chinese alder was the most valuable thing in the room which the discriminating Chimbashi could have chosen to begin his work upon.

I looked at the medicine-man's relic with increased interest. We must lock it up, I thought. A cork won't do.

The children gloated over their treasure, turning from one object to another. The smell of camphor pervaded the room. The purple emperor was being measured against the papilio. There was talk of a division of spoils. A communal collection was so dull. Val offered Irene the whole of the museum, even the purple emperor and the shoe made by the lunatic at Colney Hatch, if she would let him keep the papilio and the blue bird-winged butterfly and the dead-leaf insect for his very own. Irene, of course, rejected this offer with proper scorn. He threw in the Goliath beetle, but she laughed derisively, like a little box-wallah. She had a better idea of a deal. Val might keep the blue bird-winged butterfly and the dead-leaf insect if he gave her the papilio in exchange. "That's two for one," she conceded generously. The rest of the things they could divide, and draw lots for the first choice, like picking sides.

And so they bickered and chaffered. Chimbashi, of course, was indivisible.

Val picked it up again. "Let's wish for something," he said.

Irene jeered at his innocence.

"Don't be so silly. It's no good wishing if it's not your own shadow."

"My turn." She seized it from Val and pressed it to her eye like a telescope. "I wish Uncle Bliss could see it," she said.

Just at that moment we heard a boom in the hall. It was Ursa Major. The Brebis hurriedly snatched a book from the shelf, as if to cover her flight, and slipped through the conservatory into the garden. One might almost call it a scamper.

"Hullo! What have you got there?"

The children were triumphant. I believe they thought Uncle Bliss was going to be jealous, or "J," as they called it. However he admitted that it was quite a good papilio. And he told them how he had seen clouds of them about his camp, especially when his pots and pans had been scraped and were put out in the sun to dry. They were attracted by bright things. The blue bird-winged butterfly, too, and the dead-leaf insect were as common as cabbage-whites in Africa.

The children seemed disappointed. I disliked Uncle Bliss intensely.

But worse was to come. He derided Chimbashi. He said that it must have been a miserable specimen of an antelope. And why a single horn?

"Why didn't she send you the whole head while she was about it?" And he told them that he could give them a much better head, not that he *would* give them one. That might have been more palatable.

"But it belonged to a witch-doctor, it—"

Uncle Bliss generally listened to Irene, but this time somehow she couldn't get her meaning through to him. Impossible to make him understand the sacredness of Chimbashi, his magic attributes, his amazingly romantic history.

Val interposed stalwartly. "Please look inside, Uncle Bliss, and tell us if you can see the shadow."

"Shadow! There's no shadow except what you put into it. Depends how you hold it. Of course, if you go and shove your silly little head between it and the light there is bound to be a shadow."

And he did not even pick it up and look inside. Uncle Bliss was certainly not "in a good shape." It was the first time I had heard him snub the children. What had he come for, I wondered?

He had come to see me, it seemed, and about a lawyer. More litigation. He had just lost another big libel suit. Enormous costs. He wanted to change his firm of solicitors. They had landed him with a bill for over three thousand pounds. And now there were more legal complications about the purchase of the Clapperhouse. "They're a lot of saurians. Do you know what I had to pay for a stamp?" Also there was trouble with the workmen. "They don't know on which side their bread is buttered, but I'll show them!" Uncle Bliss was minatory in the shadow of these catastrophes. He shook his fist at them.

We walked up and down the garden path between the shrubbery and the summerhouse, while he expatiated upon the obstinacy and stupidity of lawyers, and how costly it was to him.

"What I want," he said, "is a man who will do what I tell him, and not argue about it, some one I can leave in charge."

"Are you going away?" I asked hopefully.

"Yes, to New York."

Uncle Bliss' new quest was the dinosaur's egg. It was on sale in the United States.

"I found a cable waiting for me when I got away from those pestilential teetotallers last night. There are other bidders."

"I suppose you will have to pay a pretty stiff price for it."

"Five figures, perhaps. But I won't let it go whatever it costs."

Here he stopped and began to puncture the gravel absent-mindedly with his walking-stick.

"Five figures! Yes. I'll find it. It's an investment. But I am not going to stand any more of their nonsense at the Clapperhouse. Seventy pounds for drains! Enough to feed a rhino for six months. And now they want to repair the roof. Say the rain is coming in. Let it come in. Servants' bedrooms! Let them sleep somewhere else. There's room enough. Saxby has just sent me in his estimate. Enough to pay my taxidermist's wages for a whole year."

Uncle Bliss was moving round in a slow circle, the sub-conscious part of him occupied with some design he was pricking out on the gravel.

"Saxby must go," he exploded. "He's about as much use as an anthropoid ape. Anyhow, I can't afford him. That's what I came to talk to you about. Lawyers! I want an economical man. And he must be able to look after an estate without pouring money into the drains. Now, what about your solicitor at Homerton?"

"Borett, you mean. He couldn't possibly take it on. Much too busy."

Borett was an old friend of mine. He wouldn't thank me for introducing Bliss in a business connection. I could imagine that he would very soon find a polite way of sending him to the devil.

"Why don't you advertise for an estate agent?" I suggested.

"I wanted you to help me."

"I am afraid I can't—" I began.

But Uncle Bliss interrupted me with an explosion of grunts. I cannot be sure of his exact words, but it sounded very like, "Then do the other thing."

"How long do you expect to be away?"

"In America? The inside of a month. Not more."

Uncle Bliss stepped off the gravel on to the grass, and surveyed his design, a fearsome creature like a gigantic lizard with a huge toothed beak and wings.

"What about the pterodactyl?" I asked him.

The pterodactyl, he told me, would have to wait. Until Christmas, perhaps. It would mean fitting out an expedition. And from New York he was going straight to the Pyrenees. He intended to be at Luchon before the end of October.

Luchon! It was one of the Brebis' haunts.

"Not baths!" I gasped.

"No, funguses. That is to say, a particular fungus. Amanita Caesarea, if you want to know." He described it. "Orange-red cap, yellow gills, frilled ring on the stem—"

"I didn't know you collected funguses."

"I collect everything."

There was nothing vulgarly sensational about Uncle Bliss' subjection to the tyranny of objects. He seemed to want this fungus every bit as much as the dinosaur's egg or the pterodactyl. In fact, he was putting off the pterodactyl for it. It was the children's museum again on a large scale, the lunatic's shoe, the envelope with forty-five postmarks on it, and now the Goliath beetle and the papilio. A more robust and adult curiosity, perhaps, but with little more science or method in it.

"It will look well on the drive," he said, "if I can get it to seed."

The vision of the orange cap and yellow gills had exorcised financial and litigious vapours.

"And while I am about it there are two plants I want to get the roots of, Monotropa and Lathræa. One ought to find them in the beech-woods at Luchon."

We had started our promenade again, and Uncle Bliss stopped to transfix a toadstool with the ferrule of his stick.

"Saprophytes both," he added, I supposed with reference to these plants of the Pyrenean beech-woods.

We were standing by the summer-house now, and I heard a nervous sheep-like cough inside.

Silly Brebis! She was quite safe. Why did she give herself away? I believe she thought saprophyte was a word that ought not to be overheard by a lady. I remember feeling rather doubtful about it myself when I heard Uncle Bliss use it in a figurative sense.

"Hullo!" said Ursa Major. "There's some one inside."

He kicked the door open, and discovered an elderly, rather frightened-looking lady with brown eyes and a Roman nose, and her hair pulled tightly back into a bun behind, sitting bolt upright in a deck-chair.

"You haven't met Mr. Bliss?" I said to Aunt Hudson, and introduced them.

"Who?" said Ursa Major.

"Miss Hudson. Irene's godmother. You must have met at the christening."

Aunt Hudson with a brebis-like movement slowly and stiffly propelled herself up out of her chair. It is a difficult movement to accomplish with grace, even if one is an agile person.

Irene's godfather and godmother shook hands.

"Yes, poor Dickenson, I never saw him again. He died when I was in Brazil."

Uncle Bliss' voice became quite gentle; he seemed lost in reflection. Dickenson was one of his earliest loyalties. Aunt Hudson subsided into her chair again, and began fingering her book.

I began to hope that the Brebis was going to escape without a scratch. There were risks, of course; still I could not decently detach Irene's godfather from Irene's godmother two minutes after they had been introduced. So, searching fatuously for common ground, I told the Brebis that Uncle Bliss was just going to the Pyrenees, and I told Uncle Bliss that Aunt Hudson had just come back from them, or not exactly the Pyrenees; it was Dax this year, wasn't it? But last year, and most other years, it was the Pyrenees.

"Were you at Luchon?" he asked her.

"Yes, last year."

"And Eaux Bonnes?"

"How high is it?"

"How high?"

"Yes, what's its elevation?"

"Oh, it's quite a long way up. I think it must be nearly three miles uphill from the station."

"But how high is it above the sea?"

"The sea isn't anywhere near."

"God bless my soul," said Uncle Bliss. "Do you know how high Mount Everest is?"

"Twenty-nine thousand feet." Aunt Hudson was relieved at this chance of displaying a little learning.

"Twenty-nine thousand feet above what?"

"Above where it starts from, I suppose."

"Above the sea." Uncle Bliss explained with singular patience. "You measure mountains by their elevation above the sea. Perhaps you remember the trees. That would give you some idea. Were they chestnut, beech, or pine?"

But Aunt Hudson could only remember a monkey-tree in the hotel garden.

"Can you tell me which side of the railway it is, east or west?"

"I am sorry, I don't understand."

"Humph!" growled Ursa Major, "you wouldn't. Perhaps you can tell me how it stands to Eaux Chaudes?"

"Oh, that's quite simple. The same charabanc takes you to both."

The Brebis was becoming ruffled and confused. She was sitting bolt upright still in her deck-chair with her book in her lap, a finger marking the place, looking up

apprehensively into Uncle Bliss' biscuit-coloured beard
and purple face, as a sheep sometimes surveys a dog
through a hole in a fence. It seemed a long while, but I do
not think Ursa Major had been baiting her more than forty
seconds when I took him by the sleeve, and, exercising my
counter-boom, bawled into his ear, "Come to the library.
We'll look it up in the map."

But how to get the Brebis safely back into the home
pastures? One could not leave her in that perplexed ovine
attitude, suspended between retreat and defiance, peep-
ing through the hedge, tapping the ground with her foot,
so to speak. I tried to think of some conclusion to Uncle
Bliss' catechism which would leave her more appropriately in possession, less like a brebis who had been dragged
through a bush.

"You're going to let me drive you to the bazaar?" I
reminded her. "You know Angela is lunching with the Sellingers?"

The Brebis hesitated. She was very nervous about driving, so nervous that she had not trusted herself in a high
two-wheeled vehicle for over twenty-five years; but as I
was such a very safe driver, and Joan so very quiet and
sure-footed between the shafts, she was going to take her
courage in both hands, just for once, and drive with me in
the dog-cart to the Sellingers'.

The Brebis laid down her conditions. "If you promise
to be very careful, and not to use the whip, and to walk
downhill. Joan doesn't stumble, does she?"

I couldn't promise about the whip, as Joan might go to
sleep, and then she would stumble. As to the other conditions, I could be conscientiously reassuring.

"I am going to be very brave," the Brebis said, "and it
will be tre*men*dously exciting.

She was quite the bell-wether now, no longer a baited
brebis, entangled in brambles.

I ought to have left it at that, but I was fool enough to ask her what she was reading.

Aunt Hudson picked up her book, which she had snatched from the shelf when she heard Uncle Bliss in the hall, and looked at the title. She had not the vaguest idea what she was reading. It was a novel by Martha Caraway.

"I was just choosing one," she explained.

"You like novels? Eh?"

"No," said Aunt Hudson, "I can't say I do, not enough to read them seriously. I read one sometimes for an hour after dinner to pass the time when I am not feeling intellectual."

"And what do you read when—"

"The map's in the library," I bawled at him. He was going to say "when you *are* feeling intellectual," but I was just in time. He turned to me and shouted, "I am not deaf." For once his dynamic resources yielded to mine. I morally propelled him through the door. But it was difficult to dovetail Ursa Major into an apologetic exit.

VII

THE ANTELOPE'S HORN

In the library I conveyed to Uncle Bliss that he would be more welcome if he did not bully my guests.

"Bully your guests? Who?"

"You were not very polite to Miss Hudson."

"Not polite. That's a pity. Stupid woman. She knows nothing. I was telling her; that's all."

I was surprised that he was not more resentful, but he answered me absentmindedly, without giving the matter a thought, as he turned over the pages of the gazetteer. "She reminds me of a pigeon," he continued. Then added ungallantly, "with the brains taken out." Trifles like the susceptibilities of Miss Hudson, or my opinion of his behaviour to my guests, did not come into the focus of his preoccupation.

I rather hoped that he would go off in a huff. It would have meant that we should have seen less of him, perhaps nothing at all. Anyhow, what with the dinosaur and the mushroom and the pterodactyl, the tranquility of Homersfield for the next few months at least seemed to be assured.

While he was determining Pyrenean altitudes and directions, I took the opportunity to find out what a saprophyte meant, and was relieved when the dictionary told me that it was nothing more opprobrious than a vegetable organism which lived on decaying organic matter. Not a bad term of abuse! I wondered if the Brebis would have the curiosity to look it up too.

It had been a tempestuous morning for her and all of us, and I don't wonder she was not herself at lunch. The Brebis was accustomed to respect and a number of small attentions from the family, and she had been spoken to scoldingly as if she were a little girl who had forgotten her catechism. She admitted that she was "feeling at a very low par." She attempted to evade going to the Sellingers', but I thought it would be good for her, and coaxed her to come with me. The bazaar was for a pious object; Renton Magna Church was to have a new organ; all the clergymen in the neighbourhood would be there. She hesitated. Was I quite sure that dreadful man would not be there? I told her that it was very unlikely, and if he did happen to be there, I would smuggle her off at once. In at one gate and out at the other.

"In fact," I said, "I do not think we are likely to see much of Uncle Bliss for a very long time."

"He is going to New York, Aunt Huddy," Irene volunteered.

"And to Africa," added Val.

"And to the Pyrenees."

"Oh, my dear," said the Brebis, "how mercifully distant."

The children had been talking to Uncle Bliss. They met him outside the gate, and he got off his bicycle to say good-bye, and he gave Irene a shilling.

"He was not half so cross," Irene said.

"He was in a much better shape," said Val. "I think it is because of the dinosaur's egg. Daddy, what does five figures mean?"

"Five figures means having everything you want, everything that money can buy, ponies, dogs, fishing-rods, cricket-bats, lovely presents for Mummy, Persian carpets so soft that you can't hear when anybody comes into the

room. It means turning bad land into good, stocking the
Homer with trout, making ugly things pretty, poor people
comfortable, and workhouses unnecessary. If you have five
figures and miss a train, you can order another one all to
yourself, or an aeroplane if you want to get anywhere in a
hurry; you can fly to Paris after lunch and come back with
marrons glacés for tea; or you can keep a yacht and go anywhere you like—up the Amazon where there are butterflies
as big as birds, and birds as bright as butterflies, and no
people at all; or to Monte Carlo, if you prefer society;
and if you have rheumatism, you needn't go to those horrid French baths, you can have the water brought to you.
Five figures means leading a quiet life or an eventful one,
just as you choose; telling other people to mind their own
business and not to poke their noses into yours; marrying
a princess as beautiful as Mummy, if you could find one,
which, of course, you couldn't, and buying her a new pair
of seed-pearl earrings every day; and generally behaving
like a fairy godfather or godmother, and giving everybody
you are fond of, whether they deserve it or not, a perfectly
scrumptious time—"

"What a bee-*ut*-iful picture," said the Brebis.

"Or if you prefer it, instead of enjoying all these good
things, you can become the sole possessor of the only
dinosaur's egg in the world."

"Has Uncle Bliss got five figures?" Irene asked.

"He has got six. Very nearly seven, I believe."

Val, after a process of mental subtraction, arrived at
the conclusion that if Uncle Bliss bought the dinosaur's
egg he would still have two figures left, and that would be
enough to buy nearly half the other things as well.

I admitted the substantial accuracy of this calculation.
Val had, if anything, underestimated Uncle Bliss' resources.

"He could buy a motor-car," Irene suggested, "and sell
his bicycle."

Then Val had a brilliant idea. Supposing the egg hatched. The new dinosaur might have half a dozen more eggs. Then Uncle Bliss would be the richest man in the world. Six eggs at five figures. That would be thirty figures.

The Brebis' arithmetic was a little better than this. "Six figures is a hundred thousand pounds, isn't it? My dear, what wealth! And isn't it rather miserly of him not to keep a motor-car?"

The children's loyalty was up in arms. Misers were associated in their adventure books with hangmen, spies, informers, and such mean fry, not with explorers and big-game hunters. Irene defended her hero.

"He gave me a shilling," she announced, blushing generously.

Val thought that he was going to get one too.

"He put his hand in his pocket, and kept it there quite a long time, as if he was thinking of something else. But when he pulled it out there was nothing in it, and he told Irene to give me half hers."

"He must have hated parting with that shilling," I said.

"Then you really think he *is* a miser," the Brebis said.

"No, he is a collector," I explained, "and that means he is not a distributor. The difference between a miser and Uncle Bliss is that one collects money and the other dinosaurs' eggs and pterodactyls. When you get into the habit of collecting banknotes or extinct animals, it hurts frightfully having to spend a shilling on anything else."

Irene was so sorry for Uncle Bliss that she wished she had not taken the shilling, but she quite saw the point when I explained that that would have hurt him more. What was to be done? She couldn't give the shilling back.

"I know," she said; "I will offer it as a subscription for the dinosaur's egg. Of course, he can keep the whole egg, but that little part of it will be mine.

"Half of it," said Val. "The other half will be mine. We each have a sixpenny share."

Irene had not thought of that. She looked at Val with the contempt of the gallery for Shylock after the fifth act. What a grasping spirit! The division of these very problematical shares might have ended in a serious misunderstanding if I had not intervened.

"No," I said, "you can't do that. Giving you the shilling made Uncle Bliss feel comfortable inside. Don't you remember what a bad shape he was in when he came and found you gloating over the things Marjorie sent you?"

"He didn't seem to like them much," Irene conceded.

"And do you know why?"

"Because he was J?"

"Yes, but J of what?"

"Of the papilio and the Goliath beetle, I suppose."

"No, you little goose, J of Marjorie, of course."

It occurred to me that Uncle Bliss would be happier if he gave some one who did not expect it a shilling every day.

"When is he going to America?" Aunt Hudson asked. "I hope very soon."

"Perhaps to-morrow."

"And we haven't seen the museum," Val wailed, "or the menagerie. He might have shown us the cages even if the animals weren't there."

"And on Monday Miss Seamore is coming, and we will have to go out for walks and begin lessons again."

"Whimp, whimp, whimp!" I bleated, which was the family word for "wail."

But I was sorry for the children. Miss Seamore was a good soul, but she quickened the fugitive instinct in the young and the old. It was the end of the holidays, and I remembered how I used to hate ends. And all Uncle Bliss' promises had evaporated in smoke, those visions of the enchanted land in which you met stuffed hippopotamuses and lionesses with cubs, and the incredible lake with its crocodiles, and turtles, and beavers, and seals, and the king penguin who would only bow when it was cold.

"He is waiting until he has unpacked all his cases," I told them, "and got things ship-shape. When he comes back from New York he will ask you to go and see them; and if he doesn't, I will take you over myself without being asked. And now if you want to know what the pterodactyl is like. Uncle Bliss has drawn a picture of it in the garden. Look for it on the gravel. A penny for whoever finds it first."

The children walked to the bazaar. Irene was in charge of a bran-pie, and Val commissioned to help in restoring the balls that were thrown at the coco-nuts. We passed them in the dogcart, and they caught us up when we had to walk up or downhill. Joan was sleepy, and I wished I had not yielded to the Brebis' entreaties to leave the whip behind. However, we arrived safely, Val and Irene hanging on at the back.

To the Brebis' great relief, Uncle Bliss was not at the bazaar. But everybody was talking about him. The dinosaur's egg was coming to Renton Parva. There was a cable from New York about it in 'The Times.' There was a photograph of the Clapperhouse in the 'Daily Megaphone,' and large headlines. Uncle Bliss had again achieved fame. The pygmy incident was recalled. He was referred to as "the famous African hunter," "the intrepid explorer." The impending purchase, for it appeared that the deal was not concluded yet, was described as a patriotic action. It was "a matter of congratulation that the relics of this fabulous monster should find a resting-place on British soil." A pleasing omission was that there was no photograph of Uncle Bliss. Reporters and press photographers had tried

to waylay him before, but he had a short way with them,
It was in an earlier phase of notoriety that he met a dep-
utation of pressmen on the doorstep of a house at which
he was staying. The door was suddenly flung open, and he
burst upon them with a gun in his hand, purple with rage,
and threatened to send them off with a charge of No. 8 in
their calves if they gave him any more trouble. Nothing of
this got into the papers.

Knowing Uncle Bliss, I was rather tickled at the idea of
taking him seriously. His only claim to respect seemed to
be that he was a man of resolution. But naturally Renton
Magna was interested, possibly a little contemptuous and
"J."

"The press does exaggerate things so," Mrs. Sellinger said.

"What is he paying for it?" Sellinger asked me. "Do you
happen to know?"

"Five figures, I believe."

"Pity we couldn't touch him for the organ."

This set Renton Magna calculating.

"Twenty organs for one dinosaur egg. Expensive kind
of fowl! Pity we can't run a dinosaur farm ourselves. Why
didn't you bring him with you?"

"My dear," said Mrs. Sellinger, "do try and be a little
more sympathetic. He is bringing it home to England, you
know."

I took off my hat to the editor of the 'Megaphone.' Is
there any village in which the blare of his instrument is
not heard?

Roger Clarkson of the British Museum happened to be
at the bazaar, the Archdeacon's nephew, and a mine of
information about dinosaurs and pterodactyls, and other
unfamiliar fowl—or reptiles? He, of course, knew Bliss,
and smiled at our notion of his scientific attainments.
Bliss a naturalist! Bliss with his extravagant and puerile
theories, the laughing-stock of learned societies.

"We all hide when he comes to the Museum. He rolled in one day, literally rolled, with the skin of a young giraffe in his pocket, which contained among other things his lunch and a folding butterfly-net; and he tried to persuade us that it was an okapi. But you can't argue with him; it only makes him rude. He still thinks he has shot an okapi. Ask him to show you the skin. Have you seen his stuffed specimens?"

Sellinger had not. He supposed the collection would soon be on view at the Clapperhouse.

"If so, don't miss it," said Clarkson. "Inflated golly-wogs. Bags of sawdust."

"Does he stuff them himself?"

"No, he has got a taxidermist of sorts. A queer fellow. I don't know where he picked him up."

"Staff?" I suggested.

"Yes, that's his name. Wears corduroys, and has got the most unholy squint. 'Bliss' Sancho Panza' we call him. He goes with him everywhere—Bloomsbury or Timbuctoo. Bliss took him to the Museum one day, to broaden his mind, I suppose; but the stolid Staff was not impressed. They stumped through all the rooms in the Natural History section. This took them about an hour. Then Bliss brought him into my office, and I asked him what he thought of it. All he said was, 'I didn't see anything there to frighten me.'"

Staff's exhibits, on the contrary, were positively startling. His British specimens might pass in the parlour of an inn. But Bliss' African trophies! Clarkson described them. A taxidermist in these days must be something of a specialist, he reminded us. A little knowledge of comparative anatomy is essential; otherwise you can't give the animal the air of being alive. The bones must be properly articulated. You can generally tell by the way an exhibit is mounted whether the taxidermist knows anything about its habits. To be really first-class at his work he must be a naturalist first, then an artist. But Staff was untrained. "He hasn't got the most elementary idea of anatomy," Clarkson concluded. "Neither has Bliss for that matter."

My loyalty was stirred at this. I don't know why, but I felt that I must champion Uncle Bliss. I was beginning to feel as sorry for him as I had been for the Brebis a few hours earlier. Why? Ursa Major was a hectoring bully. He stood as firm on his feet as a colossus. Four-square. Where did the pathos come in?

And he had the doughty Staff for his Sancho Panza. We had heard a great deal about Staff, a devoted squire, if an indifferent taxidermist. He had once saved Bliss' life. Bliss kept him on because he liked him. Also because he was cheap. Two very good reasons. I mentioned the first to Clarkson, who did not seem to understand the alliance.

"Bliss' Sancho Panza" was very apt. I had not thought of him in that light, nor of Bliss as a pathetic or romantic figure. Clarkson must have started the current of sympathy when he derided Staff, and it flowed from the squire to the knight. I told Clarkson that old Dickenson used to think a lot of Bliss.

"Yes," he said, "according to Dickenson, Bliss was a promising lad at Cambridge. Keen. What's wrong with him is that he has never grown up. An *enfant gaté*. Too much money, I suppose. Swollen head. Not that that's a bad thing. Very useful in business. Less room for other heads. But in science it won't do. There you have the anthropometric standard."

"He is not self-conscious," I objected. "I don't believe he thinks of himself in relation to other people."

Clarkson admitted that there was no vanity in Bliss. He described him rather happily as "an uninstructed appetite." Acquisitiveness was his strong point.

Sellinger defended Ursa Major. "I like him," he said. "I hope he gets his dinosaur's egg, and that Sancho Panza doesn't sit on it."

Here Lady Potter rustled past and bowed to our group stiffly.

"She has discovered that alcohol is on sale in the refreshment tent," Sellinger suggested.

"Or she hasn't got over last night."

Clarkson smiled. The Archdeacon had told him about the dinner. "I haven't met Bliss lately," he said, "but I hear his manners have not improved."

We watched our hostess of last night buttonhole the Archdeacon, and saw him turn and gaze with affected concern at the refreshment tent.

"Personally," said Sellinger, "I prefer a pothouse to a Potterhouse. A dose or two of Bliss would do Lady Potter a lot of good. Don't you agree with me? Last night was the first time I enjoyed a dinner in that house."

Instinctively we gravitated towards the refreshment tent. Sellinger was still commending Bliss when a maid brought him a telegram. It was from Marjorie.

"Miss Ismay has had an accident," he told us. "Broken her arm. Infernal bad luck! A motor smash, I suppose. We expected her to lunch, and she was going to stay the night."

"Miss Ismay is the only woman traveller I like," Clarkson observed.

Sellinger agreed. He detested the Amazonian tribe generically. "Dianas in puttees." "Mrs. Winterbotham," they say, "hammers her coolies."

"And her husband," Clarkson emended.

He quoted other flagrant examples. Lady Vertigo, who would stand on her head to collect a crowd. Miss Carmine, who collected the photographers at Port Said by wireless. Madame Waddilove, or *qu'est ce que vous aimez,* as they called her in Constantinople, the Turcophile. "She's got a street named after her in Stamboul." I wished Angela could have heard us; a pet theory of hers is the existence of the "man-gossip."

Sellinger didn't believe they really enjoyed it. "Like to get themselves talked about. Picture in the 'Tatler,' and all that. Now Miss Ismay—"

"Has a sense of humour," I put in.

"I like her laugh," said Clarkson.

"Yes, Marjorie is a sportswoman," our host concluded, "and remarkably good-looking too. Extraordinary thing the sun hasn't spoilt her complexion. Critchley's a lucky fellow."

Here I saw a chance of a home for Chimbashi. I described Miss Ismay's latest contribution to the museum.

"She is a great ally of the children," Sellinger said. "She was unpacking her African cases all yesterday, worse luck, or she might have been here."

I strategically unfolded the story of the witch-doctor's shadow in the antelope's horn. Then I asked Clarkson if they were interested in African talismans in the museum. Talismans and totems, it appeared, were a speciality in the ethnological section.

"I wonder if they would like Chimbashi."

Sellinger protested. "You don't mean to say that you are going to give Marjorie's present away?"

"Of course, I will ask her first."

"And Irene? She will have something to say to it. Can you see her endowing the nation? Don't tell me that she is such a precociously public-spirited young lady as all that. We shall have her going in for causes soon, teetotalism—"

"I can square Irene," I said. "That will be quite easy."

"But really, Clayton, why this sudden access of public spirit?"

I was spared explanations. The broad and kindly Mrs. Sellinger filled the door of the tent.

"Well," she said, "you are not very energetic. Why aren't you spending money?"

"We are," Sellinger retorted, putting down his glass. "How are things going?"

"Not fast enough."

We rose guiltily.

"We must make things hum more," said our host. "Let's go and have a dip in Irene's bran-pie."

We made short work of Irene's department. It was closed in five minutes, and her moneybox full. It took us nearly an hour to spend half a crown each on the coconuts. When we had released the children we made the tour of the stalls. Their pockets were soon Blissfully bulging. I remember a round table with edges like a tray and a slowly revolving beam with a feather at the end which brushed through a succession of numbered openings in the rim, wobbled, hesitated, and came to a stop in one. It was most tre*men*dously exciting, as the Brebis would say. For if it happened to be your number, you were given the choice of all objects in the stall. Irene carried off a box with shells on the lid and a comb to give to Jessie. And Val chose a tooth glass. He wanted one of his own to keep his water-beetles in. Then nobody would mind if he broke it. Jessie had emptied his last beetle with a company of newts into the sink. The difficulty among this superfluity of china dogs and india-rubber babies with glistening behinds was to find something really suitable for Miss Seamore. The children's number kept coming up, but nothing would quite do, and in the end we had to solve the problem by a tip, which they converted into a lace collar at Angela's stall.

Angela, who had accepted a lift in a friend's motor, left before us, and after a final visit to the marquee with Sellinger, I collected the children and disengaged the Brebis from a beatific *tête-à-tête* with the Archdeacon, that sworn enemy of ritualism. There were others of her "persuasion" at the bazaar, for it was an evangelical neighbourhood, and I noticed a safe-in-the-fold look in her eye when she was talking to them. Her head had been very close to the Archdeacon's. "I have had the most delightful afternoon," she said, as I helped her up into her high seat. Luckily the children walked home.

It was a lovely still September evening, clear overhead; only a single bank of clouds in the west absorbed all the fire of the sun. It was almost too bright and fiery. Angela, who liked quiet colours, would have called it loud. The Brebis and I did not spoil it by chatter; we just drank it in. It was the hour of reflection. Heavenly tranquility of a September evening, when the corn shocks standing in the fields grow spectral and ghostly, and the tawny owls call to one another, an almost human cry, and one begins to smell the dew.

The only small cloud on the horizon was Miss Seamore. Buying her presents had reminded me of what the children called ends. I hated her coming just as much as they did. No more intimate dinners with Angela when Aunt Hudson had gone! When Miss Seamore was anywhere near she was ubiquitous. And she talked incessantly and didactically. Still we had nearly five days left. We must send the children to school a term earlier. That would be a way out. Now if Chimbashi would turn his attention to Miss Seamore—

Chimbashi had been indulgent all the afternoon, but I had a suspicion that he was lying low, "a sort of feeling," as Angela says, something premonitory in the air. When I got home I was going to put him away.

Supposing he began again on Miss Seamore. A touch of lumbago, say. Nothing serious, of course. I should hate it if Chimbashi hurt her, but some small impediment to her locomotion. I thought of Marjorie. Marjorie and the witch-doctor's shadow. What a pity she wasn't at the bazaar! If it hadn't been for those African cases— It only then dawned on me, thickhead that I was. She must have unpacked Chimbashi yesterday.

It was growing dusk. A nightjar began churring in an oak coppice. The cows loomed in the mist like huge black barges silhouetted in cotton wool. Lights began to appear in farm windows. At the next rise I should have to stop and light up. Poor Marjorie! I hoped her arm would soon mend. It was absurd to think of Chimbashi waylaying Miss Seamore; he was not an ally.

Joan! Impossible! Shadow of Chimbashi! What had happened? I was lying on the road on the top of the Brebis, who was clasping Joan's neck.

An hour later Angela in one of her reconnaissances from the hall doorstep saw by the light of the moon a melancholy procession coming up the drive. The Brebis was alone in the dogcart, lying like a dislocated sack across the seat, clinging on to the rail with both hands. Her bonnet had slipped round to the back of her head, and under the string two little wisps of fluffy grey hair stuck out like sheep's ears. The muscles of her poor neck seemed to be functionless. And I was between the shafts wheeling her in. Or, there was only one shaft; the other was on the road somewhere. I had left the broken-kneed Joan tied up to a gate.

We dined alone. We had not met since breakfast, and I had the history of a full day to relate. Uncle Bliss made history rapidly; he spun it out like yarn. I began at the beginning with his brusquerie with the children and his derision of Chimbashi. Angela agreed that he was "J" of Marjorie. That would explain Irene's shilling. And she believed that Chimbashi had broken Marjorie's arm. To

Angela he was an accomplice of the Disciplinary Spirit, the providence that presided over the lucklessness of the Claytons—and their friends, standing like a signpost at the cross-roads with a finger pointing to the unfortunate turning.

"We must get rid of him," I said.

"What's the good?" She meant that even if we could depose him there would be another totem waiting to take his place. "We are not lucky people," she said. "I wish somebody would leave us some money. Is it true that Uncle Bliss has bought the dinosaur's egg?"

"He is going to New York to buy it at once. Perhaps to-morrow. And then to Africa to bag this pterodactyl. Oh, I forgot the Pyrenees. He is taking them *en route.*" I tried to remember the name of the attractive fungus.

"Chimbashi precipitated him on the poor Brebis," I added. "He put her through a Pyrenean catechism, and she obtained no marks."

Here Angela left me to see how Aunt Hudson was getting on with her soup.

"She's finished it," she said when she came back, "and would like an omelette." The Brebis was not really hurt, only bruised and a little dazed. She thought she heard Uncle Bliss' footsteps.

I was not surprised. I told Angela how infernally rude he had been to her in the summer-house.

"I had literally to drag him off."

"We really can't have him here again," Angela repeated.

"When I tackled him about it afterwards, he didn't seem to take it in. He was too wrapped up in himself. Do you know, I can't explain why, I wanted to kick him at the time, but now I am rather sorry for him."

"Yes," said Angela, and I saw that she knew what I meant. She could probably have explained it, which was more than I could.

"Clarkson was talking about him to-day. I had not realised how futile he was. A standing joke. He knows about
as much natural history as you will find in Pliny."

"Ridiculous in everything except his loyalties."

"Staff, for instance. Bliss' Sancho Panza they call him
at the Museum."

Angela admitted that Staff would make a creditable
Sancho Panza, only the knight was missing. You couldn't
have a Sancho Panza without a Quixote.

Bliss was not quixotic. I granted her the antithesis in
the ideal, but I still felt there was a lurking analogy somewhere. In the illusions, perhaps?

"In harrying Brebis," Angela suggested, which reminded her that it was time to go and see Aunt Huddy again.

We had our coffee in the library, where Jessie had lighted a
fire, our first fire. It was the first really cold evening with
an autumnal nip in the air. When Angela rejoined me, I
was piling on more logs.

"She is fast asleep," she said.

Fast asleep. I wondered what she was dreaming about.
Two guesses, I was afraid, would cover the field of the
Brebis' subliminal adventures—a rude, aggressive, bearded, purple man, and an immensely high and shaky vehicle
on the edge of an abyss. But dreams, like cocktails, are
generally mixed, and I hoped there was a little allaying
archdeacon in it.

"I wish Joan had not let me down," I said.

"Joan let *you* down? I thought it was the other way."

"Joan or Chimbashi; it is the same thing. What do you
think she is dreaming about?"

Angela couldn't imagine. Possibly Uncle Bliss.

I thought I heard a rustle of paper on the writing-table
in the corner. There was no draught. I got up and found
Chimbashi in possession. The children had left him there

in the innocent guise of a paper-weight. I locked him securely in a drawer.

Then I returned to the fire and the bellows. Angela pointed to a white-hot metallic-looking object in the embers, and I fished it out with the tongs. We examined it curiously, but could not make it out at first. It looked like a cigarette-case, but it was too big for Angela's, and I had left mine in the pocket of my coat upstairs. When we had turned it over two or three times and it began to cool, a dragon's eye under a red mane defined itself on the metal. If we had fished a salamander out of the fire we could not have been more startled. It *was* my cigarette-case, Japanese silver-work, cunningly chased. Angela gave it me. It was her pet dragon, abundant in symbolism. It breathed out fire with an enigmatic leer.

"Who put it there?"

I was on the point of quoting her familiar adage, but it was superfluous. It more than just showed. Chimbashi had a style of his own; his *griffe* was unmistakable. There was his signature in the ashes.

He had a balanced mind had Chimbashi. He dealt out malice evenly with both hands, my last present to Angela, and Angela's last present to me. And the morning and the evening were the first day.

"That settles it," I said. "Chimbashi must go."

When we had restored our dragon to the fire, its proper element, and covered it decently with ashes, Angela departed sorrowfully to bed. She reminded me to be very careful in seeing that all the doors and windows were fastened.

When she had gone I took down the folio edition of 'Don Quixote' in two volumes, with the Gustave Doré illustrations, translated into French by Louis Viardot, and began to search for the elusive analogy. But I could not find it. Uncle Bliss was a prosaic figure, and deficient in courtesy. He did not seek adventure for the profit of the necessitous. Nor was he emulous of honour. He did not care a rap whether his name was writ in bronze or water. And Dulcinea was not in the picture. Also, I had my suspicions of his liberality. If he won his kingdom, would Sancho Panza come into his island? I doubted it.

I dozed off with the huge tome on my knees open at the picture of the *grand lac de poix-résine bouillant à gros bouillons, dans lequel nagent et s'agitent une infinité de serpents, de couleuvres, de lézards, et mille autres espèces d'animaux féroces et épouvantables.* The lanky knight was on the brink ready to dig his spurs into Rosinante, but gazing at pictures in the clouds, not at the *lac effrayable* which was swarming with dinosaurs and pterodactyls—like the "black hole of death" in the Jiundu swamp. The scaly brutes had scented him, and were serpentining up the cliff.

Had I turned the key on Chimbashi? I was too lazy to get out of my chair and look. Uncle Bliss on Rosinante was becoming narrow and elongated; he and his lance were like two peers, one the shadow of the other. A saurian was turning his flank, and there was an octopus coming up behind, both big enough to swallow Rosinante, who, by the way, was looking ominously groggy about the knees.

The tome fell with a thud on the fender, and lay open at the picture of Don Quixote suffering chastisement at the hands of the muleteer. Immortal ironist!

I looked at the plate for a sign, my sortes Virgilianæ, for nobody had asked the tome to open at this page. But I was no nearer a clue. Where was the pathetic parallel? Let the pundits laugh at him as much as they liked, I could not picture Uncle Bliss lying on his broad back in the mud and being hammered by the canaille. It would be tragic indeed if there were anything infirm in the pedestal of this magnificently autonomous being.

What sort of a picture would Doré have made out of the hunter of the pterodactyl? Or Cervantes? Or Milton? I thought of Samson Agonistes. Again I nodded.

Tragedy? Sublimity? No. I was getting colder. The knight of La Mancha was nearer. Pathos. Bathos. And so in a ring. A vicious circle. The analogy evaded me.

Finally I fell asleep and entered a land where things had definite shapes, even abstract things, and you could see into them, and there were no fugitive values, or problems, or doubts. Here I bestrode the shaft of a broken cart and watched Sancho Panza sit on the dinosaur's egg until it hatched and ate him.

VIII
SENTENCE ON CHIMBASHI

The next morning Angela and Irene and Val and I held a court on Chimbashi in the garden. He had destroyed Angela's Chinese alder dress; he had caused Ursa Major to harry the Brebis; he had hurled Aunt Hudson from her high seat in the dog-cart on to the hard road, bruised and frightened her, and destroyed for ever her confidence in vehicular locomotion and in me as a driver; he had broken Joan's knees, Marjorie's arm, the shaft of the cart, and my reputation; and he had thrown the cigarette-case which Angela gave me into the fire.

The unanimous verdict was, guilty. The sentence, capital punishment. But this was afterwards commuted to imprisonment for life.

The children were quite reconciled to Chimbashi's fate. I believe they would have enjoyed making a bonfire of him—with the proper ritual, of course. For they entered into the spirit of the tribunal, and prepared the altar and the stage. This was the true romance. Were we not fighting for our lives with a malignant spirit? The court was held under the catalpa, which did office for the Juju tree. Chimbashi lay naked and exposed, and, as we were all secretly aware, impenitent, on the round green table which was part of the perennial summer furniture of the garden.

On the tray beside him were placed the customary offerings to the presiding Juju—a chicken, a plantain, and a yam. For the chicken a fowl was requisitioned out of Noah's ark; the yam and plantain I modelled out of bread crumbs. Val intermittently belaboured a tom-tom, which he had disinterred from a cupboard of derelict toys. Only the sacrificial goat was missing.

When Chimbashi's sentence had been commuted, mainly out of respect for Marjorie, as we could not very well burn her present without asking her, we carried him in procession to the attic for internment. His prison was a long box which the children called "the sea chest." It smelt as if it had once contained apples, but it was now used for storing theatrical properties. One could distinguish the glitter of a cuirass and helmet and other frippery through the cracks between the loosely-joined boards of the lid. The key was in the lock, and I opened it and held Chimbashi at arm's length over his dungeon while I repeated the spell—

"Eye of lizard. Eye of hyena. Eye of cat. Witness that the shadow of Chimbashi is interned!

"Claw of leopard. Horn of bison. Tooth of lion. Tusk of pig. Stand by me in what I am about to do!

"Eyes of the forest. Eyes of the river. Eyes of the lake. Look to it that this evil one breaks not bonds!"

Chimbashi fell without protest into the strangely assorted company of the sea chest.

But who was going to turn the key on him? It complicates matters when the prisoner is in a position to retaliate, and this was the ultimate provocation. Val and Irene boldly volunteered, but while they disputed the point I turned the key myself. Then to make doubly sure I locked the attic behind me and put both keys in my pocket. "Now," I said, "let him get out if he can."

"That's that," said Angela.

But it was not the whole of it by a very long chalk. Chimbashi had been swaddled impotently in a packing-case at Marjorie's agent's for more than a year, and it was not likely that he would expend his bottled-up malice in a few hours.

We had a slight repercussion in the afternoon. A tele-gram from Miss Seamore asking if she might come on Saturday instead of Monday. Her mother was going on a round of visits and wanted to shut up house. I read it out at tea.

"Whimp! whimp! whimp!" from the children.

This was no light affliction. Saturday was the day after to-morrow, and she was coming by the morning train.

"I am not sure that it would not have been better if we had sent him right away," Angela observed.

"The sentence need not be final," I reminded her. "Marjorie is the High Court. A word from her, and Chimbashi burns. Ashes have no shadows."

"The sea chest is not dark or air-tight enough."

She evidently thought that the totem was projecting his shadow.

"Isn't there any one we could have given him to?"

I thought of all the people I didn't like, but I was not vindictive enough.

"Mummy," said Val, "don't you think Lady Potter would like it?"

I was rather taken with the idea, but hypocritically denounced the code of the head-hunter. I mentioned the alternative of transportation to the British Museum. Clarkson seemed to think that they would be keen on giving him a home. He could not do much harm there. Too many other Jujus. In the anthropological section, I had no doubt, he would be enfiladed by rays as malignant as his own. Cross-circuited all round. He would have a struggle to live. Besides, think of the massive weight and

respectability of Bloomsbury. A rebellious sprite in room
XIII! Chimbashi would have about as much chance as a
b••• n••••• butting against the British Empire.

The attic seemed to have quietened him down a bit.
I comforted myself that his influence was declining. The
Brebis joined us at dinner, and was almost herself again.
The children dined with us, a tacit compensation for the
imminence of Miss Seamore. There was a general sense of
"as you were" in the air except that I was feeling an increase
of my malaise. Chimbashi, when I came to think of it, was
the direct agent here too. Wheeling the Brebis home had
rather taken it out of me, and I had been ordered to avoid
strain and go slow. The collective verdict of Harley Street
might be summed up in three words, "Conservation of en-
ergy." Then, perhaps in a few months— It was nearly time
for my next Board. But I never allowed myself to consider
the possibility of being turned down by the medicos.

It was a bore having to give up tennis. And I had missed
Sellinger's shoot. I was not allowed to walk up partridges
in the turnips; I could shoot driven birds, but that was
not the same thing. There remained the river, and that
reminded me; if the weather held, we were going to have a
family picnic on Saturday, a sort of annual festival at the
end of the holidays. I would take my rod, and Angela her
work or a French novel—she had just discovered Colette
Willy; and the children their lines for eels. Angela always
hoped that they wouldn't catch one. Irene did catch one
once, and cut it in halves, and the livelier half got into
her work-basket. Then I remembered Miss Seamore. How
had we ever let ourselves be saddled with the spectre?
Fatal and misplaced kindness of Angela! And how were we
to unsaddle? In voice and gait and angularity and decision she conformed to the type which French tradition has
associated, quite erroneously, with the normal English-
woman. One meets them more often on the Continent

than in our happy island. *Cookesses* is their name for them, *osseuses et sévères, rébarbatives, qui mangent à longues dents, épouvantails à moineaux.* Miss Seamore's bones hung all wrong. They were less successfully articulated than many of Staff's mounted exhibits, and her clothes were not designed to modify, or even to adapt themselves to, these projections.

I confess to a bias for pretty and pleasant-looking women, and I can bear with ugliness in its many attractive forms; it is when the outer seems to be shaped by the inner that prejudice is cruel and illogical. Miss Seamore's mind was as hard and angular as her body. She was a very literal woman, the last person in the world to see the shadow in the antelope's horn. Chimbashi would have provoked a sermon at the breakfast table, some long-winded homily on superstition. But I doubt if Irene or Val would have given her the chance. They were uncommonly perceptive young people for their years.

I had continually to remind myself that Miss Seamore was "a good soul." That was Angela's euphemism. But I was not going to let her goodness spoil our last Saturday. Something must be done to dispel the blight. I thought it all out. We should have our picnic just the same, only it must be farther afield; the Witch Pool and the Mill were too near, within easy walking distance. Now at Renton Parva, the next station to Homersfield, Uncle Bliss's station, by the way, the Homer is at its loveliest in September. Beech woods with a sprinkling of wild cherry and maple. We could go there by train. Irene and Val, when they were tired of fishing for eels, could explore their burrow by the Renton Parva beck. Miss Seamore would arrive by the train after we had left and find an excellent lunch waiting for her, and a fly at the station, and a friendly little note telling her that we had gone out for the day, and that we hoped she would make herself comfy and have a good long rest after her journey. Angela would arrange a bowl of flowers in her room.

"Don't whimp," I said to Irene.

"I am not whimping, Daddy."

She was kneeling on the edge of her chair with her arms and head drooping over the back, looking as forlorn as a robin in snow.

I explained to them that because Miss Seamore was coming on Saturday it did not follow that she would be with us officially. "Lessons don't begin till Monday, you know."

Visible levitation.

"We can have our picnic just the same."

Subsidence of humps.

"Only I am afraid Miss Seamore will be too tired to join us."

Irene and Val came up behind my chair and kissed the top of my head. I unfolded the Renton Parva project.

Impotent Chimbashi! I was warmed with a sense of deserved popularity for the rest of the evening, and if there is anything more satisfying when one wakes up in one's armchair at bedtime after ruminating the events of the day I don't know it.

Again Don Quixote lay open on the library floor, his riddle unsolved.

Chimbashi with all his ingenuity of malice was not a rain-compelling sprite. Probably he was confused in his latitudes and thought we wanted rain. He must often have been invoked in that capacity by those he was retained to befriend, "calling down the waters from beyond the white wall of the sky." Friday was the fifth day of a perfect Indian summer. As I sat drinking my tea in my dressing-gown by the open window looking into the garden, I wondered if I had said good-bye to the East. I had these doubts sometimes, but drove them out of my head. Not that I hankered after the Sudan; it paid for Homersfield. That

was all. Dear Homersfield, as the Brebis said. One need
not go farther than Homersfield for the terrestrial paradise. This morning it was at its autumnal best. A crop of
pink toadstools had sprung up in the night on both sides
of the drive. A fairy avenue. In the matter of goblins I preferred Puck to Chimbashi. The grass was half-silvered with
moisture. There was a sparkle of dew on the gossamer. In
the meadow beyond the stackyard erratic waves of darker
green marked the path of the cow called Hungry to pas-
ture. The horse-chestnut tree in the garden was flaming.
Ungathered damsons, cracked and rusty, hung on the trees
and sprinkled the clipped lawn with rusty beads. One or
two of the elms were already brandishing a yellow torch.
All the colour was in the leaves; the only flowers in the
garden were Michaelmas daisies and a few lingering sun-
flowers, great golden discs that contrived to look homely
and exotic at the same time.

Angela was in the garden after breakfast collecting
snails for sacrifice when Sellinger drove up in his car with
Clarkson. I was filling my pipe by the library window and
heard him tell her that they were on their way to a shoot.
"Poor old Bob!" I heard, "I wish he could join us."

I shouted out of the window, "Hullo, Sellinger; wish I
could. Next time, perhaps. What news of Marjorie?"

"Going strong. We heard from her this morning."

"How did it happen?"

"A case fell on her when she was packing. Jammed her
against the wall. It was her left arm, luckily."

They both got out. Sellinger explained that they could
only stay two minutes. Clarkson wanted to see the antelope's horn. "Do you still think of giving it to the Museum?" he asked me.

I told him that I was ready to forfeit all private interest
in Chimbashi if the nation wanted him. He was not popular at Homersfield.

"May we come in and have a look?"

I led them up to the attic. They were both surprised at the precautions I had taken to secure Chimbashi. Doubly locked like a Crown jewel. Clarkson turned it over and over, and examined it like a pundit.

"It's a duiker horn," he pronounced, "and it has been sealed with wax. Do you know what tribe it belonged to? Was it the Alunda?"

I told him that I could not remember the name of the tribe, but that Miss Ismay would be able to tell him. It was not a Sudan species.

Clarkson thought it was a charm against the nkala, a kind of crab with a head at both ends which killed people by eating their shadow.

"Has any one ever seen one?" I asked him.

"It is only visible to the witch-doctor," he explained. "There is a special guild of them who make a fat thing out of the antidote."

He held it up to the light, scratched the inside with his pocket-knife, and shook the loose flakes on to the palm of his. hand. "Smell it," he said. "No doubt it is the identical anti-nkala preparation. What does it remind you of?"

It reminded me of the mousey smell of crushed hound's-tongue. Sellinger sniffed it and thought he detected the savour of bats in a church tower.

"Well, that's what the nkala smells of. The diviners tell you that the preparation they use is made up of the crushed heads and claws of defeated nkalas which they have called up out of the water. Set a nkala to catch a nkala. As no one else has ever seen one the witch-doctors have the monopoly."

Clarkson asked me if I could find him a sheet of brown paper to wrap it up in.

Here was a golden chance. I was greatly tempted. In five minutes the house might be quit of Chimbashi for ever. But I decided that it would not be playing the game. Supposing Clarkson got smashed up in the train or in a taxi going to the Museum! His blood would be on my head.

"No," I said. "Don't bother. I'll post it myself."

"As you please," he said. "Perhaps a formal presentation would be better. In a fortnight or so you will get a gilt-edged letter of thanks from the trustees."

We ran into Val at the bottom of the stairs. He was being hotly pursued by Irene, and was calling out to her over his shoulder, "Devils must go. Devils must go." It was some Indian chant they had picked up—heaven knows where.

Sellinger collared him and held him up in his arms. "Yes, young man, devils *are* going," he said, "and about time too. Don't you think so, Clayton? How is Miss Hudson, by the way?"

"She is doing very well," I told him, "but what is the connection?"

Sellinger raised his eyebrows meaningly as if we shared some common secret. I had been wondering why he was suddenly reconciled to my giving away Marjorie's present.

"And how are Joan's knees?"

I pushed him firmly into the motor. "Go and frighten your partridges," I said. The dear old boy was a notoriously bad shot.

They drove off, and the children returned to their game. I saw Val dive into the shrubbery, shouting, "Devils must go! Devils must go!" and Irene at his heels, her long mane of chestnut hair flowing behind.

When I next heard their voices the bonds of fraternity were dissolved. They were quarrelling in the conservatory.

"You agreed," I heard.

"I didn't."

"You know the papilio is worth all the rest."

"You promised, if—"

The angry high-pitched voices were raised in a concert of passion. Soon they became indistinguishable. Then I heard Irene say—

"I hate you. I'd rather go out alone with Miss Seamore."

Then Val's rejoinder, "I won't go to the picnic. You'd spoil it. I am never going anywhere with you again. Never."

"I wouldn't have you, little pig."

The silence which followed this announcement was ominous. A few minutes afterwards a crimson and breathless Val stalked up to Angela in the garden. "Mummy," he panted, "please may I have my lunch brought up to me in my bedroom, and my tea and my supper? I couldn't eat it if Irene was there. I have decided never to have anything to do with her again."

"Little goose," said Angela, "stay here."

She called Irene, who was still in the conservatory. "Now, stand there. Say you are sorry. One, two, three. Both together."

They bleated, "I am sorry," but without conviction.

"One, two, three. Both together. Shake hands."

It was the limpest of handshakes.

"Now run away. If there is any more nonsense you will begin lessons to-morrow with Miss Seamore instead of going to the picnic."

The two self-conscious little figures went off in studiously different directions.

"Chimbashi!" I whispered to Angela. "He is eating their shadows. I wish we had let Clarkson take him."

We agreed to pack him and take him to the post-office after lunch.

At lunch neither of them spoke a word. Even when I told Aunt Hudson that Chimbashi's sentence had been commuted to transportation for life, and that he was going to the British Museum, they did not seem interested.

"Wouldn't Mr. Bliss have liked it?" the Brebis suggested innocently. "Why do you laugh, Angela dear? Perhaps he doesn't collect horns."

"I believe he collects everything," I said. "Uncle Bliss is very catholic in his tastes."

"How dreadful!" sighed the Brebis. "But I have always suspected it."

All this time the children were moping, as glum as two mutes. Val pecked at his food. He seemed literally incapable of swallowing anything with Irene for a *vis-à-vis*. Irene was jerky and unresponsive to the Brebis. Evidently the roof of her sky had fallen in, or the floor had given way, but that was no excuse for being rude.

"You must finish your pudding," Angela told her.

"I can't," she said crossly, "I haven't digested half of it yet."

"Then get up and digest it outside. No dessert for sulky little people."

Irene got down, red as a peony, and left the table. She shut the door with a bang, and then opened it again and closed it very gently so as to pretend that she was not in a temper. "I don't want any dessert," she said through the chink.

The Brebis looked puzzled. "What can have happened to the child?"

"What was the quarrel about?" I asked Val. "Division of spoils?"

Val's reply was a deepening crimson. His lips twitched, but no sound came out of them. To give him a chance of pulling himself together Angela sent him off with a message to Jessie. "Take a pear with you," she added tactfully, to spare him the necessity of coming back.

"No, thank you, Mummy, I don't want one."

This was something beyond a whimp.

"What can have upset them?" Aunt Hudson exclaimed.

"The dispute," I explained to her, choosing my words carelessly, "is whether they should continue to have a communal museum."

The Brebis was shocked. She hoped that I would put my foot down firmly on the idea—I quote her own metaphor. She distrusted communism and everything Russian.

"But this is a different kind of communism, Aunt Huddy," Angela assured her.

"Perhaps, my dear, but I think all kinds of communism are wrong. If you ask me, I believe it is that which is ruining France."

"But surely France is not turning Bolshevik."

Aunt Hudson qualified her statement. "It is not Bolshevik yet," she conceded, "but there are communal schools everywhere. There was one at Dax. And it is not only in the towns; the villages have them too. That is the beginning, don't you think so? Quite enough to explain all their irreligion and papacy."

I left Angela to the instruction of the travelled Brebis, and mounted the stairs to the attic. Chimbashi's hour had come. I exhumed him roughly from his incongruous company in the sea chest, wrapped him up in several thicknesses of brown paper, bound him with an old fishing-line as tightly as a spliced cricket bat, and delivered him to Angela to tie on the label and fasten off the ends.

"Now," I said as we started to the post-office, "I don't see what he can do to us."

"I don't think he will like being sent away," Angela replied.

It was only then that I remembered the circumstances of his last transfer. Marjorie had received him from her tame chief on the morning of an earthquake. I tried to conjecture what a translated African bogey would reckon as a set-off to an earthquake in quiet Homersfield, and after totting it all up concluded that Chimbashi owed us a

trifle on the balance. I hoped we had had our earthquake.
However, I warned Angela.

"'Ware cross roads!"

But there was no need. At the sight of the most innocent-looking cow coming down the road she climbed over
the nearest gate into a field. When we heard a motor we
both backed into the hedge.

Val was lying flat on his tummy on the lawn when we
started for our walk. We called to him to come with us, but
he pretended not to hear. He spent the whole afternoon in
the garden. When we came back, relieved of Chimbashi,
he was mooning about darkly in the shrubbery.

"Hullo, Val. What have you been doing?"

"Nothing, Daddy."

"Where's Irene?"

"I don't know."

Where was Irene? She was not at tea. It was the first
time in my life that I had known her miss tea. Where was
she hiding? She and Val had an uncanny gift of making
themselves invisible. Like the nkala. Was this Chimbashi's
earthquake? The air was charged with apprehension. Angela was abstracted; she put two lumps of sugar in the Brebis's tea; the Brebis hated sugar in her tea. "What can have
happened to the children?" she kept saying. Val had de-
veloped an absent-minded appetite. The door opened, but
it was only Jessie with the scones which we had forgotten.
No, I reassured myself, we have had our earthquake; this
is only a seismic tremor, part of the subsidence. Naturally
Irene would be reluctant to present herself. One remem-
bers the poignancy of children's quarrels, those disputes
that seemed the end of everything, the conviction that the
door was for ever closed. The first wounds the two little
angry animals deal one another do not hurt much; it is
after they have separated that the salt enters in. If only
the peace-breaker, the other party, would come forward,

his eyes opened, and say, "I'm sorry. I didn't mean it," all might be forgiven. But peacebreakers are hardened and obstinate. The children's meeting would be difficult. And here Val, who had stayed in the arena, had the advantage of Irene, who had gone off in high dudgeon and would have to come back. His part was the more dignified. It was for her to find her way, awkward and shame-faced, in the new dimension, while he sat still, established.

"Where *can* the child be?" moaned the Brebis.

I kept my eyes fixed on the drive. Penitent, or impenitent, Irene's entrée would be complicated by her behaviour at lunch. She had been cross and rude. It wasn't Val only she would have to face. The one sweet in her bitterness would be that she knew we were anxious, and that the longer she stayed away the more frightened we should be, and therefore the more ready to forgive. Little strategist.

"Val," I said, "what did you quarrel about?"

"Nothing, Daddy."

"Well, then, let's go and look for her."

We all four trooped out into the garden. The Brebis began to peer under the laurel bushes, one by one, methodically, as if it had been a game of hide and seek. "Where do you hide?" I asked Val. He took us to the loft above the cow called Hungry, where we found two depressions in the hay like the forms of two hares. This was their retreat when Lady Potter came, and suchlike hippogriffs, or when Miss Seamore wandered about the garden calling them for some walk or errand, outside the schedule. I envied them their gift of invisibility. Val had become very confidential. He told me how one day she tracked them to the barn and they saw her gaunt equine face raise itself through the trap-door. But it was a fruitless reconnaissance. They lay still, completely buried. I envied them their fragrant fitter. If one could be buried in hay instead of mould, death would lose half its terrors. I called Irene's name, hoping that she might have buried herself again in the hay. Val gently prodded a suspicious-looking heap with a pitch-fork. But there was no relic of Irene in the loft except her bathing-dress, which was hanging from a beam. It must have been there since August.

I could see that Val was frightened, or he would never have betrayed their secret places,—the dark hole through which they squeezed into the loft through the gable of the cart-shed, their Father Holt's chamber, the bole of the pollard hornbeam, the ditch covered with elder where the shade was so thick that nothing grew, the flat-topped straw-rick where they were as safe as on a desert island when they had scrambled to the top and kicked away the ladder and lay ready to slide down when Irene pronounced that the coast was clear. Another bolt-hole was the disused pig-sty in Farmer Stubbs' garden, which they preferred to any, in spite of the nettles, because it was trespassing. I hoped that I would find her here and that she would jump out at me with a "Boo," and clasp my knees and clamber up on to my back, and pretend that it was all a game. But Irene was not to be found in any of these lurking-places.

We returned to the house. I had a thin hope that she might have slipped back while we were looking for her, but the Brebis was alone on the doorstep. "Where *can* the child be?" she sighed.

It was getting dark. We separated to reconnoitre her favourite haunts. Val and I went down to the river—I pictured her coiled up like a squirrel in one of her hol-low willows; Angela to Cuckoo Lane; Jessie to the village; John, the Providence of Joan, to ask if she had been seen on the Renton Magna road. We knocked up Farmer Stubbs as we passed, but she had not been down to the river by his meadows. As we came back I looked for a light in Irene's window. It was dark. Angela arrived at the same moment. Irene was not in Cuckoo Lane, nor in Primrose Wood, nor

in Nightjar Coppice, and she had not been seen in the
village or on the Renton Magna road. The table in the
work-room was laid for the children's supper, but I told
Jessie they would dine with us.

"Shall I lay a place for Miss Irene too?" she asked, like
a rustic Sibyl.

"Yes," I answered shortly.

But none of us dined. We were much too miserable. For
hours I had felt that salt taste in my mouth which ascends
from the stomach to the throat, the foretaste of desolation. I remembered partings from Irene, particularly one
day at the end of my first leave when I had said good-bye
to Angela, and shut the door of her room, and heard Irene
calling me from the nursery to come back as I was going
downstairs. She toddled out on to the landing to meet me
with a hair-brush in her hand and said, "Are you going
inside the Sewdan, Daddy; then let me brush your hair
before you go inside the Sewdan." I was getting maudlin
with suspense and fear. I have only once been more frightened, and that was in the hour when the cause of our trouble first saw the light.

Angela was magnificent. She always is in the face of
big things. Not a hint of despair. As she stood in the hall,
reassuringly cool, revolving the next phase in the search,
Val came up to her and stroked the sleeve of her coat.

"Mummy," he said, "I want Irene to have the papilio,
and everything in the museum. I can start another one."

IX

IRENE DISCOVERS SANCHO PANZA

I do not believe Irene had an idea where she was going when she burst out of the room and closed the door so gently behind her. It was *Irene contra mundum,* but primarily *Irene contra Val.* The first need would be for some further assertion, something to make Val envious, some proof of worth, implicit vindication. She felt very brave and desperate, only she could not see a way of acting heroically. There was nothing within the bounds of her daily walks to inspire her. The familiar fields and hedges, cattle and sheep, were their common property, a matter-of-fact world which she would have to leave behind if she looked for individual adventure. She had no plan in her head, but abstractedly followed a path of her own across the meadows, burrowing through gaps in the hedges until she found herself in the neighbourhood of Homersfield station. Then she remembered the 2.30 train to Renton Parva. Suddenly it all became clear. She would go to the Clapperhouse and see Uncle Bliss. She would see the museum, and the animals, if they had come, anyhow the stuffed hippopotamus; and she would come home and tell Val. He should hear of all these things through her, hear, but not see. Afterwards they would go and see them together. Irene triumphant could see herself forgiving Val.

Luckily she had fourpence in her pocket to pay for her ticket one way, part of Uncle Bliss's sixpence. She had never been a railway journey alone before, and she had the train almost to herself, and felt very important.

Renton Parva Station is close to the river. In a few minutes she found herself in the scabious field where we were going to picnic the next day in spite of Miss Seamore. She had forgotten the picnic, and now somehow she could not picture herself slipping back by the side of Val again in a family jaunt as if nothing had happened. The most dreadful unretractable things had been spoken. And she had forgotten Miss Seamore. That meant the end of the holidays, and Irene hated ends.

Putting her story together from hints that escaped her afterwards I gathered that the adventure had lost some of its colour by the time she dived into her burrow. Anger was wearing off, and with it, of course, the inspiration to act heroically. Still, being a very resolute and determined young person, she went on.

The children's burrow, it should be explained, was the tangle of undergrowth through which the Renton Parva beck, or the beck as it was called for short, flowed into the Homer. This small trickle of a stream was their river of romance. It led into an uncharted country. Every holidays they had explored a little farther, but never far enough, never as far as the grounds of the Clapperhouse, which even before Uncle Bliss burst upon the family was a remote and alluring objective. Now that he was installed the mystery that hung about the secret windings of the beck became more iridescent. Did it not flow out of the lake that held the sacred crocodile? And if they followed it up would it not lead to the Abode of Bliss itself, a wonderland peopled with a strange fauna, a great house inhabited by a strange gruff man, half ogre, half fairy godfather, who was reputed to be in possession of keys that would unlock treasures that were not to be found in the British Museum? Irene was not afraid of Uncle Bliss in spite of his bear-like exterior. Besides, he had promised that one day he would show her everything. What was to prevent one day being this afternoon?

Irene crept through the alder and hazel cover on all-fours. The brambles tore at her skirt, and the burs covered her all over with sticky bristles, stuck in her hair, and pricked her through her stockings. Every now and then she came to a gap where she could peep through at the stream where the forget-me-not lingered in ferny nooks, and oak trees spread mossy arms across, and dipped yellow fingers into the ripple. Or she would find herself in open country and dive back into her burrow. For it was taboo to leave it. She would look through a window of floating seeds and gossamer on the meadows which the devil's bit scabious covered with purple. Then back into the shady underworld. It was darkest on the sandy rises under the blackthorn scrub where the rabbits lived. She sat among their burrows still as a stone until they came out and sat by her. She looked into the black eye of one which stared at her until she put out her tongue, when it lolloped off to the next hollow. They hardly took the trouble to run away, and an old blackbird refused to budge for her.

Presently she came to a clearing where a patch of water-mint by an old saw-pit smelt sweet and earthy. There was a stack of faggots, by the side of which the blackened stalks of the marsh thistle stood over her head. This was the far-thest point that she and Val had reached in their explora-tions. She remembered that they had driven a stake into the ground to mark the spot, twenty paces from the faggots in the direction of the stream, fifteen paces to the left of the track where the burrow started again after the clearing.

They had been reading 'Treasure Island.' She looked for the stake and found it untouched. It had their initials scratched on it, I. C., V. C.,—the boundary stone of the Claytonian Empire, an empire which they had sworn to extend by slow conquest to its Ultima Thule, the source of the beck.

Irene absentmindedly pulled up the terminal post as if she were going to carry it on with her. Then she turned and put it back. The beginning of the unknown was a thicket of sloes to be penetrated on one's tummy or on all-fours. Rabbit territory again. There was a continual scurry ahead, white rumps plunging into safety. Soon she came to a sort of a tunnel which led to a warren, where she sat down to rest. She was beginning to feel lonely again. Something seemed to have taken the wind out of the sail of adventure. The air was full of the complaints of injured rooks. Autumn was melancholy. Why should there be ends and complaints? She was happy enough one minute, and the next she was depressed. That was silly. She sat so still that the rabbits came out again, and she watched a trickle of sunlight steal through the cover, and glint in a cobweb, and burnish a red dock leaf behind until a cloud dulled it, and she came to a sort of definition in her mind that happy people were people who never bothered about ends, or at least not until they had come. She had often bothered about them before they came, and that was silly too. A sudden heavy tearing and flapping on the other side of the stream, as if some one were pulling off the top of an oak, startled her from her reverie, as a pair of wood pigeons broke through the foliage across the beck.

She abandoned the disturbed nook and wandered farther into the burrow. It, at least, seemed to have no end. Tea and blackberry jam and Devonshire cream were miles and miles behind. The thought of them made her feel empty inside. She began to think of Val. They had quarreled before and made it up. Why couldn't they cancel all the horrid things they had said? "Val, you are not a pig."

"Irene, I like going out for walks with you." Tentative and sheepish advances; awkward, but healing. She was glad that she had left the stake behind. Val ought to have been with her. It was mean to steal a march on him. Why not go home at once? It would soon be dark. Besides, if she got to the Clapperhouse, Uncle Bliss might be angry; he might not want to see her. Irene hesitated. She hated unfinished adventures; they were worse than ends; and she must be nearly at the end of her burrow. Why not go and spy, see the cages, peep into the windows of the house through the shrubbery, and if Uncle Bliss caught her, pretend that she had come to call? It would be perfectly true. She had come to call.

Still it would not be very loyal to Val, this encroachment on their joint territory. Irene was no longer emulous; she did not want to go home and vaunt to him. They would go together the first chance they had of escape, and carry on the terminal post with them, and plant it in the park where the beck came out of the lake. She had only to unfold the plan to Val and they would be allies again. She was on the point of turning back home when she remembered that she had only got a single ticket and would have to borrow fourpence from Uncle Bliss. That decided it. She crept on until she emerged from the tunnel, and after traversing a country rich in surprises came to a dry bank with a hazel hedge on it. There was a gap into which the burdocks had crowded. She had to part them to creep through. On the other side a gravel path led to an old cottage covered with ivy. Grey smoke was curling out of a chimney over the gable. Ivy and smoke made her feel cosy. She stole along the flecked path until she came to a border of Michaelmas daisies which half hid a tiny square lawn. The gate at the end of the path opened into the park. Irene's heart jumped to her throat. Beyond the privet hedge in the bracken she saw an antlered head moving. The herd emerged, white bellies, speckled flanks, and gazed quietly at the cottage. They must have escaped, she thought. Some of the animals had come, then. If the stags, why not the lioness and cubs? The lake might be full of crocodiles. Why had not Uncle Bliss told her? Was he keeping it as a surprise?

She became aware of something moving the other side of the border of Michaelmas daisies. She looked over and saw a white-haired old lady bending down and emptying an apronful of damsons into a basket. The old lady looked up at the same moment, and her eyes lighted on a little girl standing wide-eyed beside a sunflower, a very untidy little girl, all brown and scratched and covered with burs, and over her boots in mud, and her mouth stained with blackberries. Her eyes were brown too, and dreamy, a shade browner than her skin.

"Well, I never!" said the old lady, which was exactly what Mummy might have said.

Irene had never seen such bright eyes under such white hair.

"I am afraid I am trespassing," she said.

"Trespassing! No such thing, my dear. Not for the likes of you. But where did you drop from?"

"I came by my burrow." Irene gave an outline of her itinerary.

"Well, I never!" the old lady repeated. "No wonder you look like a little pincushion. Come inside and let me brush the burs off you. But I dare say you'd like a cup of tea."

Irene followed her into the cottage. The kettle was steaming and singing, shouting, one might say, with joy and promise. Never had she felt more like tea. And the table was spread with bread and butter, and harvest cake. This was the top of adventure. Better than Alice in Wonderland. She wished Val were with her.

While the old lady was laying a third place Irene looked round the room. Her first idea was that she had stumbled on to Uncle Bliss's museum and that her hostess was the caretaker. Every inch of the wall and all the shelves were taken up with stuffed specimens, birds and fish and animals, herons and kingfishers, stoats, foxes, owls, some of them in glass cases, some simply stuck on stands, or hanging from nails on the wall. The door of the room at the other end of the cottage was open, and she could see that the collection had overflowed into it and filled the passage between.

"I see you have got a museum," she said tactfully. It would never do to give the old lady the impression that she thought these treasures belonged to somebody else.

Facts justified her diplomacy. The "lumber," as the old lady called it, was her son's. She didn't "hold with it" herself. She liked a parlour in apple-pie order. With all that stuffed vermin about you couldn't keep a place clean.

"I think it is beautiful," Irene said.

The old lady took down a moulting owl from a shelf and held it out at arm's length for Irene to see. "I call it nasty rubbish, she said, flicking the loose feathers into the grate with the corner of her apron. "One of these days, I tell him, I'll put it on the fire."

But Irene knew she didn't mean it. Putting two and two together it began to dawn on her in whose cottage she was.

"Is stuffing his perfession?" she asked.

"Stuffing and mounting," the old lady amended. "He stuffs for Mr. Bliss."

"Not Staff?" Irene exclaimed.

"Staff, to be sure. You'll have heard Mr. Bliss tell of him, maybe. That's him whistling."

Irene heard a melodious pipe coming from the direction of the park. She listened entranced until the music

stopped and the window was darkened by a strange for-
eign-looking figure. It was Staff with his flute in his hand.

He stared in at her, and his mother introduced them
through the window. "The young lady has come to See Mr.
Bliss. From Homersfield, didn't you say, my dear?"

"Then you'll be Miss Irene," Staff said. Irene said he
spoke strangely. "And where be Mr. Val?"

Staff's erratic eyes searched the room alternately, like
an electric-torch turned on and off, as if he expected to
find Val in a corner or under the table.

Irene watched him, fascinated. But I must give her own
account of the person and accomplishments of her hero.
To begin with, he was wearing "a beeyutiful brown velveteen suit with ribs all down it." And there was "something
funny about his eyes, like a magician. He never looked at
you with both eyes at the same time, and sometimes you
didn't know which it was he was looking at you with. And
he is the most wonderful stuffer. And he plays the most
beautiful tunes on a flute, which he made himself out of
an elder stalk, and he has promised to make me one. And
he can imitate all the different noises animals make, and
make them come from where he likes. He did a cat under
the dresser, and a dog in the hall, and a hyena in the garden. Mrs. Staff says it is ventiloquising, like the man from
Masculine and Devant's."

"And where be Mister Val?" Staff repeated.

"He hasn't come," Irene said. "He is coming another
day."

"Well, I'll take you to see Mr. Bliss after tea. But you'd
better make a good tea first. You won't get none over there."

Irene was making a very good tea; she had never made
a better. And so was Staff. This was another of his accomplishments. He ate as if stuffing were really his "perfession." Nearly a whole loaf and half the harvest cake.

Irene was beginning to feel dubious again about Uncle Bliss and the Clapperhouse. Mrs. Staff looked so kind that she thought she would borrow the fourpence for the ticket from her. Besides, it was getting dark.

"I don't think there will be time to see Mr. Bliss now," she ventured. "It is so late. I am afraid I will miss my train."

Staff looked at his watch, and told her that she would have plenty of time. The supper train; that was 6.35 at Renton Parva. He could take her to the governor in five minutes. They would find him at the stables converting the loose-boxes into a menagerie. "Cages for lions," he added contemptuously.

Irene inwardly exulted. This put a different complexion on the case. "Have any of the animals come yet?" she asked.

"Come? No, and if you ask me, they aren't likely to come."

Irene's spirits fell. "But the stags have come. I saw them. They must have got out."

"Bless your heart, the deer have been in the park these hundred years. Colonel Slingsby's grandfather brought them."

"But he promised me he was going to have a lioness and cubs, and a hippopotamus, and a giraffe, and—"

"Bless your heart," said Staff, "whatever has he been filling your head with?" But, seeing her disappointment, he added, "They may come. There's no telling what the Governor'll be at." Here he reflectively bisected the remainder of the cake. "And if they do come, as likely as not he will send them away again."

"But why?" asked Irene.

Staff did not answer her question directly. But after another pause for more stuffing, he observed, "There's nothing so curious as folk."

Mrs. Staff hoped that they would never come. Putting animals into cages was another thing she did not hold with. "You wouldn't like to be shut up in a cage, I am sure, after having all the world to roam in."

This was an uncomfortable grown-up way of thinking about zoological gardens which had not touched Irene's sympathetic imagination. She carefully removed it to a corner at the back of her mind. She asked Staff to tell her the names of his stuffed animals, and to explain to her the difference between a weasel and a stoat. "And what was that angry smooth-coated animal which showed its teeth?" "An otter?" She had never seen one before. "No," said Staff. "They're not in the way of showing themselves."

He imitated the cry of the otter at night. This opened the ventriloquistic entertainment, after which Irene asked him to play to her on his flute. Staff played a meandering African tune, which converted the gamekeeper's cottage into a medicine-man's hut. Irene was perfectly content. Staff was sufficient. She had no inclination to test unexplored grades of Bliss. But the prosy side of the magician asserted itself when he dropped his flute and reminded her that if she wished to spend half an hour at the Clapper-house before catching her train, it was time to be making a start.

Irene didn't wish, but there seemed to be no getting out of it.

Staff, surveying his collection of stuffed exhibits with a revolving sweep of his operative eye, asked her if there was anything she would like to take away with her.

"Oh, but I couldn't," Irene faltered.

"There's plenty more where they came from."

Irene hesitated.

Mrs. Staff added her persuasions, "Yes, my dear, do take away as much of that lumber as you can carry. It would be a good riddance, I am sure."

Irene wavered between the owl and the hedgehog, and chose the hedgehog because of its bristles. She would not let Staff carry it for her, because she liked to feel the bristles under her arm, and to adjust her embrace so that they did not prick her too much.

"You are most like a little hedgehog yourself," Mrs. Staff said, "with all those burs on you. You must let me brush them off before you go to the Clapperhouse."

Irene presented that bell-shaped back view of little girls which is so affecting to old folk.

Mrs. Staff was such a long time pulling out the burs that it was quite dark when they left the cottage. An owl was hooting in the elm by the gate. "Can you do that?" she asked Staff; and, according to Irene, Staff hooted better than the owl. Anyhow, another owl answered him. And he called the deer to him. Irene hid behind a tree, and a large doe came and rubbed her nose against his pocket. It was just light enough to see her spots,

So more time was lost in crossing the park, and when they got to the stables they found Uncle Bliss working by the light of two hurricane lanterns.

He beamed and boomed at the sight of Irene. "Hullo," he said; "this is a bit of luck. The second to-day." Irene felt a huge bear's arm round her waist, and was hoisted up on to his shoulder. "Where's Val? What's that you have got under your arm? A gift, eh?"

"It is a hedgehog," Irene explained, "Mr. Staff gave it me."

"My little Queen of Sheba. She shall have apes, ivory, and peacocks."

"Have you bought the dinosaur's egg?" Irene asked him.

Uncle Bliss flung her into the air, and caught her, and perched her on the other shoulder. "I have," he bellowed, "I got the cable this afternoon. That was my first bit of luck. You are my second."

Irene felt very proud at being weighed in the scale against the dinosaur's egg that cost five figures. She remembered all the things which five figures would buy. "Did it cost five figures?" she asked him.

"Four," trumpeted Uncle Bliss.

"And what are you going to do with the other figure?"

"Ah!" said Uncle Bliss. "We shall see. Come to look at the treasures, eh!"

"Oh, Uncle Bliss, how lovely! But won't I miss my train."

Uncle Bliss said that he would bicycle her to the station. He turned to the men and told them to stop work. They had stopped, and were staring at him from the dark corners of the stable. The scene must have been unusual; the Governor in a new role. He was entirely unselfconscious, of course, but Irene noticed their astonishment, and felt a little shy. She heard him tell Staff to take the men to the house and give them a glass of beer. It was a "good egg" that the dinosaur had laid. It made her mount docile under her. There was no gruffness left in Ursa Major. Probably it was the first time he had treated the workmen to beer. She heard one of them wish that "the young lady would drop in every night." Now they were outside, and she heard the bolt of the lion-house-that-was-to-be grate in the catch. Staff turned the key.

I can picture the procession to the house: a lantern in front, the group of workmen with the other lantern behind, Uncle Bliss lounging bear-like in the middle, Irene swaying on his shoulders, feeling as if she were perched on the howdah of the elephant at the zoo—solid foundation of an enduring alliance, and Staff, the other loyalty, by his side, putting in some shrewd comment or playing a catch on his flute, while Uncle Bliss heaped on his subjugator honorific endearments. "My Queen of Sheba! My Mongolian Princess!"

"Daddy, why did he call me a Mongolian Princess?"

"Because you are like one, I suppose."

It was rather apt of Uncle Bliss. There was a suspicion of the little Kalmuk in Irene with her high cheek-bones and slightly slanting eyes. She had not inherited Angela's tranquil beauty. Her eyes were more quizzical, less enigmatic and reposeful than her mother's, generally alert and expectant, as if she had just seen, or was going to see, something surprising. And what with Uncle Bliss and his Sancho Panza she had had her full share of surprises to-day.

They missed their train, of course. Irene could not go without seeing the stuffed hippopotamus. As it was there were a thousand things she hadn't time to see. She had just a glimpse of the butterflies. Then Uncle Bliss turned out half the cupboards in the house to find the insect she dreamed about, the poisonous, eight-legged, bird-eating spider. It had become an incubus and a nightmare, but Uncle Bliss told her it was not half so fearsome as it sounded, and if she saw it she would not dream about it again. But it was not to be found. The search lost them the supper train.

Irene dined with him in state, enthroned on two oriental cushions, which were quite unnecessary, and not very comfortable, as the hedgehog which she insisted on retaining kept getting jammed between her knees and the table. Still it was more Sheba-like. She was the first guest who ever stayed to dinner at the Clapperhouse. This was Uncle Bliss' house-warming.

And a most scrumptious meal it was, by Irene's account of it. It even beat Staff's tea. Uncle Bliss discovered that his cellar contained ginger beer. And he opened a huge ox tongue, and tins of asparagus, and champignons, and stewed fruit, stores he had brought home with him from Africa. The Clapperhouse was run on the principle of the caravanserai. One may be quite sure that the hunter of the pterodactyl was not the kind of man to be out of emergency rations wherever he might happen to be. Irene tasted of a delicious dish called 'Maconochie." In fact all Uncle Bliss' dishes were new to her, except the savoury, kippered herrings on toast, which reminded her of Cuckoo Lane. And of Val. She was thinking of Val rather remorsefully when she heard—

"And what pudding does the Queen of Sheba command?"

Irene plumped unhesitatingly for trifle.

"Trifle," Uncle Bliss demanded of the flushed and heavy-handed Phyllis who thumped the dishes on the table so heartily. But she hadn't "heard speak of trifle." She would ask Mrs. Staff.

"Does Mrs. Staff cook for you!"

"Staff or Mrs. Staff. Next time you come you must try Staff's spatchcock. Sometimes, when he is not cooking, he joins me at dinner."

"What is spatchcock, Uncle Bliss; is it a bird?"

Uncle Bliss was explaining when Phyllis interrupted him with the announcement that trifle would take two days.

"Two days is no trifle," said the entertainer of the Queen of Sheba.

Solomon was in a jesting mood. That was his second joke during dinner. The first was when he discovered a large green caterpillar in the cauliflower. He described the dish as "crawly flower," and told Phyllis to take it away, after ascertaining that Irene did not want the caterpillar for her museum.

"And what does the Queen of Sheba suggest as a substitute for trifle? Pineapple? Peaches?"

"Oh, pineapple, please," cried Irene. "It is my favourite fruit."

"You haven't tasted dorian," Uncle Bliss said. "It is the king of fruits. It smells like sherry, and tastes like almonds and cream, and looks like a green porcupine. When we go hunting together we will live on dorians and lion chops."

Irene wished she was grown-up like Marjorie and could shoot lions. But Uncle Bliss was not interested in Marjorie.

"Is lion nice to eat?" she asked him.

"It's rather like beefsteak."

"How many have you shot, Uncle Bliss?"

"Twenty or thirty."

They talked lions over their whisky and ginger beer. Uncle Bliss told her how Staff had saved his life from one. "He knocked it on the head with the butt of my rifle when it was eating my hat. The lion ran away, but I think it was his eye that did it. Staff has a very useful eye."

"Is Staff very brave?"

"Very brave indeed."

"I thought so," said Irene.

"And now we must be getting home," Uncle Bliss concluded regretfully. "Have you had enough to eat?"

"Yes, thank you," said Irene. "I am abserlutely replete. Let me kiss the top of your head, Uncle Bliss."

Ursa Major bowed for the salute. His bicycle was in the hall. Irene clambered up on to his broad back, the hedgehog under her arm. Sancho Panza's hedgehog, by the way, was the only material spoil she carried home from her raid.

X

THE ABODE OF BLISS

"Mummy," Val was saying in the hall, "I want Irene to have the papilio and everything else in the museum. I can start another one."

Just at that moment we heard the iron clank of the gate in the drive, then a high-pitched treble voice, followed by an unmistakable boom.

"Well, here's your little rosebud. Safe and sound, eh! Missed the supper train."

We met them on the steps, Irene still pick-a-back. Uncle Bliss strode beaming into the hall.

I think Angela and I concealed our relief, and appeared to be expecting her. Of course neither of us demanded a word of explanation. The situation explained itself, as the French say. The stage clue to it was that Aunt Hudson, realising that the suspended pulse of life was throbbing normally again in the house, slipped away, fearing ursine encounters.

Irene threw one arm round Angela's neck and hugged her; the other still embraced the hedgehog, which had become a useful stage property. When she unclasped and slid down, she went straight up to Val and held it out to him.

"Look what Mr. Staff has given us for our museum," she said. Nothing could have been more Sheba-like.

Val bled his finger on the hedgehog manfully.

I admired her economy of phrase. *Our* museum. The plural possessive pronoun contained the whole alphabet of reconciliation. And it was done so gracefully—like Uncle Bliss' Mongolian princess.

Poor old Val! Irene, the peace-breaker, had had all the fun and all the adventure, while he had been mooning in the garden, and now, it seemed, she was going to have the glory. So illogical are the awards of destiny.

But Val never turned a hair. He admired the hedgehog, and pricked another finger, like a young Spartan. Communism was restored.

Irene began to retail her adventures, rapidly, breathlessly. They chiefly concerned Staff—Staff and the owl, Staff and the doe, Staff and his flute, Staff and his "ventiloquising." Too much Staff, I thought, for Uncle Bliss. I detected a queer look on his face. Could he be "J"?

He turned to Val. "And where has Val been? Why didn't you come with Irene?"

"We lost each other," Val replied truthfully, upholding, with pink standards, the Claytonian honour.

"Well, well!" said Uncle Bliss. "You must both come to-morrow. You and Irene. Why not the whole family, eh?"

He looked at Angela, and Angela looked at me and the children. To-morrow was the picnic, but there was no question which would be the bigger treat. Besides, restitution was due to Val.

"Come to lunch," Uncle Bliss suggested. "Sample Staff's spatchcock."

"Do, Mummy. Please do. Uncle Bliss will give us Maconochie and pineapple. Won't you, Uncle Bliss?"

Irene gave us to understand that Uncle Bliss' repasts were something quite super-terrestrial. The dinner had been "heavenly."

Uncle Bliss was visibly elated and flattered. "Trifle shah be prepared for the Queen of Sheba," he urged gallantly.

It was an urbane and conciliatory Uncle Bliss. What spell had the child cast over him? Angela was reminded of Calidore bringing home the Blatant Beast. That was our new name for Ursa Major after the harrying of the Brebis, strictly between ourselves, of course. But Irene had tamed him. Butter would not melt in his mouth.

"It is very kind of you," Angela said, "but I am afraid we should be too many. We are having a picnic by the river to-morrow. Couldn't we come and see the museum afterwards?"

Uncle Bliss accepted this change of plan with becoming protests. The children were crestfallen, but only for a moment. Irene's bright invention flashed across the impasse like a kingfisher over a muddy ditch. "The burrow!" she cried. "Let's all go by the burrow."

The adventure would balance the loss of Uncle Bliss' lunch, even the Maconochie and pineapple. Again she saw herself in the role of pioneer, this time a leader with a retinue, bursting through the burdock cover into Staff's garden, beckoning us to follow, introducing us to Staff's mother, emerging from the cottage with the old lady's benediction and more stuffed vermin under her arm, and Staff playing us across the park like a drum-major to the steps of the Clapperhouse. And that would be only the beginning.

When Angela had shepherded the children to bed Uncle Bliss joined me in the library for a whisky-and-soda. I noticed an arrested movement of his hand to his breast-pocket. For once in his life he had forgotten his flask. The enchantress again? However, he emitted no sound of disgust and gulped down my whisky with admirable self-restraint, as if it had been his own. "Something like a peg, Clayton," he said. And he commended my long tumblers, the Sudan tumblers, as Angela called them, designed for an African thirst. "If there is one thing that annoys me it is the way they have in these hotels and restaurants of giving you a whisky-and-soda in a wine-glass as if it were a short drink." Uncle Bliss entertained a profound contempt for Britons who drank like foreigners. Vermouth and liqueurs he associated with light women. As for cocktails they were a symbol of national degeneracy.

The mention of cocktails recalled New York and the dinosaur's egg, which Irene's exploit had driven out of my head.

"We thought you would be on the way to New York," I reminded him.

"New York's off," he announced triumphantly. "I bought the egg this afternoon. Had a cable."

Uncle Bliss refilled his tumbler. "Bit of an escape too," he added. "I had forgotten America was dry."

I congratulated him on all counts. "Where are you bound for next?" I asked him. "The Jiundu swamp?"

No. He thought, the Pyrenees. The pterodactyl hunt would mean a lot of "bundobast" and delay. The beast was not likely to become extinct after having survived since glacial times, whereas the first severe frost might nip off his precious fungus, Cæsarea, or whatever it was called. In the meanwhile he wanted to find some one to leave in charge while he was away.

"It ought to be easy enough," I said. "Have you tried an advertisement in 'The Times'?"

"I was thinking of you, Clayton. Why don't you give up the Sudan? Supposing you fail at the next Board. It is a toss-up, it seems. What are you going to do then?"

"I don't know," I said, "but I'm not going to give up the Sudan until the Sudan gives up me."

Uncle Bliss stared at the bottom of his glass. Then after a pause he observed, "It would be pleasant finding young people about when one came home."

I was sorry for him. He had not a grownup friend.

"I was going to suggest five hundred," he said, "but I could raise it."

The offer would have been tempting if it had come from any one else. Supposing the Medical Board did spin me again, if I were agent for the Clapperhouse estate I could still keep on Homersfield; otherwise I should have to sell it. But business relations with Uncle Bliss were, of course, impossible.

"I am sorry," I said, "but for many reasons I am afraid I cannot take it on."

"Well, if you won't, you won't, I suppose, and that's an end of it."

Uncle Bliss emptied his tumbler and emitted an ursine grunt, which, so far as I could interpret it, was contradictory to the mood, or shape, in which he had arrived charioted by Irene. However, he did not tell me to "do the other thing."

The Brebis did not feel at all equal to the burrow; nor to any road for that matter, or method of progress, or avenue of approach, that had at the end of it the Abode of Bliss. Neither was Angela a burrowing person; brambles and burs, and gaps in hedges, and muddy ditches she abhorred. So it was decided at breakfast that they should spend the day at Homerton shopping, and have lunch at the dear square opposite the little restaurant in the cathedral where Aunt Hudson could see the Chapter and the minor canons coming in and out, and tea at the confectioners' in the market-place where they made the most lovely little tapering coconut cakes, white at the top and brown at the base, like Fujiyama. It would be quite an adventure for them, and in the evening they would have a carriage to take them and their parcels from the station to the house. Angela would buy the Brebis a sachet, and the Brebis would buy Angela a bag. She was always buying new

ones or having them presented to her, and they seemed to
give her pleasure, though what she did with the old ones I
was never able to discover, for a dead donkey is not so rare
a thing in my experience as a discarded bag.

So we all had adventures after our kind. Our first one
was an unexpected and entirely unforgettable glimpse of
Miss Seamore. We had forgotten her existence, and were
sauntering along the bank of the river in the second meadow from the station when the train clanked and rattled
over the Homer by the iron bridge. It was the train that
crossed the one we got out of at Renton Parva. As usual
it was almost empty, but not quite. I felt a tug at my
coat and heard a h—sh in Val's scouting whisper. The children had taken cover. In a second I was flat on the grass
beside them behind an alder bush. The parrot-like head
and beak of the governess protruded from a window on
our side, crowned with a little round, hard, incongruous
hat. I could distinguish—characteristic insignia—the hat
pins, like enormous knitting needles with inflated amber-
coloured bulbs at the end, which fastened the super-
structure inflexibly to the severely plaited top-knot, part
of the armour—offensive or defensive?—of this bird of
prey. We could see Miss Seamore quite plainly, but she
could not see us, though she was staring straight into our
bush. I clasped Val's bare knee. It was all-of-a-tremble
with excitement. He was feeling that sense of power—
vestigial instinct of the hunter—that comes of watching
without being seen. It is strong in Claytons, I think. I
have even felt it in towns when looking out of the window at a person in the street who is unconscious of being
observed.

For the moment Miss Seamore was our victim. The
children had cut a notch in their tally of the head-hunter.
To the cave man within them her unconscious passage at a
mere bow-shot from where they lay hidden meant an arrow

in the heart or flank of the image. Thus we started on our expedition propitiously.

In the account I have given of Irene's first penetration of the Renton Parva beck territory the details are borrowed from the second day's reconnaissance in which Val and I followed her. As to the moods and humours inspired by the adventure I received no direct confidences; they came to me by suggestion. We halted where she had halted, and explored the alleys she had marked by arrows scratched on the ground or by the white notches she had cut on the blackthorn stems with her pocket-knife; only here and there where the tangle was thickest I was allowed by virtue of my infirmities and less accommodating bulk to steer a parallel course coastwise in open country, but always within halloa. Not that I was insensitive to the attractions of the burrow. Following up the windings of the beck was a delightful bit of pioneer work. In the sloe thicket where Irene had sat with the rabbit I felt exactly like an explorer in darkest Africa, and when we came to the patch of reeking watermint by the faggot stack and measured twenty paces—Irene's paces—to the hidden terminal post, I felt like Balboa, or Pliny the Younger writing his report for Trajan, a humble scribe adding his footnote to the extension of the Claytonian empire.

Val carried on the terminal post, as was fitting. But here we entered blackthorn cover again, and finding the jungle too thick for me I left the children to cut their way through like Stanley on the road to Ujiji, and discovered a more middle-aged path by a hazel avenue on high ground above the stream. I lay in wait for them where the tunnel emerged at a spot where I remember being posted with a gun in my teens when old Slingsby owned the estate. Irene pretended that they were not ambushed. Val swore he spied me first. My "Doctor Livingstone, I presume," was an old chestnut in the family. The children knew all about that descent to the port on the lake embowered in palms. Many a time had they awakened Ujiji to the news that a caravan was coming, and peered into the palms to try and make out in which hut lived the white man with the grey beard whom they had heard about on the Macararzi.

"Unfurl the flags and load your guns!" cried Irene.

"Ay, Wallah; ay, Wallah, bana!" echoed Val.

We drew Staff's cottage blank. Irene burst through the burdock clump like a little naiad, Val and I at her heels, just in time to see Sancho Panza slip out at the gate at the other end of the garden. He had seen us. We saw him look over his shoulder furtively, and take a sharp turn behind the privet hedge on the park side as if he were taking cover. "Daddy, he saw us." Irene was incredulous. *Her* Staff. She would not believe that he did not want to see her. It was our first check. The door was open and the fire burning in the kitchen, and the smoke from the chimney floated away between the trees, but the cottage was empty. No Mrs. Staff. No stuffed vermin to carry away under one's arm.

"He will ask us to come in afterwards," Irene explained apologetically; and she did not qualify her faith with a "perhaps."

So, unheralded by Sancho Panza and his pipe, we crossed the park to the lake, where we found that no preparations had been made to receive the beaver or the crocodile; the foundation stone of the palace of the King Penguin was still unlaid. It seemed to me rather an inhospitable sheet of water, homely but exclusive, not prepared for exotic guests. The cindery grey of the willows, the aspens trembling, the sedges leaning forward in a row, the startled grebes and waterhens were familiar to Renton Parva; somehow I could not fit them into the picture of Uncle Bliss' zoological gardens, with flamingoes and adjutants. An alligator's nose under a hawthorn, especially in May time, would be horrid. But for a long time I had shared Angela's belief that there wasn't going to be no zoo.

Val produced the terminal post, the broken end of a water-level marker with black lines on white paint, which they had picked up after a flood. They drove it into the soft squashy turf, where the beck oozed out of its bed of brooklime and water-cress, more a spring on the edge of the lake than an overflow, the sort of place where you are disappointed if you do not flush a snipe. Val was afraid that somebody would pull it up, but Irene said that she would tell Uncle Bliss about it. She seemed quite satisfied that a word from her would be enough to preserve their boundaries.

Val remarked on the barrenness of preparation. "He hasn't begun, Daddy."

"Fish ponds!" I reminded him.

The word had come to denote a philosophical school of thought in the family.

"But he means to," Irene amended.

Generally speaking, she was the less sanguine of the two, rather inclined to be a little unbeliever, but her newly-acquired ascendancy over the providence of the Clapperhouse had reversed the roles. I wondered how long it would last.

But here was the providence himself. Val was the first to spy him lounging towards us from the direction of the stables. Uncle Bliss was wearing the same grey suit in which he had lunched with us little more than three months ago, the trousers very baggy at the knees and very tight underneath, looking as if the calves would burst them, and the pockets mysteriously bulging—but bulges now had merely an objective interest. I had never seen him in any other suit, except the portentous swallow-tails he wore at the Potters'.

The Queen of Sheba was immediately enthroned on his shoulders, which, it seemed, had become her privileged mode of progression. A brawny hand was extended to Val.

"I was looking out for you," he said to me. "Expected you hours ago. And how's my little rosebud?"

"Very well, thank you, Uncle Bliss; and how are you?"

"As fit as a trivet," Ursa Major replied courteously.

"What is a trivet, Uncle Bliss?"

"Ah, there you have the advantage of me."

"Have you got one in your museum?"

"We shall see. If not, we will send for one. Is it the Queen of Sheba's command?"

Uncle Bliss seemed to have set permanently into a good shape, like a blancmange. One does not buy a dinosaur's egg every day.

"Now, where is Don Quixote?" I asked myself as I surveyed our muscular and confident friend, four square, fortified at all points, and so little of a visionary. A barrel of cement could not be more impervious to rubs. Where did the pathos come in?

He escorted us across the wasted park, past the sawpits with their rotting cross-poles, the hollows where the Scots firs had been felled, the tumbledown lichened barns of the Out farm, and the straggling unkempt hedges which marked land that had been enclosed in Slingsby's father's time. It was once all park. The wilted regiments of ragwort and thistles depressed me. I had no ambition to be Bliss' estate agent.

Even from a distance the Clapperhouse was in a visible state of disrepair. Its square spacious ugliness reminded me of a Turkish cavalry barracks. However, there was plenty of room to put things in, and that was what Uncle Bliss bought it for—a sort of dump. The place never had any aesthetic pretensions.

To the children, of course, the interior was a terrestrial paradise, the pleasure dome of Kubla Khan; but I am afraid it is necessary in the interests of the prosy and literal Muse I serve to correct Irene's appreciation with an adult view of Uncle Bliss' museum. My first impression was of lumber run riot, the kind of nightmare Mrs. Staff might have if after a repast of pineapple and spatchcock the stuffed-vermin-holding capacity of her cottage were to swell and increase to the proportions of the Albert Hall. Many of Uncle Bliss' exhibits were stowed away in packing-cases, but enough had been exhumed to prepare me for the chaos of unrelated objects that has since become notorious. I think we were the first visitors to see the Clapperhouse Collection in embryo.

Irene constituted herself assistant showman. "The hippopotamus is at the door," she whispered to Val as we entered. And there it was standing, or rather squatting, to receive us. One could see that Staff had had no hand in the hippopotamus. Uncle Bliss had gone to one of the best taxidermists in South Africa, who had mounted the beast in the attitude in which it had fallen back bellowing, with its head up, into the water. The *vis-à-vis* of the pachyderm was a magnificent polar bear (purchased) with a cub. Uncle Bliss introduced them. "Ursa Major and Ursa Minor. What are you giggling at, young man?" Next came a lion which looked as if it had died of mange, shot by Uncle Bliss, cured by Staff. A South American jaguar rubbed shoulders with a Tibetan kiang. Strange stable companions. A snow leopard (Ward) consorted with a Devonshire badger (Staff) and a giraffe (Staff), as if the animals in the ark had changed partners in some country dance. It was the kind of museum Alice might have seen through the looking-glass, beasts from all lands, some innocent and familiar, others strange and fierce, looking as if they had come out of the Apocalypse, wyverns and basilisks perhaps. "The owl and the panther were sharing a pie." I was quite prepared to meet the griffon and the mock turtle on the stairs.

But the best view of this still life menagerie was from the centre of the hall. When I took my stand here and looked round at the four walls I was reminded of a great khan in the Yemen, camels stalled beside little donkeys, only the animals all had their rumps to the wall, and were staring out at me. One had to move circumspectly. The caravanserai was crowded with tables on which loose objects were strewn promiscuously, and cabinets with glass tops, among which it was difficult to pick your way, an equally heterogeneous collection, while under the stairs alligators and cuttlefish and sharks and other sea monsters and stuffed cetacea were hanging from hooks and chains in the ceiling like objects in a Dutch interior.

On the stairs Staff's exhibits were given a prominent place. They all looked very sorry for themselves about the muzzle; hairs had dropped out; hardly one had good ears. There was a giant eland standing on its four legs as stiff as a towel-horse, and a cracked rhino hide thrown over an erection that looked like parallel bars. Staff could make a flat skin, but he had never planed one in his life; Uncle Bliss' coolies must have carried double weight. Clarkson was right. Inflated gollywogs and bags of sawdust. And he had no idea of mounting. None of his bones were properly articulated.

Uncle Bliss took us to a wing of the house which had once been the servants' quarters, a warren of bedrooms fitted with cupboards with glass doors, and chests of drawers which emitted a smell of camphor and decay. In the passages there were broad open shelves littered with fossils, skeletons, flint implements, sea-shells, and a variety of dull colourless objects in bottles, out of which the spirits had evaporated. The whiskers of a civet cat brushed a plaster cast of the Neanderthal man. It was not what you might call a systematic or educative collection. The student of comparative anatomy would have found it lacking in plan. There was no grouping of objects which together told a tale. Darwin and Mendel might never have existed. And if you occasionally ran up against a skeleton of one of the higher anthropoids, a gorilla or a lemur, at a corner of the stairs or in some alcove where a knight in armour ought to have stood, you might be quite sure that Uncle Bliss had not stuck it there with any highbrow scientific intention. The student might look in vain for a key to the essential features of the order Primates in the Clapperhouse Collection. I remember Clarkson telling me how Uncle Bliss had withered him when he suggested a card catalogue. "Card catalogue! Card fiddlesticks!" he replied. It certainly was rather a stupid question to ask him.

As a corrective to this confusion there were collections which he had bought in the gross, so to speak, arranged and complete, which could not help being instructive. This explained his loans all over the country. One cabinet showed the life history of various insects. He had bought it from a collector in Amsterdam. But the thing which ravished the children was the case of assimilative insects displaying their protective resemblance to a background of leaf and bark. Uncle Bliss was not a bit fussy. They were allowed to touch as well as see. They felt the praying mantis, and then the leaf or twig it straddled. Irene discovered a replica of Marjorie's deadleaf insect. In the case of Congo specimens a blue-roller bird was snapping up a green mantis, in spite of its wonderful make-up in imitation of its surroundings.

The butterflies were magnificent. Some of the species from Brazil outshone Marjorie's papilio. I believe the Clapperhouse Collection is still famous for its lepidoptera.

Among other treasures we were shown the only complete set of extinct British coppers. What it was worth I cannot say; perhaps five figures, if one can put a price to things unpurchasable. But to do Uncle Bliss justice, he valued things more for their rarity than for what they would fetch in the market, though this, of course, threw a glamour over them when he first bought them. Acquisitiveness was his strong point, a certain dogged combativeness in the face of competition. Clarkson had been contemptuous about "Bliss' uninstructed appetite and long purse." He was tenacious too, though the glamour of acquisition seemed to wear off. When he was rummaging for Irene's spider in what had been the housekeeper's linen locker, he fished out a cardboard box containing two Great Auk's eggs.

"Hullo," he said. "What have we got here? I had forgotten these. I must put up a stand for them in the hall."

Now there are only sixty-seven Great Auk's eggs in all the museums and private collections in the world—any dealer can locate them for you. Uncle Bliss must have spent more on them than on the dinosaur's egg. But the paint had worn off the toy.

What did he value most?

Irene asked him, and he led us to an alcove by a bow window, his holy of holies, where hung the okapi skin.

"I shot that before it was known to science," he said proudly. He took it down and ran his finger over the mite-infested pelt.

"By the way," he said to me, "do you know Clarkson? I showed it him. One of our arm-chair zoologists, British Museum. Doesn't know the difference between an okapi and a giraffe. Why they put him there I can't think. Specimen, I suppose. Stercoraceous fellow! Troglodyte!"

Our attention was diverted by a heavy regular footstep in the corridor. I could tell by the expression on Irene's face who was coming round the corner.

It was the adored Sancho Panza. Uncle Bliss turned to him, still stroking the skin.

"You remember the man in the Museum, Staff? Lives next door to the mummies. Ought to be shut up with them."

The okapi skin served as a context, if any were wanting, to recall the arm-chair zoologist.

"Why, yes," Staff said. "Not likely to forget him neither. Him that mistook the occupi for an amateur giraffe."

"Exactly," said Uncle Bliss. "Immature giraffe."

"It would take a rare ignorant kind of man to understand him," Sancho Panza observed tolerantly, and added, "There's nothing so curious as folk."

This last remark, a favourite aphorism of Sancho Panza's, was addressed to me. It was our first introduction.

Uncle Bliss omitted the formality. And there was no need; he introduced himself. The squire was as natural and unselfconscious in his relations with the world as the knight. There was something uncanny and intriguing about Staff, a curious incongruity in the way he walked and looked at you and talked. Everything that seemed most characteristic in his self-expression was out of keeping, irreconcilable almost, with his appearance. In feature I should have put him down as a Mediterranean type. A Catalan, perhaps. Clarkson's word was Dago. "Furrin-looking" was the Homersfield term. But his amazing squint made specification difficult.

He had a high forehead and very long black hair which stood straight up and curled over like pothooks where the parting ought to be, a frame to his squint. In spite of his sallow southern look his speech was laconically English; yet his operative eye, when it did flash on you, was like an electric torch. His walk, an absorbed stride, as if he were counting his steps, was certainly not Latin. Nor was it English, but that may have come of flute-playing.

He turned from me to Irene, who was watching him admiringly. "I saw you come along by the cottage," he said, "but I didn't want to greet you afore I had the flute. I've cut it for you proper."

He extracted the flute from his pocket and handed it to her. It was an elder stalk newly stripped of its bark, white as baby flesh. "And where be Master Val?"

Staff and Val shook hands. Irene spluttered gratitude. Staff told them that his mother would be expecting them over at the cottage when they had seen Mr. Bliss' curiosities. I thought I detected a suspicion of contempt in the way he said "curiosities."

"There'll be more varmin for you to carry away. Maybe Mister Val would like to choose something."

Uncle Bliss was moving his feet impatiently.

"But I dare say it'll be supper-time afore you've seen all he"—Sancho Panza nodded familiarly at Don Quixote—"has got to show you."

Squire and knight seemed to be on terms of equality. There was no class consciousness about either; as regards rivalry I was not so sure. Staff was a bit too free a distributor for Uncle Bliss' taste. And that flute of his had captivated Irene.

Obviously it was not Sancho Panza's day. His rustic shrewdness seemed to tumble to the fact, for he said, "It won't do for the young lady to miss the supper train again," and took himself off without a formal goodbye. Presently we heard his diminishing flute under the window.

We very nearly did miss the supper train. By the time we had finished tea, stewed pineapple, a tin of mixed biscuits, and Mrs. Staff's harvest cake, there was no time left to see the birds and the marine shells. The last half-hour was spent in looking for the spider and the trochil, the bird that picks crocodiles' teeth, which Val had read about in some book of travel. Its impudent daring teased his imagination.

Both were found, Val's trochil and Irene's poisonous, eight-legged, bird-eating spider, which disturbed her sleep. But the beauty of it was that it hadn't any legs left; Irene had to take them on trust. And as for eating birds, it looked as if a bird had eaten it. No wonder Uncle Bliss had been a long time finding it. He held the bottle up to the light, and revolved it slowly, so that we could count the disjected parts of the spider as they chased each other round the glass. Val reckoned that there were eighteen of them. Possibly legs. The fearsomeness of the insect had not survived dismemberment.

Solomon presented the bottle to the Queen of Sheba, or his little Arachnophobe, as he called her. "Take it home with you," he said; "then you won't dream about spiders any more."

"Oh, thank you, Uncle Bliss."

The gift was hardly in the category of apes, ivory, and peacocks. Still, as an antidote to nightmare, especially in the form of arachnophobia, I have no doubt it proved "a sovran remedie."

And now it was Val's turn. I can imagine that his heart leapt. If there were any balance in the distributions of Providence, Uncle Bliss was going to give him the trochil.

"And what would Val like?"

The encrimsoned Val was, of course, inarticulate. For a golden second, I believe, he thought that he had been given the freedom of the treasure-house. I wanted to pull his sleeve and whisper in his ear, "Val, old man, don't forget the fish ponds."

What was Uncle Bliss going to do? I felt for him in his difficulty. The last time he exercised his avuncular bounty he had settled the problem by the simple expedient of

division. Irene's shilling had split up easily into two six-
pences. Was he going to apply the same principle of bisec-
tion to Irene's spider? If not, what Solomonian shift would
he contrive to make things even?

I might have known that Uncle Bliss was not easily cor-
nered. The problem now was one of even-handedness. He
carefully detached from the shelf a bottle which contained
an insect even more dismantled than the spider. It was a
scorpion. A scorpion for Val, and a spider for Irene. That
made things square. There was nothing to choose between
their part in the impoverishment of the treasure-house.

"You like scorpions, eh?"

Val appeared to be delighted with the gift. You would
think he had emptied the whole cornucopia.

We had to run to catch the supper train. Luckily it was
a few minutes late. Uncle Bliss saw us to the drive gate.
Altogether it was a day to mark with a white stone. The
spoils, perhaps, were hardly worthy of the raid, but if the
children were disappointed they were too loyal to show it.
They held their bottles tight and upright so as not to let
the stoppers fall out, spilling the seeds of scorpions and
bird-eating spiders in quiet Homersfield.

In the train and most of the way home from the station
Irene chattered about Sancho Panza, who had promised to
"larn her" the flute.

Poor futile Don Quixote!

XI

CHIMBASHI AT BLOOMSBURY

Evidently Chimbashi was quiescent; we were outside his radius; his ghost was laid. I hardly gave him a thought the day we went to the Clapperhouse, and that was the very first day after our fright. When we got home we found that Sellinger had called, and left a parcel for the children. It was the most fearsome-looking Tibetan devil mask, to which he had attached a label, "Warranted tame. Won't bite." They hung it up on a pole in the work-room, and it nearly frightened Jessie into a fit. The gift was intended to console them for the loss of the antelope's horn. It was like old Sellinger to think of that. But we had forgotten Chimbashi, and, what was more important, Chimbashi had forgotten us.

The removal of our African bogey was a positive purgation. He seemed to have carried away any germs of mischief there were about as well as his own.

Everything began to go smoothly again. Lady Potter called when we were out, and we missed her. That was a bit of luck. And the children were very welcoming to Miss Seamore, whom they found waiting for them in the hall. This was not hypocrisy, but remorse. I felt a twinge of it myself. It was quite a different Miss Seamore, subdued, almost responsive; the awesomeness had evaporated as out of the eight-legged spider. Even her looks had improved.

It is most illogical, but there are people one dislikes more at a distance than when they are living in the same house with one. I remember my antipathy for Miss Seamore used to increase towards the end of the holidays; then when she came back, I felt that I had been an unjust brute.

The passage of Chimbashi seemed to have put us all in our very best shape. Probably those Juju men knew what they were worshipping. He was their adaptation of the ill wind proverb, the soul of goodness in things evil, the uses of adversity, which, like the toad, ugly and venomous, conceals a precious jewel in his head. Chimbashi had absorbed all the malice in the air—like a sponge. Swept the place as clean as the lubbar fiend. And now we had got rid of him. Here was a thesis for some Spook Society. There was an order of goblins known to the early French necromancers as *follets buvards.* Gervase of Tilbury (Otia Imperialia) gives an account of "the drudging golbins, or Portunos, freaks among spirits who do play their pranks in those unsubstantial bodies, which they assume by God's permission. As soon as the doors are shut the goblins warm themselves at the fire, and take frogs from their bosom, which they roast on the embers, and proceed to eat . . ."

One could not expect Chimbashi, coming from darkest Africa, to be so amenable as the drudging goblin, Milton's lubbar fiend, who, in return for a certain license of mischief or a warm corner by the fire, used to do odd jobs for the housewife. No doubt the medicine-man knew how to control him, but that was in his own *milieu;* at Homersfield it might have been dangerous to keep him too long.

I broached my theory of the *follets buvards,* or sprites absorbent, to Angela.

"Wait and see," she said.

Angela's rationalism is a bit shaky when it is a question of a malicious agent. Chimbashi fell in with her idea of a punitive order of things.

The only lasting ill effect we could trace to housing him, so far as I could see, was my health. I had lost vitality, and was feeling confoundedly tired. I found myself sitting down instead of standing up to shave, and wishing that one went downstairs instead of upstairs to bed, a condition of feebleness that dated from the Sellingers' bazaar. It had been a bit of a strain wheeling the Brebis home. She was most concerned about it. "My dear," she said, "I am afraid it must have been a Herculaneum effort."

Chimbashi, of course, had upset her, and so was at the root of the evil, but when Angela implied that he was the agent of the Disciplinary Spirit, I took up the other line of argument out of contrariness, that it was all a chapter of accidents. Chimbashi just happened to be there.

"You don't really mean you believe in him?" I asked her.

"Have you forgotten how jumpy you were at the crossroads?"

"I like that," I said. "Who climbed the gate when she saw a cow?"

"You remind me of the lobster," she retorted.

"What lobster?"

Angela quoted my favourite lyric—

"When the sands are all dry, he is as gay as a lark,
    And will talk in contemptuous tones of the shark.
But, when the tide rises and sharks are around,
    His voice has a timid and tremulous sound."

"A fig for Chimbashi!" I said. "I have the greatest contempt for him. The first chance I get I will go and grin at him in the museum."

"I wouldn't if I were you," Angela said.

The first chance, as it happened, was the day I had to go up to town to confront my Medical Board. I was not going to let them turn me down this time. I had been lying

low, storing up vitality, putting on weight. I had hardly been out of the garden since our visit to Uncle Bliss.
The little twinge Chimbashi administered had made me
careful.

It was ages since I had been in town, and I looked forward to the jaunt. It would be jolly lunching at the club.
One never knew who might turn up—fellows one had not
met since school or Cambridge, ship companions, men
in one's own service. Probably I should hear some Sudan
gossip. One was rather out of the world in Homersfield.

I had to get up early and leave before the post to catch
the breakfast train. When I looked in to say good-bye to
Angela, I did not remind her of my project of grinning at
Chimbashi. I might not go near the museum, so I thought
it better to say nothing about it. But I was as good as my
word. Something, not exactly curiosity, impelled me.

Depression settled on me directly I had given up my
stick and received the round green label for it from the
janitor—horrid rite that deprives one both of support
and respect. I was in no hurry to find Chimbashi or his
friends. Anthropology rather bores me; and in a very few
minutes I found that I had drifted into the Assyrian Tran-
sept and the Nimrud Gallery—haunts of mine in early
days, when I had a great longing to be an Assyriologist,
and dig up the despatches of Khammurabi in cuneiform in
their clay envelopes and decipher them. That was in the
days before I thought of going to the Sudan. My boundary posts, stones, and terminal posts were Sumerian and
Babylonian; my spiritual adventures with Layard rather
than with Cortes and Balboa or modern African explorers.
Val and Irene had not felt the pull of antiquity yet. Here
was the stele inscribed with Khammurabi's code of laws.
I knew my bearings in the Babylonian room. It used to
stand in Esagila, the temple of Marduk in Babylon. The
king of Elam bore it off to Susa after the sack of the city,

and there it lay among other vanities, unconsidered lumber, which, no doubt, the people of Elam didn't hold with, until de Morgan dug it up 3000 years afterwards. It was his find that made me want to be an excavator.

Then I found myself among the tablets of Ashur-bani-pal, 20,000 of them from his library at Nineveh. If I had stuck to my hobby of Assyriology I might have been able to decipher them, and to roll you off a list of the most trustworthy houses in Babylon when Esharhaddon was king, or the catalogue of plants which Khammurabi ordered for his botanical gardens, or to read Nebuchadnezzar's decision in the case of the corrupt assessor, or what the baker at Lagash had to pay for adulterating his flour. It seems that archaeology was a science in Nineveh. Ashur-bani-pal, the bibliophile, was as curious about the past as a Cambridge professor, only instead of Greek and Hebrew he studied Sumerian, which had become a dead language, and sent out scribes to the ancient cities of Babylonia to collect rare and important books. Those human-headed bulls once stood at the door of his palace to prevent evil spirits getting in. Chimbashi must have run the gauntlet in Bloomsbury. That omen tablet recorded the dream of a Chaldean astrologer. Was there ever a time when men did not cajole spooks and dream? Or play with heraldry? Those eagles and lions were the arms of Lagash which flourished 3000 years before Balshazzar saw the writing on the wall.

I turned to familiar friezes. A king was pouring a libation on a lion which had fallen to his bow; Esharhaddon II. received the ships that were coming in from Tyre and Sidon. And here was a procession of foreigners bringing in a present of apes to Ashur-bani-pal. How far had that porter carried his ape? From Africa, perhaps, and it was perched on his shoulders with its belly pressed against the top of his head; its fore-arms scratched the man's forehead, while its hind-legs were dug into the nape of his neck.

And what did Ashur-bani-pal, King of Assyria, want with
the ape? He was a collector, I suppose, a sort of glorified
Uncle Bliss. The habit seemed to be as old as time. What
did Solomon want with apes and peacocks? A curious instinct, this of collecting. A sort of grown-up childishness.
That was a profound aphorism of Staff's: "There's nothing
so curious as folk." You would think that Solomon might
have known better. Why, even I in my small experience
had come to learn that one's comfort depends on not
accumulating things. Why did Angela collect china for
Jessie to break? Whimp, whimp, whimp! *Vanitas vani-
tatum!* Vanity of objects, and collectors and collections of
objects! The place was getting on my nerves. I felt as if I
had been talking to one of the most dismal of the Hebrew
prophets, or reading Ecclesiastes. I must find Chimbashi.

I was a long time finding him, a long time even before
I could discover the quarter of the museum in which he
ought to be. I thought of looking in on Clarkson, but I
had registered a silly oath not to ask the way. All this took
me at least half an hour, but when I did come within his
radius I was drawn to him like the man at Maskelyne and
Devant's to the hidden thimble with his eyes blindfolded.

I found the innocent-looking Chimbashi in a glass case,
a nonentity among spooks, ignominiously labelled and
shelved with a lot of other totems as impotent as himself.
The most ossified anthropologist would not have stopped
to look at him.

Well, we had settled Chimbashi's business! I left him
there with his companions "to dry rot at ease till the Judgment Day." I put out my tongue at him like a Tibetan,
and turned my back. I was not in the least interested in
the company he kept, or in anthropology, or in primi-
tive man. How these pundits run folklore to death! Too
many pedants. Too many theses. Too many ramifications

of the Golden Bough. I looked at my watch. It was time for lunch. Why had I wasted my morning at the Museum?

The club soon put me into "a good shape." London had lost much of the romance with which I invested it in extreme youth, but I still found it a pleasant enough caravanserai; that is, if one didn't try to sandwich too much of it between the bread and butter of life. And if one didn't go sight-seeing, poking one's nose into museums. The club was always a good draw. I felt home-like directly I got inside. It was agreeable to be remembered by the hall porter when one had not been near the place for years, and to find the same old fogey in the same corner of the reading-room reading the same paper. They told me he was a bore, but what did it matter? He never buttonholed me. One sometimes hears men grumble at Service clubs. Every one is of the same type, they say, and they complain of the sameness—I am not sure that the word is not narrowness—of outlook. But I do not agree with this highbrow point of view. I like my club. You hear less politics talked in it than in any other in London, and I have never listened to a discussion on psycho-analysis or the merits of a minor poet. As for the soldier man, is there any one more responsive, or easier to get on with, or more individual under the skin? If you cannot get him to talk, you may be sure it is your own fault.

While I was hanging up my coat I was greeted by Tubby Hughes. That was one old friend. And while I was washing my hands in the next basin to Tubby, I clapped on the back by another.

"Hullo, Clayton!" I heard behind me. "I thought you were in the Sudan."

It was Scatters Marshall. He condoled with me. "It was bad luck missing that Mongalla shoot. You had to give it up, I hear. Had an extension of leave? Seeing the Board this afternoon? I suppose you hope they'll pip you?"

"Not quite. I have had nearly two years."

Tubby raised his head from the next basin and spluttered, "He doesn't know when he is lucky."

He and Scatters had just burst upon London out of the Nilotic mud.

"Let's make up a table. I saw Rowlandson in the hall."

We did. It was more or less a Sudan table. Tubby Hughes, of my service,—he and I had spent a week ibex-driving with the Hadendowa soon after I joined up; Scatters Marshall, the only man who had found a way to make the Dinka work; Duncan of the Intelligence, who could speak Arabic in twenty-five different dialects. And we were joined by Boomer Smith, fresh from Amritsar, where he had had to stand by with his regiment while the Akali Sikhs and Mahants took it in turn to butcher one another. None of these men were born old or codified; they were certainly not of one type; nor was their humanism glossed over by the Oxford manner.

The talk veered from theatres and Hurlingham to shikar, Africans, and Asiatics. Duncan's last exploit was to arrive at Khartum by the Felata pilgrim route from Bornu disguised as a barber. I asked him why he had chosen hair-cutting as a profession. The only reason he gave was that he thought it might come in useful. One learnt a lot; the occupation demanded a certain amount of ritual. I suspected that he had chosen the role because it offered the most chances of giving himself away, but this was a point that he did not emphasise.

"How long were you on the trek?" I asked him.

"Eighteen months. A little more."

Here Boomer Smith, beside whom Uncle Bliss had a voice like a sucking dove, drowned our African talk.

"I'd rather deal with a lashkar of Orakzais and Afridis any day than with the Singhas. You never know where you are with them."

"Quite," said Tubby Hughes, who had served in India as a subaltern. "I don't like their cry. I remember one of my corporals asked me whether they were cheering or jeering, and I am blessed if I could tell him. Queer-tempered fellows."

"Eighteen months?" I said to Duncan,

"Yes," he said. "And six months I was laid up in a hole that hadn't got a name, poisoned by a suspicious husband. The wife's looks would have been enough to secure me a verdict in a Christian country. I had to wait until another pilgrimage came along. But it was all experience."

"What on earth did you do all the time?" I asked him.

"Simply vegetated. The difficulty was in keeping one's temper. I believe the poison made me a bit peevish. You see, if you hit one of these fellows, you had to kill him, or he would kill you. And if you did finish him off, there would be his pious relatives to settle accounts with."

"You would have got through to Mecca, I suppose, with that first lot."

I believe it would have been quite easy. Duncan's main difficulties must have been at the start. He would have covered his tracks before left Bornu. In Khartum no one would have suspected him. But I was not fated to hear the end of his story. Boomer broke in—

"Were you saying that you had been poisoned, Duncan? Same here. In the Abor show."

Tubby hoped that in the next war he would be on the Abor front. "Just the kind of warfare I like. Up against bows and arrows. Better than those damned H.E.'s."

Boomer had his doubts. "I am not sure I wouldn't prefer the Somme again," he said. "You can't see farther than that wall, mind you, and when their arrows are fresh, they only give you five minutes—five devilish unpleasant minutes, too. Luckily my man was a bit slack about keeping his venom up to date."

A discussion arose as to whether the Shilluk who hunted the hippopotamus with the spear poisoned their weapons. Rowlandson had seen them at work. It was a form of sport that needed courage. One had to be as nippy as a torero. "I saw them finish one off," he told us, but added modestly, "I was up a tree."

"Any news of the spook-beast?" Scatters asked Rowlandson.

"The *lau?* Why, yes. There was a scare the other day in a village of the Bahr-el-Ghazal."

"Has a white man seen it yet?"

"No, only that Dago. I forget his name. The half-caste Portuguese engineer at Ennobio."

"What *is* a *lau?*" Boomer inquired.

Rowlandson enlightened him. "The *lau* is a composite beast; it is reputed to have a bit of the bird, snake, and lizard in it, like the wyvern in coats-of-arms; but, according to the most trustworthy accounts, the python element predominates. White men have seen its trail, and have been puzzled by it."

"Yes," said Scatters. "Gregson told me that it left a furrow like a tumbril dragged along without wheels."

I had forgotten the *lau,* of which I had heard rumours from time to time. The Sudan, it seemed, had its pterodactyl, too. I told them about the legendary beast of the Jiundu swamp and Bliss' proposed expedition.

"Do you mean Pygmy Bliss?"

"The man who bought the dinosaur's egg?"

"A bit touched in the head, isn't he?"

"A tough nut, I should think."

I had not realised Uncle Bliss' notoriety.

"I wonder if there is anything in it," Scatters reflected. "Bliss' beast and the *lau* may be cousins."

Rowlandson thought there was. "There is hardly a corner of Africa where you don't hear some yarn of the kind.

You remember the story of the brontosaurus which was supposed to haunt Katanga? And there is the flying reptile of the Libyan Desert known to the Senussi as the *issula,* own brother perhaps to Herodotus' winged snake. But it is generally in swamp forest like that Jiundu morass you mentioned. Much the same country, I should think, as the *lau's* habitat, difficult to explore. It would be exactly the kind of place you would find a prehistoric survival. If any exists."

"The natives all seem to agree about it," Scatters said.

"Yes; there is plenty of presumptive evidence. The Dinkas describe it as having a bunch of tentacles on its head, a thick wiry net of hairs which it darts out to entangle the bird or fish it feeds on."

"Or man," said Tubby. "I think I shall give the *lau* a miss. I don't fancy being stalked by one. Not my idea of shikar."

The general verdict of the table, I think, was: Difficult to dismiss as untrue.

Scatters and Tubby went off early to Ranelagh; Boomer had a train to catch; and I was left alone with Rowlandson, who treated me to one of his jeremiads on game extermination. In five years there wouldn't be a Giant Eland left in the Sudan. That was cattle disease. But the curse of the country were the Yanks and Cockneys. Cook's tourists. They get fitted up in Khartum, rifles and everything. All they had to do was to walk on board.

"I saw a steamer a party had hired, gramophones on deck, tables laid out with sandwiches and short drinks, English-speaking boys, broadcasting apparatus. And the beggars pepper elephants and giraffes from the deck, fire into the brown. I believe they carried a machine-gun. What's the good of game preservation laws? The most thumping fine is about as much use as a sick headache. The profiteer pays up smiling. The other day Government confiscated and auctioned a fellow's heads and skins. He bought them in. Six months' quod in Khartum gaol is what they want."

Rowlandson gulped down his cognac and lighted another cigar. "Well, good-bye, Clayton. I must be off. Got an appointment with Ward. Good luck with the Board. I hope we go out on the same steamer together."

I still had half an hour before I need leave the club. I had been as happy as a lord at lunch, as if I were already back in it all—the mud, the sand, the sun, the mosquitoes, the flies. The glamour of the Sudan was revived. I kept the thought of the Board under a tight valve. The undercurrent of misgiving was like an ache which one forgets when one is excited. Duncan had disturbed my contentment with the vegetable existence more than any of them. When Rowlandson left, I thought I would go up to the library and look up his line of pilgrimage on the map. I was a bit vague about the lie of Falata and Bornu.

But I found the stairs a serious proposition. I had to stop and rest at each flight as if somebody had tied a weight to my legs. Had Chimbashi got in a Parthian shot? By the time I reached the top I was certain of it.

I remembered that the Board met in a room at the top of another three flights of stairs, and that there was no lift. Obviously strategy demanded a slow and cautious approach if I was going to arrive with my pulse in order and all my breath. So I left the club without satisfying my curiosity about Duncan's itinerary. Now I come to think of it, I have never repaired that omission. For in the next quarter of an hour the thing happened which made it necessary to rearrange my future completely, and Angela's, and the children's. There was no bluffing the medicos. The Board decided that the Sudan was out of the question. They prescribed a temperate climate, a very uninteresting diet, and the negation of all but the mildest activities. So that was that. I could imagine Chimbashi grinning in his glass case.

In the train I reviewed the situation, my mind revolving like a caged squirrel. Up and down, round and round. A whirligig of emotions. One of the sensations that kept coming up was relief. No more suspense. The thing was settled. I had been trying to fool myself into the idea that I was fit for work. I suppose I had known all the time that I was not, but it was the Board's business, not mine, to discover that. In the meanwhile, with the aid of the philosophic portcullis trick, I had been chewing the lotus contentedly all these months. "I'll put my stake on red," I had said, "If black turns up, what does it matter? Why fuss?"

Still the financial side of it was rather a poser. How were we going to live? I should have a small commuted pension, probably in a lump sum. We should have to sell Homersfield, of course. Then there were Angela's shares. Amalgamated Moonstones. A bit shaky, but she insisted on her 7 per cents. They brought her in £47 a year, less income tax. Now, I supposed, they could not make us pay income tax, as we had no income. Silver lining No. 1.

I reckoned it all up. We should have less than three hundred a year. We might live on that in France, if we were careful, with exchange at eighty. The Board had advised the south of France. I could not see myself and Angela going the round of Dax and Ax and Aix with the Brebis. In the Riviera, of course, living would be too dear. Besides, we both hated it. The Basque coast appealed to us more, but I had heard that it was getting just as expensive, or worse. Still, there were other *gites,* and France would be the very thing for the children's education. By Jove! that reminded me. We should have to leave Miss Seamore behind. Silver lining No. 2.

France was an attractive idea, but after a year or two the children would have to go to school; then the fees would eat up the whole of our income. That would mean living on capital. How many years would it be before we had spent it all? After more involved calculations I worked it out at eight, possibly nine. And what should we do then? What do people do when they have used up their capital and find themselves on the unemployed list? There must be thousands in our place, with even less to fall back upon. They would probably think us rich. Yet they managed to knock along somehow. This was a mystery which had often puzzled me. People talked casually of the workhouse as a refuge, but I could not think of any one I knew personally except a few philosophic Homersfield friends who had been reduced to living in one.

The train pulled up opposite a murky-lighted street, rows of mean dismal little houses all exactly alike. I had never explored slum realities, but the word "tenement" called up an alarming picture. The squirrel in its cage started its revolutions again. Up and down, round and round. I remembered a recipe an optimist once gave me for the compression of hump. I will not answer for its morality, or even its efficacy. One had to count up one's escapes by thinking of people less happy than oneself. Item: the tobacconist's assistant in his upright coffin in the Underground. Item: the teacher in a Spanish school. Item: the prisoner in the condemned cell waiting to be hanged. Item: the Chinaman in his Sorrow Cage.

There were worse things than being penniless. One might be tortured, or burnt, or periodically chastised, or bored, or suffer other barbarous treatment until one's affections and appetites were slowly atrophied. Maupassant has a story of a peasant woman who bullied and starved her husband when he became too weak to work and earn wages. In some countries when one ceases to be useful to Society, one is put away. Or one might be blind.

Imagine not being able to see Angela! Or lose one's curiosity, or one's interest in the interior life. By the time we got to Renton Parva I was beginning to think myself an uncommonly lucky person. Angela and the kids were as fit as three trivets.

After all, it is not much fun trying to do things when you don't feel up to it. There were hundreds of books I wanted to read, and I could sit down to it now. French literature alone; I had hardly touched it. And I could work up medieval history. I might get some publisher to give me translating work.

As we drew into Homersfield I saw the lamps of the dog-cart in the station yard and a silhouette of the resurrected Joan. Angela was on the platform. There was no need to break it to her. My forced grin was enough.

Angela, of course, was angelic. She didn't wait for me to tell her. She knew. I am afraid she embraced me on the platform. "I am so glad," she said; "I couldn't bear to think of you going back to that horrid Sudan."

Silver lining No. 3.

We had left the station lights behind when I heard her say something about Miss Seamore and finding her a new place. "I suppose we ought not to be glad," she murmured. Then she prepared me for bad news. "Amalgamated Moonstones. I had a letter this morning. They are not paying dividends."

Poor Angela.

"You didn't go and see Chimbashi?" she asked me, after a silence so pregnant that I knew what was coming.

"I did," I admitted.

It just showed. But Angela was much too chivalrous to say so.

XII
THE SIMPLE LIFE AT NURIEN

The exodus from Homersfield was not the dismal event I had feared. The thing I dreaded most was the sale of the place and the warehousing of the things we could not bring ourselves to sell, but we were able to let the house instead of selling it, so in name at least it was still ours. The Whittakers, our tenants, very old friends of the Sellingers, kept Jessie and the cook, and John and Joan, and promised to look after the garden and not to break the china. Sellinger brought them over to see us two or three times, so they became sufficiently friends of our own to volunteer these assurances. Angela had every reason to feel comfortable about her treasures. There were not going to be any children, or dogs. And Whittaker was a bibliophile, so our books were safe.

To Val and Irene, of course, who had few memories of ends, the exodus meant very little. Their only cross was that they wanted to take their museum to France, but had to leave it behind. I sympathised with Miss Seamore when she received their airy goodbyes. But partings of this kind rarely have any significance for children. A week, or a month, or a year, mean much the same thing. We had let the house for four years, and they quite thought we were coming back again.

Anyhow, the excitement of travel left no room for homesickness. I was still young enough to wish that one could look out of both windows of the train at the same time, and the children were old enough to enjoy the "furriness" of it. I remembered my own schoolboy holidays in France. At Nurien everything was strange. Not only the people. Even the dogs were different, in the way they walked and in the way they looked at you, a sort of Gallic consciousness, as different from English dogs as Frenchmen from Englishmen. The French horse, with its strange headgear and collar exalted like a horn, no doubt had a French way of thinking. And the smells were not the same. That early morning smell of the streets, a fragrant blend of newly-ground coffee and caporal, mingled with the exhalations of the boulangerie, was new and delicious. Val remarked on the absence of pillar-boxes and policemen. It was delightful to go to the tobacconist's for stamps instead of the post-office, and to watch the old lady serving other old ladies—who were

sometimes bearded—with snuff over the counter; and on the way to peer into the half-Moorish wistaria-hung courtyard with its stone troughs like fonts, and oleanders planted in tubs under the balconies; or to explore the cobbled alleys which led down steps and through arches to the stream where the washerwomen beat clothes on flat stones. The out-of-doors laundry, with its public washing, seemed an expression of the agreeable intimacy of the easy-going responsive Nurienais. The children soon made friends. There was Henri, the pharmacien's son, who knew a few words of English, and wanted to acquire more, or to parade those he already had; and M. Bruneteau, the notaire, whom Val found fishing, and who inducted him into the art of catching trout with the gentle *asticot*. He became an occasional visitor with other acquaintances Irene and Val picked up in odd places, among whom was

M. Minicot, the dwarf, but he only came to the window, like a bird.

Dwarfs, and other human freaks, added to the excitement of Nurien. The first time I saw M. Minicot I took him for a witch. He wore a cast-off tulle hat with faded roses in the brim, and a soiled lace fichu which reached almost to his waist, and an apron drawn tightly round the lower part of him like a skirt. At a distance his appearance was rather terrifying. The beard one might have passed; it was a common appendage among the Nurienaises, and the pipe in his mouth. What frightened me was the moustache, thick and white as lamb's wool, surmounting the fichu, and serving as a foil to the roses in the hat. But the sinister impression vanished on nearer approach when one perceived that he was a man, and that it was a whim of his to masquerade like this. M. Minicot had the trustful and engaging smile of the honoured indigent. And he wore his strange plumage as if it were natural. This alone gave him a certain dignity. He would come to the window like a bird while we were having *déjeuner,* and bow to us in turn, Irene first. Crumbs, I supposed, were the attraction.

And nearer home there was Louise. It was Louise with her honest, brown, horse face and slow smile—if you can imagine a horse with a smile—who decided us to go to Madame Brun's, or Sam Suffy, as the house was called. Our choice of apartments was limited at Nurien. Madame Gerontiat's windows looked out on the Route Nationale, and offered a fine view of the drinking fountain and the plane-trees and the statue of M. Boudin, but they were hot and stuffy, and there were noises late and early in the street, and in the summer a hubbub of char-a-bancs carrying tourists to the Cirque at the spectacular end of the valley. Madame Leblanc's house was more secluded. Her windows looked on to the courtyard of the Hôtel de Ville, but Angela didn't like the smell. Madame Brun's windows

at first didn't open at all, but when they did open it was
on the quiet Rue Saint Béat, a feeder of the market-place.
The street had no particular shape. It was broad here and
narrow there, with kinks in it and projecting angles, and
alleys leading into culs-de-sac. The houses displayed a
great variety of roof, some with the mansard slope, others
pure Béarnais with bellying curves like sails, the most
sightly roofs I know; but in colour they were all of the
same satisfying pigeon-grey, house and church; and this
gave the town an individual, cosy, self-contained look,
which did not belie its nature.

Sam Suffy and Louise between them captured us at
once. Angela was determined that those windows should
open, and the brawny Louise accomplished the feat, as she
accomplished most things. The verandah of the first and
second floors at the back looked over the houses beneath
on to the valley—as generous a view as you will find in
France—and admitted as many *courants d'air* as we chose.
Our abode was well named. Sam Suffy, we discovered, was
a corruption of *Ça me suffit* (*gallice*, the Abode of Bliss).
We did not know that we lived in a house whose name was
a joke until Louise explained why so many people grinned
as they passed our windows. Nor did we understand why
Madame Brun's house dog, a brown Pyrenean wolfhound,
who frequented the hall or doorstep, was sometimes called
Vichy and sometimes Nero. Angela's theory was that it
had been born at Vichy, and that its real name was Nero.
Irene worried it out of Louise. You called it Vichy at a distance when you had a bone to give it. Vichy, in fact, was
vocative, Nurien for *Viens ici.* Thus the children learned
French. It was not the French of Paris, still it was good
enough.

We wanted them to become bilingual. This has always
seemed to me the ideal education for an English boy or
girl up to the age of twelve. "Better than a private school,"

I used to say to Angela. It was my business to preserve the illusions. We lived in the present. We probably both wondered a dozen times a day what we were going to do about their education, but we left it out of our discussions. Still my boast of the advantages of Nurien over a private school was not all make-believe. What would I not have given to be able to talk French, or to follow it when spoken quickly, without translating it in my head, searching for phrases, and worse, having to think of the correct sound of words familiar to the eye only? At both my schools a boy who talked French like Froggy would have been kicked.

Angela used to laugh at my accent, and my ear was so bad that I had not the patience to listen to voluble French for more than two minutes at a time. When M. Bruneteau or Mademoiselle Lory came to see us I used to become half hypnotised with ennui, and the effort of pretending to follow what they said. They talked and talked, and would never go. It was like listening to the rumble of an interminable train which one had to be polite to, although one was feeling train-sick. It was all my wretched ear. I loved the people and the country, and the language, so long as I had not got to listen to it or talk it, but could read it in peace. When it was a case of a difficulty in a book, Angela had to come to me. The children had her ear. They very soon learnt to use verbs reflexively, roll a sufficient "r," and put in an occasional subjunctive—and quite naturally. Irene acted as interpreter for the Brebis when she visited us, and afterwards for Uncle Bliss, and sometimes for me. She learnt to talk patois too without serious damage to her French of Nurien.

They had regular lessons, of course. Mademoiselle Lariot used to come every day. But for the first month or so French was a game. What more fascinating dictionary than a shop window! In the Rue Saint Béat we had a ferblanterie, a serrurerie, and a bourrellerie; and in the market-place a vannerie, chapellerie, rouennerie, and a pépinieriste. One had to look into the window and guess the inscription over the shop, or if the window was blank one had to look at the description and guess what was inside. Sometimes we were all four stumped, and had to consult Contanseau, as when Irene came in one evening and asked, "Daddy, what are *sons?*"

I have described the Rue Saint Béat as quiet. This was true of six days in the week, but on the seventh, Tuesday, it became the debouchement for all the traffic from the west of the valley into the market-place. This disturbance of tranquility added to the attractions of the street. We enjoyed the din, the bêlement, mugissement, beuglement, grognement—here was another exercise in French—of lambs, calves, and pigs. Market at Nurien was as different from Homerton as the Café Dodet from Homersfield Bell. From early in the morning until mid-day the procession filed through the Rue Saint Béat—lambs carried on asses' backs, two of them in a sack on each side of the saddle, bleached faces looking out as if they were going to be sea-sick; peasant women bringing in their tall, lean, chestnut-fed pigs from some distant village, generally one woman to a pig, sometimes driving it, or more often leading, walking backwards with a deceitfully extended palm, and repeating, "Viens, viens, m'petit." Best of all were the Pyrenean bullocks in their light, clean, white or grey blankets, and coiffure of sheepskin, yoked in pairs to the carts, gentle-eyed, buff-coloured, and moving in perfect step. The master of the team walked solemnly in front, the guiding rod of hazel on his shoulder, or balanced erect in his hand, the docile bullocks following. The carts they drew carried pigs or calves. There was the little charrette, balanced on two low wheels, occupied by a single oscillating sow; and four-wheeled boarded waggons with a dozen calves in them, standing in rows, rump to rump, and looking out gravely at the street. The peasants, gaunt, clean-shaven, hawk-like Béarnais, came in on foot, or in small carts drawn by donkeys or mules with enormous ears.

There were no flocks. The sheep had gone up to the high pastures, and the cattle which were not in carts were mostly led. The boucherie Mallet was round a bend of the street, mercifully hidden from our window; but M. Mallet would descend to a point within observation and accost the farmers as they brought in their stock. An old man would come along leading a single calf, its neck in the noose of a rope. M. Mallet would stop him, and they would chaffer. "Eight hundred francs for that!" M. Mallet would laugh at the demand as he pinched and pulled the calf, but after a little palaver he would bend quickly and brand his initials on its coat. Then he would take the still expostulating peasant into the buvette and stand him a byrrh, leaving the calf tied to the rail *beugling* piteously. Irene would run across the road and stroke it. Calves' lips and noses are dewy, and fragrant, and inviting; calves' eyes large and black and full of expression, but happily neither accusatory nor apprehensive. Val would offer it a lump of sugar, which, of course, it declined.

The boucherie Mallet was to become a familiar interior. Louise was too occupied to do the marketing, so we had to go to the butcher's and grocer's ourselves. Angela at the butcher's was unthinkable. I offered to go instead. But no, she insisted that it was the housewife's work. She was learning *faire les économies,* an art in which I was unteachable. So we went together. Never before had her eyes rested for more than a moment on the suspended carcasses. The ribs of the beast, we discovered, were chops. *Détails horribles.* Madame Mallet at the counter received us with becks and smiles. A strong and beefy woman with a damp pink complexion like meat. Such at any rate were her arms and neck and cheeks, and one could imagine that the raw pink tints, most apparent at the opening of her bodice, extended to her boots. A necessarily carnivorous woman, I argued in her defence. She worked like a harpy, springing from carcass to carcass, cutting, chopping, pounding, patting, and sawing, yet with a courtesy and an air of obliging which made her occupation appear almost human.

Madame Mallet was the busiest woman in Nurien; the boucherie was always crowded. And how expert an anatomist! I watched her fascinated, and tried to recognise in the disjected members dishes familiar at restaurants. I noticed that even the head and feet were sold, and some of the customers were served with "inners." These were generally soft and splashy, and could be distinguished from the "outers" by their iridescent tints of glazed lead or putty. Angela insisted that her two kilos should be solid. When Madame Mallet plumped them down on the marble counter—triply enfolded, it is true, in sheets of La Petite Gironde—she dropped them into her exquisite bag, the one the Brebis had chosen for her at Homerton the day we explored the burrow and the treasuries of Uncle Bliss.

So together we learnt *faire les économies*. But the interior of the boucherie Mallet soon destroyed our appetite for meat. Our visits became less frequent. I think the "inners" would have frightened us away permanently in any case, but the end was precipitated. One day as we were leaving the shop we saw a calf lying at the bottom of a gig outside with its neck and four feet tied up into a ball, and its nose poked into a basket of quivering raw veal. The contact of the quick and the dead was too much. After that we passed the boucherie Mallet with averted eyes. Madame Mallet regarded us reproachfully at first, and then not at all, and to avoid either unpleasantness, we used to make furtive detours to the market-place by the Allée du Panier Fleuri.

The vegetarian epoch continued for a few weeks until the Brebis came, and Louise was relieved by a *femme de ménage.* During this period we had no meat in the house except ham. Not from the charcuterie; there the risks were equal, or worse, a literal casting of swine before pearls. The pig makes a horrid corpse. We bought our ham at the grocer's in clean slices, which carried no reminiscence of pig.

Angela was never separated from her daintinesses, not even at Sam Suffy. She never had to drink out of a thick cup, but carried about with her the two Spode cups and saucers, with sugar-basin and milk-jug to match, in the osier tea-basket, the one which used to do duty at the Witch Pool; and she took her own bedspread and pillow and quilt with her everywhere, and the dress cover to protect her garments from the least speck of dust, and the shoe-bags, a different one for each pair, and her nighty-case to keep her nighty in during the day. All this ritual of specklessness seemed to me right and proper in Angela, who at Homersfield used to accuse me of leaving my pyjamas on the bathroom floor. Unhappily we had no bathroom at Sam Suffy, but had to learn the art of washing in sections, as was the mode in the country of our adoption.

At Homersfield Angela's vulnerability to the lesser plagues earned her from me the title of "The Knight in Chain Armour." "Why is mummy like a knight in chain armour?" Irene and Val gave it up. "Because she will stand up to a dragon and succumb to a mosquito." But at Sam Suffy there were worse than mosquitoes. During the summer verminicide became a necessary item in the "bazar." However, Angela grew philosophic in adversity, and though she didn't like having her chair or bed kicked, or having her meals served on coarse crockery, or being waited on by clumsy servants, she became very fond of the heavy-handed, heavy-footed Louise, and suffered her gaucheries patiently. For myself there were compensations in the simple life. It was a relief to have only two suits, or one like Uncle Bliss, and never to have to put on evening clothes or a starched shirt. I had long suspected that one's comfort depended on having few possessions.

Angela thought this a pose.

"I don't mind possessions," I said, "if I have anywhere to put them, but it is the very devil having to pack them and cart them about."

Angela agreed that we *must* have a house.

We were sitting in a plot she had fallen in love with in the chestnut woods above the town. Obviously this was the site, a hayfield which was also a park and a glade in the forest, and which commanded a view of the length and breadth of the valley. The chestnuts were distributed in scattered clumps. For some reason the trees chose to grow in outcrops of rocks, though the turf all round was smooth. This gave the glade the appearance of a gnome's parliament, with its sylvan furniture of desks and tables and footstools, covered with grey and green moss and lichen, like script, or frost on the window-pane, or patterns of moonlight. It was the kind of glade Titania might choose to play in. We saw it first in the season of foxgloves and pennywort. The ground sloped to an abrupt terrace at our feet. It was a bit too stiff a slope for a house; to level it would mean quarrying.

I pointed out this practical difficulty to Angela.

"We can avoid that," she explained, "by having one storey behind the other. The first floor would be like a bungalow, almost all verandah with trellised roses. We might just squeeze in a dining-room and kitchen."

"I don't think there would be room," I said. "Not on the same terrace."

Angela pointed to an adjacent level under the very biggest chestnut-tree. "If not, we could build the kitchen there," she suggested, "like a cook-house in an Indian compound." Whatever happened, she was not going to scrap her verandah.

"And the bedrooms?"

"They would be in the terrace behind. You could get two in. Instead of quarrying we could build steps up to it with a pagoda roof like the ones you see over the gates in the farmyards."

I asked her where the bonne was going to sleep, and she discovered another level spot under another tree, not too distant. Our terraced mansion was going to be as scattered as the gnome's parliament, it seemed. I am not sure that some of the smoother rock slabs didn't come into the inventory of furniture.

In her most Utopian schemes Angela had an eye for the economies. She reminded me that the wall of our enclosure was already built. That alone would save two or three thousand francs. And what a wall! How valiantly the foxgloves crowned it, and the pennywort scaled it, and how intimately the toadflax and the maidenhair had established themselves in the crevices. It might have been a Devonshire wall. One would have to wait fifty years at least before a new wall became a garden like that.

"I don't see any water," I observed ruthlessly.

"We could bore an artesian well."

Angela's dream bungalow would cost as much as was left of our diminishing capital to build. And how were we going to live in it when it was built? I asked myself, not Angela. A nightingale was singing in our prospective garden, and we could hear the serin finches in the pines over the wall. I had a feeling that statistics would be inopportune.

"I wonder who it belongs to," she continued. "We mustn't let him know we are going to buy it or he will put up the price. It is generally the way."

I agreed that it would be better to make the offer through an avocat, and thought of all the other houses and sites for houses she wanted to buy. There was the one in the island of the Gave de Nurien which you approached by the one-arched ivied bridge. And there was the house the curé had moved out of at Palomières, embowered in glycine; the church underneath it was thirteenth century, and the garden, when we saw it, was a blaze of lilac and horse-chestnut blossom. And there was the forsaken water-mill which straddled the beck at Lys-Argenteil, and looked as if it had been built as a temple for the genius of that dimple of a valley; not to speak of all the farmhouses, and barns that were convertible into houses, which were irresistible for one reason or another.

Here the terrain and the view were equally satisfying to our pastoral souls. The woods all round us were chestnut, and above them were the pines, and we could see the same zones repeated on the opposite slope, and the white and grey farms in the clearings, some of them so vertical that one wondered the buildings didn't start sliding down. We thought we could distinguish the cattle in the high pastures, which were lighted by an unearthly radiance, a sort of fire-mist. It was a bewitching evening. Below us the white mist was curling up the trunks of the poplars. The valley would have been incomplete without poplars. They give the ranged and ordered note which makes the lowlands appear homely to the shepherds when they bring the flocks down.

"You see," said Angela, "if we built on my terrace plan, the verandah and all the windows would face the valley."

I did not remind her that they would also face the prevailing wind from the snows, which, to use the mildest word, could be punitive in winter.

She had forgotten the Disciplinary Spirit. Or perhaps she thought this was a case in which it might be circumvented. Angela was a stern realist when it was a question of possible or probable things; a pessimist, one might say. It was only when she set her heart on the impossible that she became a visionary. She was wrapped now in the mists of illusion, as still as a flower. By the curve of her neck you would think she was watching a robin.

She broke the silence at last. "When shall we go to the avocat?" she asked.

"Oh, any old time."

"There would be time before dinner."

When I protested at this precipitate commitment to direct action she said, "I don't believe you really want the house."

I assured her I thought it the most seductive project.

In the game of make-believe Angela could give points to Irene. And she was so serious about it that she often took me in. Her own self-deception—while the game lasted—was complete.

As we descended the path through the chestnut wood, she fell to examining the economical side of the problem. A possible recovery in Amalgamated Moonstones was one solution. Then we had shares in French National Premium Bonds. The bank had warned her that neither they nor Government were responsible for notifying the results of drawings. She would send for a list of the past issues and look through it; we might have won a million without knowing it. Even if it were only a small sum it would come in at St. Sebastian. Angela had become possessed of a roulette board and an infallible system. Directly she could scrape money together she was going to St. Sebastian to try it. When the children had gone to bed she would put away her knitting, or her Zola, or her Mirbeau, or her latest discovery in the most naked and stark of the naturalistic school of writers, and take out her roulette board. She would sit over it for an hour, pale and intent like a priestess. I would hear the marble spin and rattle and stop;

then her "Rouge, Pair, Passe," or "Noir, Impair, Manque."
She looked more and more reposeful as she ticked off her
winnings on the bridge-scorer. "Ten thousand." "A hundred thousand." She never lost. "It is perfectly safe if you
have capital."

With the narrowing of the margin between us and des-
titution Angela became more optimistic. How much did I
think the ground would cost? Five francs a square metre?
The farmer ought to jump at that. His hay was thin; it
couldn't bring him in much. And stone ought to be cheap.
And as we were building on rock, there would be no foun-
dations to pay for. And we could let the house in the season. She knew a lady who built a villa in Biarritz and got
back the whole of the interest of the money she spent on it
in a three months' lease. It would be an investment.

An investment of what? The completion of the house
seemed to depend on contingencies connected with moonstones, systems, premium bonds. But the important thing,
she insisted, was to buy the ground at once. The price
of land was sure to go up. Then if we couldn't build, we
could sell at a profit. Whichever way you looked at it, it
would be an investment.

"But, of course, if you won't risk anything—"

I am afraid Angela despised me as an unadventurous
spirit whose sails were never to the tempest given. A financial coward. I remembered the advice of the bookie—"If
you don't speculate, you can't accumulate." I had become
a clog and an impediment.

Angela was thinking aloud in six figures—francs, of
course, not pounds—when we found ourselves under the
limes of the Place Dodet, and remembered with a twinge
of disappointment that it was not our night at the café.
In addition to the market-place, Nurien had two small
squares—the Place Helder and the Place Dodet. The plane-
trees outside the Café Helder were cut candelabra-wise, *en*

berceau, while the branches of the limes outside the Café Dodet were trained to curve downwards, *en voûte.* Sometimes we had our coffee at one, sometimes at the other; only in June, when the limes were out, we deserted the Helder for the Dodet, drawn there by the fragrance of the bloom, like moths.

This evening the smell of the limes was delicious, but unfortunately it was Wednesday; and Tuesday, Thursdays, and Saturdays were our nights. We had decided that we could not afford the extravagance of the café more than three times a week. But, of course, we broke our law. "Let's put off the house for a bit," I suggested to Angela, "and go to the Dodet to-night." It seemed an economical move. A drop from six figures to one! We were richer by 300,000 francs. Besides, the limes pulled us by our noses. We were seduced from piety like the man of God in Anatole France who succeeded in guarding his eyes, but left his nostrils undefended, and so was betrayed by a whiff of mignonette.

We were in complete accord about the suggested change in our budget as we threaded the Allée du Panier Fleuri to Sam Suffy. After dinner were we not going to have our coffee and armagnac under the limes at the Dodet, although it was not our night? That was something tangible to look forward to, whereas houses take the devil of a long time to build.

I liked the company at the Dodet. It was even freer of social superstitions, if that were possible, than the Helder, though the coffee was not so good. You might find M. Minicot there, strayed from the Hôpital des Pauvres to spend the last franc Angela had given him; and at the next table, as likely as not, M. le maire. M. Minicot would bow to us with a grave smile. I half expected him to take off his tulle hat with the roses on the brim, and to remove the pipe from his mouth. That he was able to retain both without discourtesy only showed that he belonged to a privileged order, like folk in a work of genius who are different from other people, yet consistent enough with their own world. One meets them in 'The Midsummer Night's Dream' and in 'The Tempest,' and occasionally in the Pyrenees.

Undoubtedly June was the month for the Dodet. The evenings were longer. We spent the best hour of the day there, "the blue hour after sunset," as the poetical Italians call it; and we would often stay on through the bluish-grey pigeon-coloured hour after that when the sky becomes the colour of the roofs.

Madame, the *patronne,* who flitted from table to table, would visit us in our turn, and give us the gossip, and inquire after the children, and compliment us on their French. They were beginning to speak *couramment,* she said. She never resented being called Madame Dodet by them, though obviously her café was named after the square. If "the blue hour" had passed, it would be time to order another drink. Angela found the armagnac too bitter. Madame recommended Cherry-Rocher, and pointed to the advertisement on the wall—

> "Hiver, je te vois approcher,
>   Sans redouter tes heures grises,
> Puisque, grâce à Cherry-Rocher
>   C'est toujours le temps de cerises."

What a beautiful language is French! Even their advertisements can be poetical. *Sans redouter tes heures grises.* What a wistful line! Here was a Gradus ad Parnassum on the walls of an inn.

And if there were no poets at Nurien there was a historian. M. Estombert unlocked the archives for me. I had just begun to be bitten by Froissart, whom I had only glanced at in Berners' translation. I discovered that Sir

John had been to Nurien with Gaston de Foix. No doubt it was in the castle over the Gave that he read him his book, "whiche boke was called the Melyador, conteyning all the songes, ballades, rundeaux, and vyrelayes, whiche the gentyll duke (Wenceslas of Boesme, duke of Luxenbourge and of Brabant) had made in his tyme, whiche by imagyna-cyon I had gadered toguyder, whiche boke the erle of Foix was gladde to se." The vines in the valley under the Ab-baye would be trained on little mulberry-trees in symmet-rical rows as to-day, and the fourteenth-century antiquary would be interested in the Roman baths. Armagnac, I be-lieve, was served at Gaston de Foix' table, and no doubt when the Earl and Froissart rode through Nurien, mine host would broach the local variant of Cherry-Rocher.

I looked at Angela. She had forgotten hers; her glass was untouched. Her detachment from the scene was as complete as M. Minicot's. She sat there looking like a white wood anemone lost in a cabbage patch.

"What are you thinking about?"

"The next incarnation," she said, "I should like to be a pig."

"In the chestnut woods?"

She was looking out on the blessed valley from the win-dow of her dream bungalow.

"Did you like the Cherry-Rocher?"

"We won't have to cut down a single tree," she an-swered irrelevantly.

"We have had our extravagance," I reminded her, but she was not listening.

"It will be lovely in June. We will come down here every night after dinner."

"I thought we were going to let the house in the summer."

She looked at me so reproachfully that I was quick to add, "But we will have to see the avocat about the price of land."

Of all our evenings at the Dodet I enjoyed the one most on which we broke our law. But in bed that night I lay awake worrying about money, thinking out plans— how we were going to double our capital independently of moonstones, systems, and premium bonds, how long it would be before we had nothing left, how we were going to avoid sending the children to the *école communale*. It was fortunate that the clock of the de Hôtel Ville had a pleasant chime.

XIII
THE FIFTY-NINE DAYS

By the time Uncle Bliss came to see us, the children had enough French to enjoy his vagaries. His contempt for the language was as complete as the Victorian schoolboy's. Travel had not made him cosmopolitan.

The shame-faced hesitations which Val and Irene must have noticed in their father were absent. Uncle Bliss didn't mind making mistakes. This made him all the more fun. He spoke almost fluently, translating the English words as they came into his head without an attempt to turn a phrase, and, of course, with a total disregard for the foreign vowel sounds. When he was in a good temper he spoke to our allies as if he were a grown-up person addressing well-meaning, but unintelligent, children. And when they were stupid and could not follow him, he used to shout at them as the Arab yells at the Nasrani, attributing lack of understanding in the niceties of his tongue to deafness. You would think that it was the French who were *dépaysés,* not Uncle Bliss.

It was a characteristically noisy arrival. I heard the din as I was shaving upstairs. The children met him at the station, and brought him to the house in a *fiacre.* Vichy examined him, and apparently refused to pass him—Uncle Bliss never could hit it off with dogs; he was suspect of the whole tribe. Vichy barked as if the house were being burgled. I heard Irene's high-pitched voice, "Nero, Nero, allez coucher!" Then Uncle Bliss' bellow, "Remouvez le chien toute de suite. Entendez vous?" Barking redoubled. Then Louise, equally loud and commanding, "Monsieur, do not raise your cane; you make him more feroce." Whereupon the latrations died down to an intermittent muffled growl.

I heard him tell Angela that he had come by the "Trane de Lucks from Paw." Pau, I suppose he meant. His luggage was at the "consign" (gallice, *consigne*). He had told the porter he would fetch it *oon otre tom.* Uncle Bliss pronounced "temps" as if it were the alternative to Dick and Harry. Then in a few minutes, after a brief fracas with the *cocher,* the house was as quiet as if it had never suffered this tempestuous invasion. The children had carried him off to explore the town.

Madame Brun had cleared out her spare room for him. I began to wish that we had sent him to an hotel. But Angela reminded me that he was an out-of-door sort of person, and in the unlikely event of his having changed his habits I could become an out-of-door sort of person in my turn. Tranquility seemed to depend on a sort of Box and Cox existence.

We met at lunch. He greeted me boisterously.

"Glad to hear you are stronger, Clayton. How far can you walk? Three miles, eh? Well, we shall have to leave you behind."

I had to content myself with the consolations of infirmity.

He turned to Angela. "I like your quarters," he said; "but if you take my advice, you will poison the dog."

Irene defended Nero. "He won't bark at you when he knows you, Uncle Bliss."

"Well, well! We'll see. We can always go to the chemist's. What's the French for poison?"

"Poison," said Irene.

"Poison? I thought that was fish. She knows the French for everything. Can't stump her. What's the French for boiled eggs?"

"Œufs à la coque," said Irene proudly.

Madame Brun had seven ways of preparing eggs, one for each day of the week. Uncle Bliss happened to arrive on the day which called for the least culinary invention.

"I don't like eggs laid by the cock," he observed. "Tell them to try the poulet." He was Madame Brun's lodger, you see, not our guest. "Still," he added, "Unœuf is as good as a feast."

Ursa Major was in a sportive mood. He had already visited the chestnut woods, and was loud in his praises of Nurien. His only regret was that he was a bit too early for the funguses; and the saprophytes were disappointing; Lathræa was over, and Monotropa not out.

"How long are you going to stay, Uncle Bliss?" Val asked him.

"Fifty-nine days," he announced without hesitation.

My heart fell.

"Why not sixty?" Angela suggested politely.

"Because there are fifty-nine walks."

Uncle Bliss was systematic. He thrust his hand into his capacious breast pocket, and pulled out the local guide.

"59

    Itineraires autour de Nurien.
        29 Promenades.
        14 Excursions en voiture.
        16 Ascensions."

"Who would like to come with me?"

"Oh, Uncle Bliss!" Two of us had no doubt. The children's passion for the extension of *orbis notus* at the

expense of *terra incognita* was as strong as when they
carried the terminal post to the source of the Renton
Parva beck. We had a large scale map on which we marked
our encroachments with flags. Our joint excursions were
limited to the chestnut level and the villages and farms
scattered in the woods on a mercifully terraced incline.
Here the blend of the *soigné* and *sauvage* enchanted
Angela, who preferred dimples in landscape to chasms,
and I had come to share her pastoral bias. When I had
legs I was enticed by Alps and crags, but being deprived
of them I had arrived philosophically at the conclusion of
our great-grandfathers, that mountains are best seen from
below, preferably through, or under, arching branches—in
spring through cherry orchards for choice, or other blos-
soming fruit-trees, and in autumn through beech or chestnut. Our sylvan fountains and gnomes' parliaments were
worth all the cascades, gorges, grottes, cirques, frowning
precipices, torrents du diable, and other such diablerie in
the Pyrenees.

We were afraid Nurien would be crowded in the season—Angela does not suffer *foules* gladly; but the Route
Nationale passed under the town. We never met a *foule*
in the forest. The local variety was disgorged from char-
a-bancs at the spectacular end of the valley. We always
intended to join in the procession and gape at the Cirque,
the lion that roared loudest in our neighbourhood, but for
one reason or another we never did. For all we knew, the
foule may not have been such a *foule* as it looked.

Naturally the children were more adventurous. Uncle
Bliss would take them beyond the radius of our half-inch
to the kilometre map. I believe the diplomatic Val enticed
him into the *librairie* with that design. But first of all
they ticked off the promenades nearer home. Angela and I
would start with them, and we all carried our own lunch,
but we would soon be left behind. Angela would find a

new glade, and quote Celia in the forest of Arden, "I like this place, and willingly could waste my time in it." Or it would be a new site for a house with the rock garden already built and planted. Or we would stop and pass the time of day with some farmer. They were all friendly, and knew us, and we could wander where we liked. There was no such thing as a hedge without a gap, or a wall without a hole in it, and we were often invited to walk through their hay, which was generally cut when knee-high, and yielded a second crop, and sometimes a third. The only penalty we had to pay was being barked at by dogs. Every farm had its good barkable dog (*bonus canis latrabilis*) of the genus of Vichy, who would escort us yapping at our heels to the next property, if its owner was not by to call it off. But soon even the dogs came to know us, and ceased to bark. Uncle Bliss, however, was never exempt. We could follow the course of the explorers for a kilometre or two after they had left us, and knew by the alternation of bark and yelp when he was throwing stones.

We wished he wouldn't stone the farm dogs, who were only doing their duty. That streak of inconsiderateness might lose us friends. It would spoil the geniality of our walks if the farmers ceased to look up from their work and say, "Bon jour à tout le monde" when the English family passed. Luckily, Uncle Bliss did not repeat the same promenade twice, or he might have poisoned our relations with them. He had already frightened M. Minicot away.

The first time the dwarf looked in at our window during the fifty-nine days, Ursa Major nearly jumped out of his chair.

"A cagot!" he exclaimed. He was convinced that he had discovered the Pyrenean variety of pygmy. Luckily M. Minicot didn't understand.

"Who's got a tape measure?" he bellowed. "I'll measure his cranium."

"You'll do nothing of the kind," said Angela.

But Uncle Bliss had risen in his excitement, and was already at the window, tapping his head and pointing at M. Minicot's. "Mesurer la tête. Oon franc," he cried, and pulling the coin out of his pocket held it out to the dwarf.

M. Minicot showed signs of flight. Uncle Bliss, fearing that he was going to lose him, outroared Boanerges. His hairy red face and beard were within an inch of M. Minicot's silvery white locks and moustache. It must have been a terrifying apparition for the dwarf. He recoiled with an inarticulate animal cry, pulled his hat over his eyes, turned, and stumped down the street, thoroughly frightened, without his franc.

Uncle Bliss threatened to follow him to the Hôpital des Pauvres and perform the operation there.

"If you do," Angela said very quietly, "you won't come back here." She was white with rage.

"Not measure his head," said Uncle Bliss. "Why not? He will think it is for a new hat. 'Pon my word, I have a good mind to give him one."

Angela made no reply.

If I had been Uncle Bliss I should have felt like a dirty moraine under a glacier. I believe he was a bit disconcerted, but he did not allow us to see it.

A blight fell on the party for the rest of the afternoon. Angela would not let the children go out with him after lunch. He was not a fit companion for them. "I suppose he will go to the hotel," she said, "after the way he has behaved." She revived the title of the Blatant Beast.

Uncle Bliss had not been in such disgrace since the harrying of the Brebis, but he did not go to the hotel. He joined us at dinner in his very best shape. He had found an early specimen of Clathrus Cancellatus (the *clathre grillage* of the French), allied to our British Stinkhorn, and with an equally disengaging smell. When Louise left the door open we felt it—the smell—coming downstairs from his room. Even Nero on the doorstep thrust his nose farther out into the street. Angela recommended Madame Brun's vegetable garden as its resting-place for the night. Ursa Major politely concurred. Her wish was fulfilled as soon as it was spoken. The *clathre* was transferred to the potager then and there by his own hands. That transforming fungus, or magic mushroom, aptly named cancellatus, had converted the ursine into the urbane. You might think that Uncle Bliss had swallowed it. The cagot was forgotten, and Angela's displeasure.

He returned from the potager in his fairy godfather mood, and began to discuss new expeditions.

He wanted to take Angela and me with the children to the Cirque in a car. He turned to Val.

"You like travel, eh? What are you going to be?"

"An explorer," said Val.

"An explorer. That's right. Just the man for me. Collect orchids and butterflies. I can't be everywhere at once, you know. Where would you like to go? What do you say to Java?"

Val wanted to go where the shells he saw on Madame Brun's mantelpiece had live fish in them, and were really rainbow-like when they came out of the sea.

"And where would the Queen of Sheba like to go?"

The Queen of Sheba wanted to go to Mexico. She had been reading 'Montezuma's Daughter.' And she wanted to wander in forests that were so thick and tangled that you never saw the sun.

"She shall have ivory, apes, and peacocks," Uncle Bliss said.

The next morning we started on our promenade to Tire-Lire and Balandrou as if nothing had happened. Ursa Major might never have outraged the decencies. When the

exploring party left us, barks, not yelps, marked their penetration of *terra incognita*. Evidently he was not throwing
stones.

Angela's discipline was salutary. Fifty-nine days, I reflected. By the time he has finished all his promenades and
excursions and ascensions, butter won't melt in his mouth.

"What's the number of this promenade?" I asked Angela.

"Seven," she replied. Calculation was easy. Uncle Bliss
arrived on 21st June. "The longest day in the best place,"
he remarked pleasantly at lunch. This fitted in with his
system of economy. I noticed that he had not renewed his
pepper-and-salt suit, which he wore every morning and
evening, long days and short days. I believe the only thing
he bought during his stay at Nurien was the fifty centimes
book of Itineraires. But it would soon be time for the
excursions *en voiture*.

"Do you really think he will run to a car?" I asked her.

Angela thought he would. She explained the unthrifti-
ness as a vagary of the collecting habit. Some of the excursions were marked in the book as too long to be made on
foot, and an automobile was recommended.

"I am afraid I don't see," I said, scratching my head
figuratively.

"He is collecting itineraries in the neighbourhood of
Nurien," she explained.

"Oh, be he? I see," I quoted. "And he won't be happy
until he has them all in his pocket. He would rather collect itineraries than money, in fact."

"He collects one for the other."

This tolerant interpretation put Uncle Bliss' niggardli-
ness in a new light.

"Why on earth should one be sorry for him," I said.
"He is quite happy."

"He has never grown up."

That absurd elusive Don Quixote analogy came into my head again. Any one less visionary, yet—

I put it to Angela. "Why does he remind me of Don Quixote?"

"A prey to chimeras?" she suggested.

Wineskins and windmills; okapis and pterodactyls. We were getting warmer.

I gathered that the pterodactyl hunt was going to land him into "five figures." For some obscure reason he had put it off for more than a year. He was becoming secretive about it; perhaps he was afraid some one would steal a march on him. He hinted at the discovery of another habitat farther inland than the Jiundu swamp. When Irene asked him outright if he were going to start in the autumn he spoke of delay at the armourer's. We supposed that the steel cage and the specialised fishing and netting contraptions which he had spoken of at the Potters' would take time. Vickers-Maxim, I believe, had the commission.

In the meanwhile, like Angela and myself and all sensible people, he lived in the hour. Sufficient for the day were the promenades and excursions thereof.

Angela was right. When it came to the excursions *en voiture,* Uncle Bliss reconciled himself to the expense of a car. He could be as thorough in his extravagances as in his economies when they fitted in with his system. He even insisted on a five-seater. I joined in some of these expeditions, and was glad of the chance of investigating the haunts of Froissart and Gaston de Foix. We went as far west as Orthez, and as far east as St. Bertrand de Comminges, well beyond the prescribed itineraries. One day Irene went alone with him to the botanical gardens on the top of the Pic du Midi, and acted as his interpreter; they got on famously with the French botanist. Sometimes

Angela joined us, but more often she stayed at home, deterred by the *foule*. Ochlophobia, Uncle Bliss called it. He was always ready with the apt technical or scientific word.

I was rather puzzled by his relations with Angela. He used to take a constitutional every morning before the daily excursion to look for her earring, which she had lost in the chestnut wood on the site of the problematical villa. Angela, like the lady in the story who was slighted by the duke, had a habit of losing her earrings. It was a recurring tragedy. The ears they dropped from were like fresh shells just washed up by the sea—in the state Val wished to discover shells in the far islands he was going to. Anything less subtle than pearl or coral or opal would have profaned them. No wonder she could speak French with ears like that; her accent became better and better, until at the end of our first year at Nurien she spoke so well that I couldn't understand her.

But it was not Angela's coral-like ears that impelled Uncle Bliss on his morning constitutional; nor was it altogether his obstinate hunting instinct. I have a suspicion that he looked for Angela's earring because he wanted to measure M. Minicot's head. With this end in view she was a person to be propitiated. The quest of the earring was a sort of insurance policy, a storing up of merit against certain wrath in the event of discovery. Angela was the only person he was in the least little bit afraid of. On the fifty-seventh day or thereabouts, he found the earring, and was most deservedly popular; and on the afternoon of the same day he measured M. Minicot's cranium, having first squared the dwarf—a sanctioned extravagance—and the *directeur de l'hôpital*. I found this out quite by chance, and did not tell Angela. Probably she will hear of it for the first time when she reads these memoirs.

On the evening of the fifty-ninth day, having completed his last excursion, Uncle Bliss left us, and the morning after that the spare room at Sam Suffy was made ready for Aunt Hudson. It was a close thing. The Brebis, hearing how narrowly she had missed ursine encounters, nearly had "a vertigo."

Aunt Hudson stayed with us more than fifty-nine days, though Nurien was not such a safe and happy retreat as Homersfield. As ill luck would have it, she arrived just in time for the Fête Dieu. Early in the morning they began distributing bundles of palms and evergreens at intervals along the pavement. A cart loaded with planks drew up opposite the buvette in the Rue Saint Béat. The Brebis from her bed watched, at first unsuspiciously, the erection of a street altar. Louise came bustling into her room with brusque apologies to hang a white sheet from the two corners of her window. Madame Brun waddled across the street to the platform with a basinful of roses. Soon I heard a tapping at Angela's door, and the Brebis' nervous cough. "My dear—" Then the door closed on a muffled conference. There is no telling what dreadful things may happen to you in France. I remembered a scene in a novel in which an equally unsuspicious English lady looked out of her hotel bedroom in the square at Auxerre and saw a man guillotined.

The Fête Dieu was not as bad as that. Still something had to be done to get the Brebis away. And dispatch was called for. Before ten o'clock the altar cloth was laid, the flowers arranged, the candles lighted, and a red velvet hassock placed on the pavement for the priest to kneel on. Angela proposed a walk in the woods. She was careful not to use the word "picnic," but tactfully suggested by way of an afterthought that it would be better to take sandwiches with us. Thus the Brebis was seduced into a Sunday picnic.

We were none too soon. As it was, we encountered a
choir of little girls coming out of one of the religious
houses dressed in sacrificial-looking white robes which
almost touched their feet, and wearing crowns of red roses.
What would her feelings have been if we had met the
whole procession, headed by the Suisse in his parrot-like
red-and-gold uniform and tricorne hat carrying the hal-
berd, and the sacristan with his cross on high, and the two
abbés bearing the host in its canopied litter, and worse—
the multitude of "innocent little mites," some of them
barely five years old, with their brassards and pompons,
and surplices, and cassocks, and other secular and idolatrous trappings?

There was no separation of Church and State in Nuri-
en. Even the Mayor and Sheriff joined in the procession.
A cheerfully devout people. We were reminded of it at
intervals during the afternoon by the gaiety of the church
bells, a rhythm peculiar to the valley. The Brebis nibbled
her Sabbath-breaking sandwiches to their mingled chime
and toll—tirralirra, bom bom, treble and base, tripping
and halting, like letting a sound out and drawing it in.

Aunt Hudson was not insensible to the pastoral charms
of Nurien, only she wished we were back in "dear safe
Homersfield." From her point of view, Nurien was the very
worst spot we could have chosen. The whole district was
"tainted." To reach it by train one could not avoid passing
through Lourdes. She had looked out of her carriage window and seen the grotto with its daylight illuminations,
and the queue of credulous sick and crippled in their chairs
and litters waiting their turn at the rails. What with the
chapels and crucifixes and calvaires, there was no spot on
which her eyes could rest without pain. Idolatry disfigured
the landscape. So long as Aunt Huddy remained with us,
this spiritual bunker, lying right across the foot of the
valley, blocked all excursions in that direction.

"My dear," she sighed, when we had run the gauntlet of the dismantled altars and street decorations and were safe again in Sam Suffy—"my dear, why *don't* you come home and live in England?"

"Exchange," Angela explained. "We cannot afford it."

The Brebis was terribly worried about our financial position. "I can't *think* what you live on."

"Capital," said Angela.

"But if it doesn't last?"

"It will last six or seven years if we are careful."

"But, my dear, what *are* you going to do about the children's education?"

"There is always the *école communale.*"

The Brebis looked wounded. She made such a bad shot in putting down her teacup that she almost missed her saucer. But Angela's smile reassured her.

"My dear, it is very wrong of you to tease me."

In spite of Aunt Hudson's annual visits to the baths, she knew less about France than Uncle Bliss. She still thought that the *école communale* was a nursery of young Bolsheviks, and that a *chapellerie* was a building associated with religious rites, and that the Hôtel de Ville was a place you could put up in.

"How I wish I had not bought an annuity!" she sighed. "You must have *ca*pital."

"Don't worry, Aunt Huddy," Angela said. "Something will turn up. We will scramble through all right."

But the Brebis' eyes were moist. I believe she was afraid the children would become "tainted."

XIV
NEWS OF THE "TERROR-DACTYL"

Uncle Bliss was not a good correspondent. He wrote to Irene once on the voyage, and again soon after landing. It was only a moderately interesting letter. No news of the pterodactyl yet, but he had found two fleas on the ear of an ant bear which were totally new to science. Evidently the bug-hunters had got hold of him.

Months passed and we heard no more beyond an occasional paragraph in 'The Daily Megaphone.' One morning we saw the headlines: "Intrepid African Explorer." "Lost to the World for Six Months." The vague inaccuracies which followed, pointing at the imminent discovery of a "Monstrous Winged Reptile," told us nothing that we did not know, except that the 'Megaphone' staff had scented "a story." No clue was given as to the source of the information. Obviously Uncle Bliss had not taken the Press into his confidence; and he would be cut off from communication with the coast.

The next message, though more sensational, was equally unauthenticated. Bush telegraphy, perhaps. "Fabulous Monster haunts Equatorial Swamp." "Gigantic Prehistoric Survival." "Pterodactyl not Extinct?" "To be brought Home in Steel Cage." Half a dozen headlines with very little text. The communication concluded with a life-history of the pterodactyl up to the mesozoic age, contributed

by Professor Bronte Saurus of Stuttgart University, and
a brief biography of Uncle Bliss, with a reference to the
purchase of the dinosaur's egg, and a more guarded one to
the pygmy incident. The detail about "the steel tank, 12
ft. by 8 ft., fitted into segments for porterage," must have
leaked out through the manufacturers. Any one who had
dined at the Potters' the night Uncle Bliss in the first glow
of inspiration had thought out his plan of campaign aloud
could have given them better copy.

It was not very creditable to the enterprise of 'The Daily
Megaphone' that we received our first definite news of
the pterodactyl hunt through Marjorie. She was staying at
Pau on her way home from Uganda, and wrote suggesting
that she should come over and spend a night with us. She
hoped that she would see the children before they went to
school. A postscript added: "Your Ursa Major is returning,
seriously ill, I am afraid. I met Sancho Panza at Mombasa.
But I will give you all the details when we meet."

Sancho Panza, if he had been corruptible, might have
made a small fortune out of 'The Megaphone.' The squire,
however, had the same contempt for publicity as the
knight. The reporters failed to get a story out of him. A
few days after we heard from Marjorie 'The Megaphone'
announced Bliss' return. "Seven Months in Equatorial
Swamps." "Wounded Winged Monster Escapes." "Famous
Hunter Fever-stricken." "Landed in Ambulance." Again
the text was little more than a paraphrase of the headlines.
Uncle Bliss, apparently, had scotched the pterodactyl, not
killed it. The dramatic thing was that he had seen it at
all. We wrote to Sellinger for news, and waited with great
impatience for Marjorie.

It was delightful seeing her, and hearing her jolly
crow-pheasant laugh again. Madame Brun put her up in
the spare room. Vichy passed her. True, he barked, but
approvingly; and the children met her at the station in

what Angela called "a hurricane of excitement." Of course, she brought them presents. They had begun to collect another museum.

On the whole, Marjorie was reassuring about Uncle Bliss. He was very bad at Mombasa, but then, of course, one always is with malignant malaria. It plays with you, like a cat with a mouse. The doctor of his ship seemed to think that the sea voyage and a week or two's rest afterwards ought to set him up.

She met Staff quite by chance. He was pointed out to her as Bliss' servant by the friend she was seeing off on the coasting steamer. That was the first she heard of his being on board. Her own boat sailed a day or two later.

Staff was leaning over the rails, the picture of woe, gazing into the water. He wore a corduroy suit and a round leather hat, like a beret, though it was 103° in the shade. Marjorie recognised him at once from Claude's description. The squint would have been enough. "He looked like a witch-doctor who had swallowed his totem."

"Do you remember Chimbashi?" she asked me.

"The eleventh commandment in the Clayton family," I reminded her, "is not to go near the anthropological section in the British Museum." I inquired for her arm.

"Oh, my arm is all right, thank you. Chimbashi has done it good."

"Well, I introduced myself," Marjorie continued, "but couldn't get him to talk at first. He retired into his shell, all but one eye, so to speak, which looked at me suspiciously. I believe he thought I was a newspaper woman. Sancho Panza's squint is embarrassing. When I told him that I knew Renton Parva and was a great friend of Irene and Val, he opened out at once, and wanted me to go down and see Bliss. He thought it might soothe him. 'He keeps calling out for Miss Irene,' he said. 'But mostly he talk random.'

"I saw the ship's doctor, but he told me Bliss was not in a state to see any one. He had just come round from a spell of coma, and was subject to delusions and loss of memory, but he thought that would pass with anti-malarial treatment. He was pumping in quinine. Intra-muscular injections. Staff said that he had had malaria off and on for six months. He tried to get him back to the coast, but couldn't 'turn him from that there dratted terror-dactyl.'"

I could imagine that Bliss was difficult to turn. "Did Staff describe the 'terror-dactyl?'" I asked Marjorie.

From Staff's account Marjorie concluded that the terror-dactyl was an enormous amphibian python, a sort of fresh-water sea serpent. This was disappointing, as I was prepared for a description of an apocalyptic beast, "each eye as large as a windmill and more fiery than a glass furnace." But Staff's story was credibly matter-of-fact. "No; he didn't see no wings. And he didn't see no legs, nor tail neither." Only its head was above water. The stolid Sancho Panza was not impressed by the terror-dactyl. He denied all its fantastic attributes.

The whole hunt seems to have been a chapter of misadventures. Uncle Bliss' porters did not "precede" him, as he boasted was their custom. And worse, the country was impossible for wheeled transport. The lorry and the Vickers-Maxim outfit, which must have eaten up a considerable fraction of the "five figures," had to be left behind at the coast. So there was never any hope of bringing back the pterodactyl alive.

They were several months locating the beast. Staff spoke disparagingly of its habitat. "It was a rare unhealthy sort of place." He could not put his finger on it on the map. There were natives, of course. They wore their hair in knobs and horns, and filed their teeth; he dismissed them as "nasty." He could not tell Marjorie the name of the tribe, but she gathered that they were a pretty low lot, as they ate chimpanzee. Even the Mbongwe eschew chimpanzee. It was most unfortunate for Uncle Bliss that this particular tribe feared the devil in the form of the kongamato, which is the local name for the pterodactyl. They feared it more than they feared Uncle Bliss. The legend ran that if the kongamato saw you first, at however great a distance, you died; whereas if you saw the kongamato first, it died: but as nobody except Uncle Bliss was willing to put this legend to the test, it was necessary to conceal the object of their expedition, and to be diplomatic in their questions about the reptile as if it were a creature they wished to avoid. Thus "the n••••••s"—Staff applied the word indifferently to all Africans from the Hadendowa of the Sudan to the Kafirs, and the blacks of Guinea—enrolled themselves unsuspiciously as beaters.

The chief's name was Shindy; Staff remembered that, because it was apt. He beat the big war-drum, the hollowed base of a tree. The others beat smaller drums, or blew horns. When they all turned out for a beat, the banging and braying was enough to scare the devil. Bliss' usual plan of operations was a drive. He would take up an advanced position on some island, while the natives formed up in a line of boats and beat along the channels. It was all bog and swamp and decaying vegetation, which gave off a putrid smell, a paradise of snakes and vermin. Sancho Panza's "rare unhealthy sort of place" was probably the most pestilential hole in Africa. Bliss was soon attacked by ague and cramp, and had to be carried when he was not paddled, but he had his daily beat all the same.

After about a hundred days of this they came across the track of the kongamato. The first native who saw it set up a terrific hullabaloo, whereupon the whole tribe swung round their dug-outs and made for the village. Bliss' boatmen were for joining in the *sauve-qui-peut,* but he and Staff seized their paddles, whereupon they boldly threw themselves into the water, swam to the nearest craft, and scrambled on board. So the knight and the squire were left alone. Here, perhaps, is where Don Quixote comes in.

"They made straight for the island where the hullaba-loo started. Staff said the kongamato had left a trail 'as if you had dragged a barrer along.'"

"Without wheels," I emended.

"Yes," said Marjorie. "How did you know? And a coating of slime like the saliva of a snail."

I told her about the *lau*. "The Bahr-el-Ghazal variety leaves a furrow like a tumbril. Staff is probably nearer the mark. He doesn't exaggerate. But please go on. What happened next?"

"They waited by the spoor until dusk, and then they saw it swimming round and round on the far side of the pool and bending its head, first to one side and then to the other, as if lost."

"What was it like?"

"You know the poise of the head of a water-snake, a sort of blind inquisitive peering. They always give me the creeps. You don't know how much they see. Well, it was like that, only simply gigantic.

"I feel as if I had seen it myself," Marjorie continued. "If I had been Uncle Bliss, I think I should have gone straight home—not because I was afraid, though it is quite likely I might have had cold feet. I mean, I should have felt that the kongamato was not my affair; I couldn't have put myself in those relations with it. I have had this instinct with ordinary animals like lions when they did not know I was watching them. As for drawing a bead on the pterodactyl—"

I think I knew what Marjorie meant.

"Suppose some one were to take you on a visit to Mars—"

"Quite," I said. "The worst possible introduction would be to begin by putting out eyes with a pop-gun."

"It is not exactly awe. That doesn't explain it."

"Self-respect," I suggested, "human *esprit-de-corps*. One wants to show that it is not done."

With creatures nearer one's own plane one is not troubled by appearances; they know. Marjorie, by the way, had given up shooting altogether.

I don't suppose it occurred to Uncle Bliss that one ought to be on one's best behaviour with the super-normal. His one preoccupation would be to shoot the kongamato before it could get away.

The beast continued its melancholy and unsuspicious parade safely out of range until it was quite dark. It was in deeper water on the edge of the forest. This was evidently its beat. Uncle Bliss' plan was to make a wide detour so as to get on the land side of the brute without alarming it, and to lie up until it came within range. They made the journey in the dark. It took them several hours, wading most of the time, and pushing and dragging the dug-out; but first they lighted a cordon of fires wherever they could find a dry patch on the village side of the swamp, lest the pterodactyl should take it into his head to decamp in that direction.

It was dawn before they were in position, and they lay in wait all day. One point Sancho Panza seems to have established in the natural history of the pterodactyl is its regular and crepuscular habit. Just before dusk it raised its head again in almost exactly the same place—an enormous head, like a crane—the mechanical variety. Staff said it had red eyes which didn't move. It was facing them, looking straight into their bush, but he thought it was blind. For a few seconds it made no movement, but held its head poised about ten feet above the water; it might have been

asleep, it was so still. Bliss gave the range at two hundred
yards. Then it began its sorrowful inspection of the landscape before starting on its rounds. It moved in widen-
ing circles, swaying its neck from side to side, probably a
habit surviving from the mesozoic age when it had sight.
Each circle brought it a little nearer. At eighty yards
Uncle Bliss, leaning his rifle on Staff's shoulder to steady
his aim—the ague still gripped him,—fired. The first bul-
let took it in the head, the second in the neck as it rose
with a convulsive leap ten feet higher out of the water. Its
head rolled over on one side, and its neck, or trunk, sank
vertically like a shaft. Then began such a lashing of the
waters as has probably never been witnessed since the days
of the churning of the Ocean of Milk in the Ramayana.

The kongamato's head was not seen again; only its middle coils continued to lash the water for some minutes.
The blood and foam reached them on the bank. Staff says
Uncle Bliss was sick, but he attributed this to the fever.
The pterodactyl didn't bleed red. The colour of the foam
where it went down
was yellowish green, "like the inside of the pods of
them water-lilies." He added a picturesque detail about a
flock of white night-herons which came and hovered over
the scum that the water gave up, like the gulls you feed
with crumbs from Waterloo Bridge.

Staff avers that the kongamato cried out before it went
under. When Marjorie asked him to describe its cry, he
said he couldn't put a name to it, but it was "most like a
siren, the kind you hear in shipping yards."

I told her that the Bahr-el-Ghazal variety bellows. The
Shilluks say the sound is like a bull calf.

The body of the kongamato was never recovered, nor
even searched for. It took Sancho Panza all his time getting his knight home. Before they reached the village,
Uncle Bliss was wandering.

"Didn't he shoot anything else?" Irene asked.

"He shot a hippo or two for Shindy, to keep him warking," Marjorie quoted.

It seemed that the two fleas from the ear of the ant bear "totally new to science," were the only material results of the expedition.

Sancho Panza spoke of the terror-dactyl contemptuously; he referred to it as "that dratted creature." The feeling uppermost in his mind seems to have been resentment, which was only natural, seeing that "the winged reptile" was the cause of his tribulations and of Uncle Bliss' unaccountable madness. Staff must have had a pretty rough time getting him to the coast. Marjorie gathered that he had had "trouble with the n•••••s." Shindy was difficult. But, no doubt, Sancho Panza's useful eye came in here. The pair of them would appear as super-normal as the kongamato. Too super-normal, perhaps. On three occasions they dropped Uncle Bliss and bolted. He couldn't walk a step, and had to be carried all the way, over eight hundred miles. Some days he was too ill to move, and kept muttering—talking random.

"Poor Uncle Bliss!" sighed Irene.

"Poor Sancho Panza," said Marjorie. "Uncle Bliss is probably up and about again, getting the cages ready for the animals so that you will be able to see them in the holidays."

They were going to spend Christmas with the Sellingers after their first term at school.

"I hope he won't hunt terror-dactyls again," Angela said.

"Sancho Panza hopes he will stay at home and hunt hares."

"That was exactly what the other Sancho Panza said," I observed.

"Of the other Don Quixote."

So Marjorie saw the analogy too.

"Staff said he hoped it would larn him."

"Perhaps it will," I said. But I couldn't see Uncle Bliss recanting. He would continue to hunt for mushrooms at the bottom of the sea.

Marjorie related this history over her coffee and rolls in the dining-room at Sam Suffy. It contains all that is likely to be known of the natural history of the pterodactyl, for, after Mombasa, Staff became even less communicative, and I never heard of any details being given to the world by Uncle Bliss. No one dared mention it, not even Irene. At the Clapperhouse the kongamato, as a subject of conversation, was taboo.

Before *déjeuner* we had persuaded Marjorie to stay with us a week. The friendly Louise added her entreaties, extolling the good air of Nurien. She touched Marjorie's elbow gently with one hand, as was her custom when she was attracted by people, and pointed out of the window, as though at the concrete desirability, with the other. Marjorie decided impulsively to hire a motor and fetch her luggage from Pau, or Paw, as Uncle Bliss called it, and to take the children with her.

"Why not stay and come home with us?" Angela proposed.

The time had come when we could no longer postpone sending Irene and Val to school. Angela was taking them the very next week, and they were going to spend a few days with the Sellingers. Marjorie was delighted with the idea of travelling home with them.

We spent most of Marjorie's week out-of-doors, and took our lunch with us nearly every day. She was introduced to all our haunts, and pronounced on the merits of the different sites for the villa, about which Angela was still hesitating. One day we went to the farm in which Louise was born and reared, and which now belonged to her brother; and Marjorie made a sketch of it for her, and

Angela decided that we must all go and live in it, and
take Louise with us back to the paternal roof-tree. It was
a seductive old farm of grey stone with a short fringe of
roof tucked in over the front gable like a matronly toupet;
while, to add to the symmetry, a semicircular bulge of
oven projected at the back, roofed in the same way.
The two ends were step-gabled, a feature peculiar to the
Nurien farms. I have never seen it elsewhere. A flat slate
is set on each diminishing stone, projecting pyramid-wise.
Marjorie thought it was a provision for cats.

"There was once a pious and seigneurial lady in the
valley of Nurien," she began, "who lost her husband in the
Crusades"; but there she stopped.

"Ye-es?" said Irene.

"Can't you go on? You ought to be able to guess the
rest."

Irene guessed that she provided for cats.

"Exactly," said Marjorie. "She became a felinophile,
which is Latin for a lover of cats. Nowadays when old
ladies feel like that, they endow homes and send round
pamphlets, 'Feed the Cats.' But if all the cats were well
fed, as they were no doubt in her time, she would have to
find another way of pampering them. So she designed the
steps to make it easy for them to get on to the roof. The
cat-gable would become a condition of tenantry."

Angela didn't like cats, but she said she would rather
have cat-gables than cats and no cat-gables.

The cat-gable roof for the villa was carried *nem. con.*
We next considered the Nurien poulailler, that curious
little outhouse common to all farms in the valley—pig-
sty, henroost, rabbit-hutch, and pigeon-house in one. The
pigs, as is appropriate, are the groundlings, and live in
small cubicles with a heart-shaped aperture in the door
for ventilation—always a heart; there is no other symbol.
The next floor, three feet from the ground, verandah and

hen-roost, is reached by a hen-ladder, where there are no steps; and the roof is the colombier with the pigeonholes inset and protruding, projecting like miniature dormer windows. Marjorie sketched it for Louise, a pig's eye and snout sticking out of each heart in parody of a love token, and Angela decided that we should have to keep pigs, hens, rabbits, and pigeons; otherwise we should have no excuse for the poulailler. Also it would be an economy, like the rock garden and the foxglove wall, in addition to being aesthetic. The poulailler would have been carried *nem. con.* if Angela had not suddenly remembered our dwindling capital. Obviously it would be more economical to return to our first project and live in the existing farmhouse, and to use the existing poulailler, as lodgers, with Louise for our *femme de ménage* blissfully reinstated. We adhered to this plan until we saw Louise's brother's wife. How one does overlook things in dreams!

Louise's brother's wife, a loud-voiced, capable, managing woman, with a figure like two pumpkins which have been blessed by the sun, was incapable of being overlooked. So we next considered the barn. Angela thought a barn would be cheaper. If not this barn, then another. There was a satisfying uniformity in the Nurien farm architecture. The barns were like the houses and indistinguishable from them at a distance, the same grey stone, immensely solid, and the same pointed roofs and grey slate tiles, Wiltshire colour. Some of them had cat-gables. And they all had the most glorious door-windows, in which four tall men could stand abreast. The whole of the hay went in here, spring and summer crops; haystacks were unknown in the valley. It would be a pity to clear it all out, Angela thought; we might leave a little in the corner for the sake of the smell. She was tired of living in lodgings, and wanted to be quite independent, and live in the country and keep pigs.

"There's our house," she said, pointing to the barn. "An outlay of fifty pounds, perhaps, and a carpenter's wages for a few weeks, and the price of a little wood."

Marjorie joined in the discussion of practical details, where the windows were to be put in, and the partitions, and the fireplace and chimney. Angela proposed making a gallery of the first floor, and a hall and library of the ground floor, pictures above and books beneath. "We could send for them from Homersfield, and the carpets. I would make the place as clean as a pin."

Val saw an opportunity for the amalgamation of the two museums.

"We could sleep in the poulailler," I suggested.

"We would have to build a little annexe for the bedrooms. But don't you think it's a lovely idea?"

I agreed that it sounded attractive. Anyhow, the barn was delightful to look at from outside.

"And if we can't earn enough money by keeping pigs," she continued, "we can live by giving English lessons to French people and French lessons to English people."

Marjorie supplemented this scheme with the suggestion that when Val and Irene came back from school with their book-larning, we should be able to open classes in arithmetic and geography as well as languages.

But the children wanted to stay behind and live in the barn, and "mind the chickens and pigs" instead of going to school. Val said, "Why shouldn't we be farmers, mummy?" And Irene said, *"I'm* going to drive the pigs to market." Arithmetic would come in there too, Marjorie reminded her.

The way Angela cast off *le souci de lendemain* was magnificent. The children believed that she would be disappointed if she did not get her barn. They had no suspicion, of course, of the too easily measurable margin between us and the doorstep. Marjorie knew, I believe. Probably that

was why Angela played the Arcadian game with such conviction; she wanted to show her that we were not worrying.

I could see that Marjorie was cogitating something.
On the way home she persuaded Angela to let her take
the children to school. "Why should you trek all the way
across France and back again when I am going anyhow, and
should love to have them with me. We could go on to the
Sellingers' together. They have asked me too, you know."

Angela agreed without a great deal of persuasion. There
were strong economical reasons, and apart from these she
had a feeling that "dear Homersfield" would be a little
melancholy with tenants in the house. She told Marjorie
that we would build her a prophet's chamber in the barn,
or annexe, with the money she saved out of her ticket.

"How sweet of you!" said Marjorie. "But you'd better
not. You'd find me a fixture."

"The fixeder the better," Angela told her. "It will be
your very own room. And when you are in Uganda we will
let Uncle Bliss in sometimes; that is, if he behaves properly, and doesn't want to measure people's craniums."

I am ashamed to say that I had not thought of Uncle
Bliss all the afternoon. We wondered why we had no news
of him. Sellinger had not answered my letter, and Marjorie was expecting to hear from Staff. He had promised to
write when she saw him Mombasa, and she had given him
her Pau address.

"I am abserlutely certain he will write, if he promised,"
Irene assured us loyally.

And sure enough there was his letter waiting for us
when we got back to Sam Suffy. It had been forwarded
from Pau, and was addressed in a curious hand to—

> Lady Critchley,
>   Ouvert Toute L'année,
>   Ascenseur,

Chauffage Central,
Cuisine Renommée,
Pau.

The post-office had chanced on the right hotel, an important item which he had omitted in the address. Marjorie opened it, and read—

"Mister Bliss is rare queer he has still got the malarier bad he keeps on asking after Miss Ireney, if Miss Ireney comes here which you say was likely you will plese inform her to visit Mister Bliss, she would do him a site of good I am thinking.—Yours kindly,

Robert Staff."

"Poor Uncle Bliss!" said Irene.

"I wish I hadn't called him the Blatant Beast," Angela said to me when we were alone.

XV
PRÉVOYANTS D'AVENIR

Sellinger's letter came the day after Marjorie and the children left. Uncle Bliss had had a relapse, but he was better again—Sellinger thought out of danger. Luckily, Cronk, the new doctor, was a good man, and seemed to know a lot about malaria.

"He was five years in Assam," Sellinger wrote, "and he has put in some research work in Nigeria. He tells me that in the majority of cases in his experience pernicious malaria has proved fatal, but Bliss is such a tough nut he thinks he will shake it off, though it is doubtful if he will ever go pterodactyl-hunting again.

"The important thing is to keep him quiet, but he absolutely refuses to have a nurse in the house. Staff is the only person who can do anything with him. An excellent fellow. Never leaves him, though personally I should not like to have that eye revolving at the foot of my bed, if I were feeling ill.

"Now for Bliss' message. He wants you to come and be his agent, to which Ethel and I add our entreaties. We shall be very disappointed if you refuse. As for Bliss, it would be an act of charity. Saxby is going in any case, and a good riddance. I don't believe the fellow is straight. Old Borett would help you on the technical side, and now you are so much stronger, I am sure you would not find the

work too heavy. I rubbed it into Bliss that you would have
to have a car, and he agreed. He wants the whole family
to come, but, of course, you will please yourself about
that. I suggested having the east wing put in order, and
he said he would have the upholsterers over from Homerton. You would be quite on your own—the best quarters
in the house, facing the lake, and the family could see as
much or as little of him as they liked, though I think the
idea of having the children about in the holidays is a great
attraction. Irene has made a conquest. I believe she could
manage him as well as Staff. Ethel always says she and Val
are the most diplomatic young people she knows. We hope
to see them both in a few days. I think you will find Bliss
has softened a great deal. He has got a trained nurse down
for Mrs. Staff—the mother of Sancho Panza—at no end of
expense. Electric massage treatment. She was bedridden
with rheumatism, but is able to get about a little now.
Whether you will be able to make him shell out for repairs
and all that, is another question. You know the state the
house is in, like a disused barracks. It wants a new roof
and drains. The farms are all tumbling down. The tenants
will be your main difficulty. They have a fair grouse, but
that is where your diplomacy will come in. If the worst
comes to the worst, you could throw it up if you found
Bliss impossible. Ethel says you won't take it on. I say you
will. It will be a great bit of luck for us if you do."

The letter concluded with a postscript to Angela from
Mrs. Sellinger, saying how they were looking forward to
seeing the children, and how desolated they would both be
if we didn't follow ourselves very soon.

Under this another postscript in Sellinger's hand:—

"Important item! I forgot to mention terms. Bliss is
offering £750 a year."

Angela was shopping when the letter came. I went in search of her, and found her buying vegetables at a stall in the market. "I have had an offer of a job," I told her. "Seven-fifty a year, motor, comfortable quarters—" Of course, she guessed who it was. She had expected it.

"But you will never be able to stick it," she said.

"We will be able to send Val to X.," I reminded her. X. was my old school.

"You mustn't think of it. You are not nearly strong enough. Besides, it would be an impossible position."

"I'll make it possible all right," I said.

We gravitated to a seat under the planes.

"The Whittakers go out next month," she reflected.

I unfolded Uncle Bliss' plan of "living in." It would mean that we should have to give up the idea of living at Homersfield. Angela's feet touched earth again, but she kept them there angelically. She thought that if we went at all, we ought to live at the Clapperhouse. We owed that to Uncle Bliss. "You see, he has no friends. It is his own fault, perhaps, but he will probably want them now, and Irene being on the spot would make all the difference. We will have to get her a new governess. After the Christmas term."

I agreed that it was the least we could do. I probably owed my appointment to Irene.

"But supposing you find him insufferable," I said. "The 'softening' Sellinger talks about is only a phase, of course."

"Of course," she agreed. "One can't expect malignant malaria to change one's spots altogether."

"There is always the remedy of Homersfield."

We spent a day or two revolving the pros and cons. Sellinger advised us to take our time. It was not a thing one could decide by the toss of a coin. Then one morning I had an inspiration. "Let's go and consult the oracle," I suggested. "Why not the *prévoyant d'avenir*."

It was an excuse for an extravagance which we had long contemplated. The oracle dwelt at Lys, a remote hamlet embowered in oaks, on the top of a hill miles away from any town or railway station. Angela had only heard of her from me, but I had seen her cottage.

"Think of the interior," I tempted her, "the kind of place you might expect to find a salamander in the fire and herbs hanging on the wall, silver'd in the moon's eclipse."

"And a broomstick much worn with straddling. But you have never been inside."

It was true. I had never been inside. Nor had I seen the sorceress. I had only seen her cottage, a fleeting crepuscular glimpse as I was whisked past in a motor; and that was twenty—to be exact, twenty-two—years ago, two or three weeks before we got engaged.

I had only seen Angela once then. It was in the early days of motoring, when people ran out of their houses to see you pass, and horses backed into the hedge or ditch, and one was either a nuisance or a show. I had a great envy to stop the car and consult the fortune-teller. About Angela, of course, and myself, whether the planets in their courses— But I was the youngest member of the party—a guest, as a matter of fact—and we were subject to periodic engine trouble, and on the point of being benighted, and my host wanted to dine and sleep at Mauléon, which I knew was impossible.

I had thought it a great bit of luck being able to explore the Béarnais country with my friends. The motor alone would be an adventure. Then two days before we started I met Angela at a tennis party.

Naturally as we passed through Lys that enchanted evening I was not in love with the machine which increased the miles between me and felicity. I might have thrown my host over; it was weak of me, I suppose, not to. I made one shamefaced effort to extricate myself, and, basely ungrateful, I was pondering another when the rays of the sun, now level with the car, caught the board over the door of the cottage, and I read the inscription, "Prévoyant d'avenir." I don't know why it was—just the hour and the place, I suppose, romance more than superstition—but I had an instinct that the soothsayer inside was the one person who could read my horoscope.

Why should she live at Lys? And why should her cottage be suddenly projected into the dream in which I was isolated? If I had seen her board up in a town I should probably have thought no more about it. But at Lys? It was not likely that she would have any local clients. That was the Greek idea: you had to frequent your oracle from a distance. These were the oaks of Dodona. I would have given a great deal to see the folk who came to consult this sorceress. But in an instant we were in the oak woods again. The place was like a small forest clearing, a dozen or more white-washed cottages on each side of the road, but, so far as I could see, no shop, not even a buvette. The only other thing I remembered about Lys was that the house next the witch's had a white cross chalked up on the door, probably a phylactery against the evil eye.

Angela and I had often indulged conjecture as to the relations between these neighbours. Perhaps we should be able to find out something.

The sceptical Angela was the last person to dabble in mysticism. I could no more picture her at a clairvoyant's than the Brebis at the confessional. She and I held spirit-rapping, table-turning, and other such abracadabra in equal derision. But she was interested in the prophet-ess of Lys. The woman's existence was an enigma. Who were her clients? I had always had an itching to be one of them. Whenever I wanted to consult the will of the gods, I thought of the woman of Lys. My youthful instinct that something really Pythian might be communicated by her

grew into what in other people I might have called superstition. This and my respect for Chimbashi were my only
concessions to the occult.

"We might meet some of the other clients," I persisted.
"And I should like to see that house with the white cross
again. I shouldn't wonder if the witch and the curé lived
next door to each other. Perhaps there is a buvette after
all. If so, we may hear some gossip."

Angela's curiosity was intrigued; the weather was pro-
pitious; we were soon committed to the extravagance. The
adventure would leave us the poorer by the cost of fourteen days of uneventful living, but it was worth it.

We left by an early train, and hired a *fiacre* for the day
from the Taverne Bernéde at Balisson, the nearest railway
station. Our *cocher* was a pleasant old Béarnais, with a set
smile and a harvester's hat. His dog, a crop-eared, red-eyed,
crop-tailed beast of catholic ancestry, but single-minded
in his attachment to our luncheon-basket, came with us. It
was twenty-two years almost to a day since I had covered
that bit of road in the motor which carried me farther and
farther from beatitude. The leaves were beginning to turn,
and every garden had its plot of chrysanthemums ready
for Toussaint. One of them which I thought I remembered
communicated that *sensation du déja vu* which one has in
dreams sometimes, and the picture brought the two drives
so close together that part of the exhilaration I felt was
like relief after suspense, as if the second drive were following on the first. I had shed the twenty-two years. And
so had Angela.

We lunched within sight of our Dodona. Lys is built
on a *mamelon*. Delightful word! Its white houses showed
through the oaks. The little stream which trickled down
to us through a chestnut wood reminded me of the beck
at Renton Parva. The brown leaves kept fluttering down

in showers, and the fruit dropping among the autumn crocuses, where they lay like curled-up baby hedgehogs on a carpet of biscuit-coloured tassels, the débris of June. They were cutting hay in the field over the beck, the third crop, knee-deep only. For the first time in my life I saw swathes of hay empurpled by crocuses.

A peasant passed with a scythe, and we asked him the name of the stream.

"Lange," he answered. Or it may have been "L'Ange."

I asked him if there were any fish in it.

"Yes, certainly," he replied. "One fishes. The stream is full of *écrivisses.*"

The word puzzled me at first. I thought of shrimps, lobsters, crabs; but I did not tumble to the fresh-water variant until I remembered the crayfish in the fountain of the Taverne Bernéde under the stuffed vulture.

"You tie a piece of meat to a string and pull it up, so," the scythe-bearer explained with an appropriate gesture.

"Yes, but are there any other fish?" I ventured.

"Certainly, monsieur; there are trout."

As he spoke I saw a fish rise under the alders on the opposite bank. It was an ideal place. "We must bring the children here in the summer holidays," Angela said; and I marked the hole from which Irene would drag up an immense crayfish, the stickle over which I should cast my fly, the backwater in which Val would dabble with the *asticot*—I am afraid his initiation into the gentle art, pace Monsieur Bruneteau, was very unBritish, but French trout are notoriously indifferent to the fly,—and the hornbeam under which Angela, guarding the luncheon-basket from nosing kine, would smile enigmatically over the last outrage by M. Mirbeau.

She was gazing up at the white houses in the oaks.

Would the sorceress have a beard, she wondered, and choppy fingers, and skinny lips, and stir a cauldron?

"Perhaps we shall meet Graymalkin and Paddock."

"What shall we ask the sorceress?"

We decided not to ask her anything. She would be certain to tell us that we were going to start on a long journey, at the end of which we should inherit a large fortune.

"I wonder if Uncle Bliss will leave Irene anything?"

"Not if he thinks we expect it."

Nice people in books do not dwell on these contingencies, but I must confess to an interest in Uncle Bliss' accumulations. I had got into the habit of waking up at three in the morning, the least optimistic of hours, and thinking about the children's future. I saw Irene, a nursery governess, wheeling a perambulator in the garden of a suburban villa, and Val behind a grille at a bank.

"Irene will marry," said Angela, reading my thoughts.

"Uncle Bliss ought to give her a *dôt.*"

"Fish-ponds," said Angela.

I reckoned up the extent of his largesse up to date. A shilling, a bottled spider minus its legs, a crushed scorpion— I am afraid impecuniosity develops a calculating disposition.

"I must give up smoking English baccy," I resolved, knocking the ashes out of my pipe. The tap-tap of the bowl against the root of our tree made a hollow sound.

"I wish we could find some buried treasure," Angela said.

She looked down at her dove-coloured stockings and shoes, and discovered a hole in the instep just large enough to admit a small mosquito. "It is dreadful having to go about in rags," she said. But in spite of her economies she always seemed to me beautifully and becomingly dressed. She was wearing a hat which she had bought at the Magasins Printemps for three and a half francs, about tenpence halfpenny, and trimmed herself. She looked bewitching in it.

I told her so, and my praise of the hat and what it framed, mingled with the music of the cow bells, the tapping of a woodpecker in the chestnut-tree, and the chatter of the stream, not to speak of the fragrance of the hay— for even September hay smells sweet—exorcised the snake in our Eden. It was impossible to indulge mercenary care in such surroundings. Besides, there was the village on the *mamelon* to explore, and the mysterious soothsayer to visit; and if that didn't add a little embroidery to the prose of life, I should like to know what did.

Twenty-two years ago, when I could not speak Angela's name without blushing like a kid, I wanted to ask the old woman up there on the hill if the stars in their courses— And now she and I had come to consult her together in the same week of September, when the chrysanthemums were flowering for Toussaint, and the chestnuts pelting the crocuses. Nothing had changed. If that wasn't something to write a poem about, I should like to know what was.

So I moralised in the manner of Jacques, or, I might say, of my contemporaries. For I lodge a sentimental Victorian bogey which I have found impossible to evict, though I have got him well under lock and key. I neither write poems nor compose them aloud, even to Angela; but three words—luckily two of them were figures, which would make it appear that I was engaged in a sum—must have escaped me, for Angel caught them up.

"Twenty-two years," she repeated. "Your sorceress must be quite an old woman."

I explained that sorceresses do not usually set up shop before the age of experience, which I believed was three-score years and ten.

In that case, Angela reminded me, the old lady, if she were still alive, must be ninety-two.

It was extraordinarily stupid of me not to think of that before. I suppose it had not entered my head that supernatural beings like witches were not eternal. My faith in this one must have been instinctive, as in matters of religion, not reasoned.

"Now I remembered," I reflected more hopefully, "fifty was the age limit at Delphi. I mean they began at fifty. By that reckoning she may not be much more than seventy after all."

We approached Lys with misgivings, but, sorceress or no sorceress, it was a perfect day. Anyhow, we should soon know.

We climbed up into the village, whither the *fiacre* had preceded us, by a lane with lopped cherry-trees on either side, hung with vines, into which the bright red bryony berries had inserted themselves among clusters of grapes with the most happy effect. We marked an avenue of toadstools, orange red caps and yellow gills, and wondered if they were the kind that had diverted Uncle Bliss from the pterodactyl. We passed a duckpond. We were on the crest of the *mamelon* now. In the grove of Dodona. Here were the white-washed buildings. On the door of the very first house we saw a white cross, and over the door of the house next to it a board. The street was deserted save for an expostulating donkey tied to a post. The only other sounds came from the ducks on the pond. "What a changeless little place!" I thought. We approached and read—

"Prévoyants d'avenir."

"It's plural," I said. "There must be a nest of them."

"The weird sisters," Angela suggested. "There are generally three."

I had forgotten Graymalkin and Paddock.

But the *étalage* in the window betrayed a small grocer's shop.

Were the priestesses lodgers? Prosaic thought!

"Veuve Felix," we read on the board.

We peered inside. At first our view was obscured by pyramids of Kub in small square packets, arrays of bootlaces, bottles of sweets, combs, hairpins, biscuits, soap, candles, espadrilles; but gradually we discerned a moving background to all this. A matronly figure of superb dimensions blocked the door between the shop and the kitchen.

Veuve Felix looked as if she did herself uncommonly well.

Slowly it dawned on us—on Angela first. "A little French," she observed, "is a dangerous thing."

Obviously it was not through crystals that our sorceress gazed into the future.

We went inside and gossiped with Veuve Felix. Angela did most of the talking. I was too occupied in watching the unfrugal folds that fell from the widow's chin in a *pente pas assez rapide,* and extended to a point a little below the middle of her apron. She ought always to sit at the door of her shop, I thought, a monument of thrift and the *bourgeois* virtues. For Veuve Felix kept a small co-operative store, and was agent for a Prudential Insurance Society.

Angela bought half the pyramid of Kub.

"It just shows," she said when we got outside.

It showed a great many things: that frugality was rewarded in the person of Veuve Felix; that Lys was a bit ahead of the times twenty-two years ago; that, as Angela had already remarked, a little French is a dangerous thing; and that further, commerce with the occult was inadvisable. But to which of these showings Angela referred I had no clue.

"Why Kub?" I asked her. "It's vile stuff."

"It's not very nice," she agreed, "but it's cheap. And it will save us going to the *boucherie.*"

So that was the end of our supernatural solicitings.

"Still," I said, "we have had a jolly day."

"Positively blissful," said Angela.

"Blissful" had become a family word through contact with Ursa Major. It could be applied with varying shades of significance, ironically to things ursine, as well as literally in its primary sense to things angelic. Thus the adjectival form of Angela and her antithesis in the order of *Homo sapiens* could be synonyms.

This may appear a pedantic excursion into domestic philology; it is none the less relevant. We had been thinking so much of the witch that we had forgotten the important decision we had come to consult her about. Angela's "positively blissful" reminded me that we were no forwarder. Should we, or should we not, pack up our things and take the next train Blisswards? The oracular inspiration was wanting. Angela said as much as we got into our *fiacre*. It was just at that moment that my eye caught the board with its inscription, "Felix."

"The oracle has spoken," I said.

"What oracle?" said Angela.

I pointed to the board. "If that doesn't direct us to Bliss, his abode, then all oracles are dumb."

"Very well," said Angela. "That settles it. To-day is Monday, to-morrow we will pack up, and we will start on Wednesday."

What a delightful thing is decision. The prophetess had cast out doubt.

"Before the end of the week we shall see the kiddies."

"And Homersfield."

"Home, Homer, Homersfield," repeated Angela.

I dismissed the doubtfully blissful considerations that had weighed with me so much, screwing money out of him for repairs, putting things straight with his tenants, keeping my temper, supporting his ursine humours; all these misgivings perished, asphyxiated in nostalgia, like moths in Val's collecting bottle.

"I shall go to Homersfield every day," cooed Angela, with the voice of a rock dove. "The Whittakers leave on the fifteenth. There will be heaps to do in the garden."

I could see her rapturously potting chrysanthemums.

"Why not instal the Brebis for a bit?"

Angela thought this a very good idea.

The Brebis, I should have mentioned, had forsaken France. Never again would she have to cross the Channel, or smell incense, or see crucifixes or calvaires, or reposoirs at the corner of the street, or processions of the Fête Dieu, or other such abominations and idolatries. Dax and Ax and Aix would know her no more. She had found a place in England with a name that ended in "wich," a much homelier termination, and the baths were every bit as good.

I claimed full marks for Veuve Felix.

"She helped us to make up our minds," Angela conceded.

I thought this inadequate. You can't expect an oracle to rap you out a plain Yes or No. It is not done. She of Lys was pure Delphi.

"She had to give it us in its Pythian wrapping," I argued.

Angela agreed that it would have spoilt it if it had been less of a parable.

Only it ought to have been in hexameters.

Prévoyant d'avenir, que veut dire ton pythien "Felix"?

No. That wouldn't do. I found the French language deficient in dactyls. The road to Balisson was strewn with broken hexameters.

"I would go to her again," I said.

We talked Homersfield most of the way home, and after dinner amidst desultory packing. The children were to spend a night with the Whittakers. They would have visited Farmer Stubbs, and the rickyard, and the Baron and Baroness Fig-tree, and the cow called Hungry, and inspected their museum, and no doubt laid night lines for eels. We could smell the water mill, and the Witch Pool, and Hungry's stable; and to these ghost smells we added another, equally homely and more persuasive, that of a log fire which we lighted in my bedroom. It was our first and last extravagance of the kind. Downstairs we had a comfortless anthracite stove, one of those French salamandres with a serpentine coil of pipe running into the wall, which emit heat without cheerfulness, and are as ugly as sin, or the kongamato, which they probably resemble. Angela in a room with a salamandre was an incongruous picture, one of the exactions of the Disciplinary Spirit.

As we drew up our deck-chairs to the blaze we heard the stroke of an axe on the terrace below. We looked out of the window and saw the stalwart Louise working by the light of a lantern which she had hooked to Madame Brun's Judas tree. She was chopping up the skeleton of Madame Brun's garden seat. Presently she stumped upstairs with the debris in her apron, and emptied it with a great clatter on the floor, bon. "C'est bon. "C'est bon. N'est ce pas. Le bon feu."

Ah, Louise! *Comme vous nous avez toujours choyé!*

Yes, a fire has a soul, and firelight is poetry, "Why does the Frenchman prefer his stuffy asphyxiating pipe?" I asked Angela.

"He would say that the open fireplace was our *goût,* I suppose, and the salamandre his *goût,* as if that was all there was in it."

Homesickness was making us insular.

"I like the lapping sound of the logs. It's like a brook."

"Like the Lange."

"Or the beck."

"And the smell is like the library fire at Homersfield."

"I wonder if Chimbashi is up to any mischief now. Does he think the gobemouches at the British Museum worth his while?"

The lapping and flickering induced sleep, in which I visited a confusion of streams, and watched Val catching crayfish in the fountain of the Taverne Bernéde, and emptying a bucket of them into the Homer, enormous fellows, ugly and deformed, climbing on each other's backs four deep in the slimy corners. I was afraid they would get into the bowls of cream which had been set in the fountain to cool. When I woke up I was asking the empty chair which had contained Angela whether it was Lange or L'Ange. When I come to think of it, I do not know to this day, and I am not likely to be any wiser until I visit that blessed spot again. In the meanwhile I like to think of it as L'Ange.

XVI
ŒUFS À LA COQUE

It was a melancholy arrival at the Clapperhouse. Sellinger met us at the station with the most alarming news of Uncle Bliss. A complete breakdown. He had had a stroke. It was peripheral neuritis, a touch of paralysis on the left side of his face and arm, accompanied by an almost complete loss of memory. He would have been all right, Sellinger told us, if only he had kept quiet, but on Monday—that was the day we consulted the oracle of Lys—he took it into his head to get up. Uncle Bliss evaded Staff, dressed himself, and went for a walk in the park. Staff found him in the stables, lying on the straw, unconscious.

Sellinger drove us to the Clapperhouse. As we drew up at the door we heard Staff's flute. "That's Sancho Panza," he said. "Cronk tells me he is worth half a dozen nurses."

I saw a nurse's head at the window. So Uncle Bliss was too prostrate to resist the invasion. I remembered that he couldn't abide the idea of having one in the house.

Cronk was there when we arrived, and he cheered us up a good deal. A patient who had survived what Bliss had been through might defeat any attack. He still had a fair amount of vitality to draw on. It was a question of storing it. "Of course, if he gets up and wanders about—" Cronk's gesture implied that he would not be answerable for the consequences. He was loud in Staff's praises. "Nobody else can do anything with him. With the nurses he is as obstinate as a mule, but Staff seems to have an extraordinary hypnotic influence over him. And no wonder, with that eye of his. He has saved his life."

"It's not the first time," I said.

If the knight were thrown, it would not be Sancho Panza's fault for not girthing Rosinante tight enough.

Cronk decided that it would be better for us not to see him until he was in a condition to recognise people. He had lost his memory about recent things, and was subject to hallucinations, a kind of divided identity, one half thwarting the other. He was in good form the day the children came over. That was before the attack.

It was a week or two before we were given a chance of seeing him. The first time he spoke to us was out-of-doors, on the drive, in the chair pushed by Sancho Panza.

Staff drew up, and Uncle Bliss looked at us, but I think without recognition. "Have you come to see the zoo?" he asked. I nodded. He did not respond to Angela's inquiries.

She and followed behind the chair like two mutes. We knew the cages were empty. After all these years the only tenant of the Clapperhouse Zoological Gardens was a flamingo, the sole survivor of a flock received by Mrs. Staff while the knight and the squire were away pterodactyl hunting. It lived in her chicken-run. The others had flown. The dear old lady knew nothing about wing-braces or tendon-cutting; and if she had known, I very much doubt if she would have applied her science to the frustration of the captive's migratory instincts.

But the flamingo, it appeared, was not our objective this morning. "Take me to the bear," Uncle Bliss said. "Have you got the plantains?"

"Ay, ay," said Staff. And he gave me a saturnine signal with the "useful eye."

The bear's cage was in the stables. We halted in front of it. There was a drinking trough and a pole with a platform at the top and some banana skins in the corner, but no bear. Uncle Bliss beckoned to Angela and pointed. She bent down over him.

"Ursa Minor," he whispered huskily, "A fastidious feeder. Likes a little marmalade on his bread. Remember that, Staff. A squish sandwich. Spread it on thick. Has Mr. Dickenson been here to-day?"

"Ay, ay," said Sancho Panza.

Uncle Bliss was back in his Cambridge days. I remembered that Ursa Minor had been his opposite number at Clare—I suppose he adopted the name the undergraduates gave it—and that Dickenson was an accomplice in saving the pair of them from expulsion.

"Where has he got to? I don't see him." Uncle Bliss stared into the empty loose-box.

"He'll be in the sleeping berth," Sancho Panza said; and he strode round to the back of the cage and tapped the wood with his knuckles, at which an angry "Woof, woof" reassured us that Ursa Minor was still in possession.

"He won't be coming out just now, I'm thinking,"

Sancho Panza returned to his charge, and they continued their melancholy perambulation.

Angela touched my elbow. "I can't stand it," she said. "C'est plus fort que moi." As we hurried back to the house we heard the cry of the hyena.

"We will have to put Irene off," she said.

We had thought of sending for her at half term. Our plan was that Kathleen Ismay, a niece of Marjorie's, should come and live with us and share a governess with Irene. Marjorie had found us a delightful woman, a friend of hers. Cronk was persuaded that the children would be an excellent tonic when Uncle Bliss was more himself. But, of course, we had to postpone the arrangement. After the Christmas holidays, perhaps.

For a melancholy month I worked hard at my Froissart, and Angela at Uncle Bliss' garden and conservatory. Sometimes John would come over from Homersfield to help. The Brebis was established there now, and we occasionally went over to see her. Once she took her courage in both hands and hired the station fly—a vehicle so low on its four wheels that its nearness to earth was a positive danger—and drove over to spend the afternoon with us. She was terribly afraid of meeting Uncle Bliss, but the poor old boy had become so tame and domestic that when she did encounter him on the drive, charioted by Sancho Panza, she overcame her instinct to run away. Uncle Bliss' vacancy at this time was pathetic; his blank stare reminded me of the face of a clock without a dial.

Very slowly he recovered his memory and the use of his legs. The first day he recognised us he asked when Irene was coming. "Three weeks, eh? We must get the place shipshape." After that he came down to lunch. There was as yet no indication of Ursa Major on the horizon, but he seemed to become more interested in things. He would notice Angela's table decorations, and potter about the conservatory with her, and admire the chrysanthemums. This was a good sign. But there were other things in which we were afraid he might become too interested. One day there was a column in 'The Times' about the *issulla,* the winged serpent of the Libyan desert, enough, we feared, to make Don Quixote put on harness again. We thought of hiding his newspaper, but decided that a press censorship was impossible. Where were we going to stop? The next morning a letter appeared on the subject containing a reference to the abortive pterodactyl hunt—unnecessarily sarcastic, I thought. This started a correspondence on fabulous prehistoric survivals. The legend of the *lau* of the

Bahr-el-Ghazal was revived. The general tone was sceptical. Bliss' name cropped up from time to time, more
often than not in an ironic context. We wondered how he
would take it. An explosion would have been a relief. But
the powder was damp; he glanced through the columns of
correspondence listlessly without comment, and would
turn from them with equal detachment to the accounts of
sales. But he didn't seem to want to buy anything.

Saxby had left before we arrived on the scene, and it fell
to me to answer Uncle Bliss' letters. They were mostly from
dealers and collectors. A settler in East Africa offered to de-
liver a giraffe alive at the Clapperhouse for fifteen hundred
guineas. For a trifle of four figures a firm in Amsterdam
was willing to part with the only complete collection of the
genus echidna. A letter from an Italian savant contained a
tentative bid for the dinosaur's egg. There were requests for
loan exhibits, and an offer from a contractor to feed the
fish-eating birds and animals of "the Clapperhouse Zoological Gardens." Orchid and butterfly collectors sought com-
missions. A specialist on arachnidae was particularly insis-
tent, and wrote twice a week repeating the threat that he was
on the eve of starting for Brazil. Most of them demanded a
substantial advance "to defray preliminary expenses," but my
secretarial work was simplified by Uncle Bliss' unalterable
formula. "Tell them," he said, "there's nothing doing."

A few months later his "Nothing doing" became *"Rien
faisant,* eh! What does the Queen of Sheba say?" as he
handed me his correspondence at lunch. The invasion of
the children marked a distinct turn for the better. I remember one afternoon, when Val spilt his aquarium into
the fender and almost roasted the newt, Uncle Bliss called
him a little batrachian and a troglodyte, after which we all
began to feel more homelike.

The children, of course, asked no questions about the
zoo. There was no talk of captive birds or beasts until Staff

came after breakfast on New Year's Day to report on the
eccentric behaviour of the flamingo. The solitary tenant of
the zoological gardens had spent a nostalgic night beating
his wings against the wire-netting of Mrs. Staff's chicken-run in a great state of agitation. No doubt, like the
prisoned crane, it felt pairing time in the islands where its
kind are, to quote Mr. Sludge, and so fell to capering by
himself on a shiny night, "as if your backyard were a plot
of spice." Staff proposed to clip its wings and release it on
the lake; but first, he thought, the children might like to
see its antics.

We all went, and were joined at the chicken-run by
Sancho Panza's mother, for whom the masseuse had been
as effective as the mud baths of Dax. The flaminger, as
she called it, was a pretty sight. He was dancing when we
arrived, or "vaunting," to use Val's expression, showing off
his grace and plumage to an imagined mate.

Staff stood by the door of the prison with the abhorred
shears.

"Pairing time," I reminded Angela.

"I should like to be a flamingo in the next incarnation," she said.

"Not a caged one, mummy."

"No, dear; not a caged one."

I think we all supported Irene's emendation. Angela
turned to Uncle Bliss, and said, "I don't think I would clip
his wings, if I were you."

"Poor thing!" said Mrs. Staff. "Let him fly away home.
He'll find the way to the sunshine quick enough, you may
be sure. Live and let live is what I say."

"And what does the Queen of Sheba say?" Solomon
demanded.

"Oh, Uncle Bliss. Please *do* let him go." Irene was
almost as agitated as the flaminger.

"Let him go, Staff."

Staff entered the chicken-run and pursued the high-stepping flamingo into a corner. He caught it by the neck, and drew in its wings, one after the other, under his arm. When he emerged with it in his embrace, and had offered it round, as the children used to say of chocolates, for us to feel and stroke, and comment on the softness of its neck and its vermilion black-tipped wings, he lifted it high, a foot in each palm, and flung it up into the air.

The flamingo had a struggle to find his wings, but never touched earth. He flew low at first; then slowly rose, his neck and legs drooping slightly, and circled round the lake, as if taking his bearings, and having determined them, made off straight for the South.

"Africa," said Uncle Bliss, and added inconsequently, "I shall buy a yacht." The instinct of liberty was contagious.

"Wings or sails? If you were offered one or the other, which would you choose?" Angela asked Val.

"Wings," said Val.

"Sails for me," voted the more practical Irene. "I should like a yacht."

"Where do you think he will spend the night?" she asked me as we returned to the house.

I pictured him standing alone on one foot by a rain-fed pond in the desert of Las Hurdes, Salamanca way, too tired to caper. In a day or two he would inhabit the swamps of the Nile, or perhaps the Niger—"the singing river," as the Touaregs call it, where all the nights are "shiny." There he would caper.

The thought of the flamingo among his mates reminded me that the Clapperhouse Zoological Gardens were now tenantless. The yacht seemed to me a very sensible idea.

Uncle Bliss' ursine humours were softened, but one could never quite depend on him. Even in his most domestic moods he was sometimes crotchety and difficult, as when Aunt Hudson remarked, "Isn't it wonderful to

think that Irene will be fourteen on Friday," and he corrected her brusquely. "I don't call it at all wonderful. It
would be wonderful if she was not fourteen on Friday.
Why should the hands of the clock hold back for Irene?"

But Uncle Bliss did not forget Irene's birthday. He came
down to breakfast for the first time. And, what is more,
he was the first down. He was reading 'The Times' when
Angela and I came into the room, and barely looked up
from his paper to reply to our congratulations. However,
he gave us two of his gruff "good mornings," one for each
of us, instead of one between us, and this seemed to mark
an occasion.

We noticed something funny about the breakfast-
table. Our first impression was that Phyllis had been dec-
orating it with stray objects from the museum. The vase
of hyacinths was not in the centre, and overtopping it,
in the place where it ought to have been, was a wooden
erection like an enormous candlestick with a bird carved
on it in crude relief, its feet on the base, and its beak
upright supporting the cup. A similar ornament stood on
Val's plate. The cups contained the two eggs which Uncle
Bliss had disinterred from the cardboard box in the housekeeper's locker when he showed us his collection. "Great
Auks' eggs." I said to Angela. "Two of the sixty-seven in
existence." The grey spheroid object in Irene's place, crad-
led in a huge calabash once a fakir's begging-bowl, was
unmistakably the dinosaur's egg.

Uncle Bliss looked up from his paper. "How do you like
Staff's work? Not bad, eh!"

We admired Staff's egg-cups, while preserving a proper
reticence about their contents; it was for Uncle Bliss to
enlighten us. The Great Auk figured on the stand might
equally have been a goose or a flamingo. I noticed that
Staff had tactfully omitted a representation of the saurian.

Just then the children burst into the room. Uncle Bliss dropped his paper to receive their salutations. "I am very glad to see you down, Uncle Bliss," said Val. "You will soon be quite well, won't you, Uncle Bliss?" said Irene. "Isn't it a beautiful morning for your first breakfast downstairs?" Were there going to be any birthday greetings? I could see that Irene felt there was something incomplete in her reception.

Then they saw the table.

"How lovely," Irene began tentatively.

"Oh, I say! Uncle Bliss!" exclaimed Val.

Uncle Bliss rose from his armchair. "What have we got for breakfast, eh?" he said, airing his French. "Œufs à la coque? Queen of Sheba's birthday, I suppose."

The children were wisely silent, waiting for him to be more explicit.

"And he hasn't forgotten Val, I see."

But who was "he"? Solomon or the cock? "Forgotten," too, was tantalisingly
ambiguous.

Irene and Val were in a "flurricane" of excitement, but admirably non-committal. I suspected that they were inwardly repeating "Fish-ponds! fish-ponds! fish-ponds!" in tune with their heart thumps. Val was the first to pull himself together.

"Have you really brought them down for us?" he asked diplomatically.

"Brought them down" was good. It might mean anything. It might refer to the simple act of conveyance as if the eggs were on exhibit, a seasonable table decoration. Or it might mean the other thing, the mere thought of which they were keeping tight down under valves. The Disciplinary Spirit had taught them that things like that simply didn't happen.

Still it was quite safe to admire the eggs objectively.

Uncle Bliss looked from one to the other quizzically. "Well," he said, "let's have œufs à la something else." The œufs à la poulet, as he called the scrambled variety, were getting cold.

The children were very silent during breakfast, almost monosyllabic. This I attributed to the disyllabic chorus which was going on inside, "Fish-ponds! fish-ponds!" Irene appeared so occupied with the recitation that I half expected her to repeat it aloud.

"Unœuf is as good as a feast, eh?"

"It is much better, Uncle Bliss."

"Good egg, would you say?"

"A very good egg."

"A birthday œuf, eh?"

This was positively cruel.

All the while our eyes kept wandering to the other *œuf à la coque,* which he seemed to have overlooked, the Great Auk's egg in the middle of the table overtopping the hyacinths in the huge wooden cup in which Sancho Panza had enshrined it. This unappointed egg was even more inexplicable and enigmatic than the other two. On the whole, it lent itself to the decoration theory.

We had got to the marmalade stage before Uncle Bliss appeared to notice it. "I see there is another egg," he remarked. "Whose shall it be?"

We all looked at him blankly.

"Who's going to have it?"

Was he in earnest or only pretending? In either case it was difficult to offer any suggestion. But the silence we were all too tactful to break he shattered himself.

"Fish-ponds!" he bellowed, leaning back and slapping his knee.

I nearly jumped out of my chair at this interjection. So he had found us out, had he? "Fish-ponds" was his

catch-word too—for designing people. He had been laugh-
ing at us in his sleeve all the time.

"Fish-ponds!" he repeated. "Come, what have you got
to say?"

It was a dreadful moment. I remembered Angela's "Not
if he thinks they expect it." The children looked as if they
had been caught Sabbath-breaking in Cuckoo Lane. I hope
I only looked astonished, and not as if I had been surprised hugging a guilty secret. My instinct was to blurt
out, *"Am* I of a calculating disposition?"

Angela, of course, preserved her composure. Her fresh
shell-pink colour never deepened. "Fish-ponds?" she repeated gently in the same voice in which she asked him if
he would have brown bread or white. "What have they to
do with the egg?"

"We will play for it, of course," said Uncle Bliss. "Fetch
the fish-ponds, Val. In the drawer under the Ovis Ammon
head." And he began to clear half the table. "Take care of
your dinosaur's egg," he said to Irene. "Don't drop it. It's
brittle."

"My dinosaur's egg, Uncle Bliss?"

"Why, of course. Whose else but the Queen of Sheba's.
And Val's Great Auk's egg. Now we will play for the other
one."

He arranged the fish on the table, and distributed the
five rods. Soon we were engrossed in the absorbing game
to which he had inducted us at Homersfield the day when
he quarreled with Angela's method of planting androsace,
and left us mysteriously bulging. Nearly four years had
passed since the myth of Irene's godfather materialised.
This was a new avatar, but with many of the old attributes.
The children could not compete with him at fish-ponds.
They were too excited; their rods wobbled. Uncle Bliss, on
the contrary, was as firm as a rock. He kept his left arm—
the one which had been affected—pressed to his side; the

other moved with the mechanical certainty of a crane; his hook slipped into the rings automatically. Of course, he swept the board. Nine out of a dozen. Angela was next with two.

"I'll toss you for it," he said to her.

Angela protested.

"Heads or tails?"

"Heads."

"Heads it is."

"Well, that's the lot, "Uncle Bliss remarked, as if relieved.

This amounted to a recantation. He might have said in so many words, "I declare myself indifferent to dinosaurs, pterodactyls, and the whole generation of winged reptiles."

"It just shows," Angela said.

"Eh," said Uncle Bliss. "What does it show?"

But Irene saved her from the perplexity of definition by approaching him from behind and kissing the top of his head. "Thank you most awfully, Uncle Bliss."

When I reach this point in my history, and the younger generation say, "Yes, but please go on. What did it show?" I come out with the time-honoured closure, "The dogs are scattered, having had their evening meal," which is the Indian way of saying, "And that is the end of the story."

For additional
stories of adventure, fantasy,
mystery, fright, and fun, visit
CoachwhipBooks.com

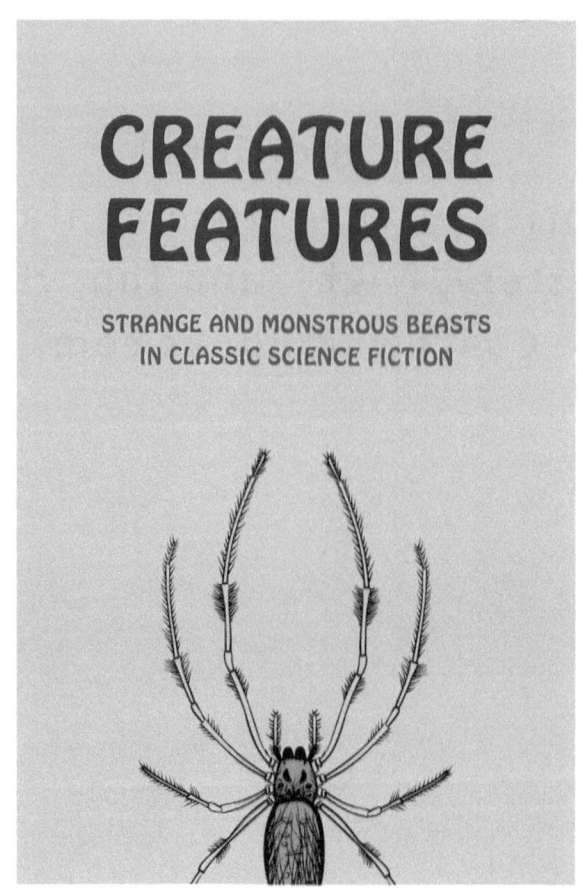

Details at
CoachwhipBooks.com

Available from your favorite online retailers

zoologica
fantastica

Details at
CoachwhipBooks.com

Available from your favorite online retailers

Details at
CoachwhipBooks.com

Available from your favorite online retailers

Details at
CoachwhipBooks.com

Available from your favorite online retailers

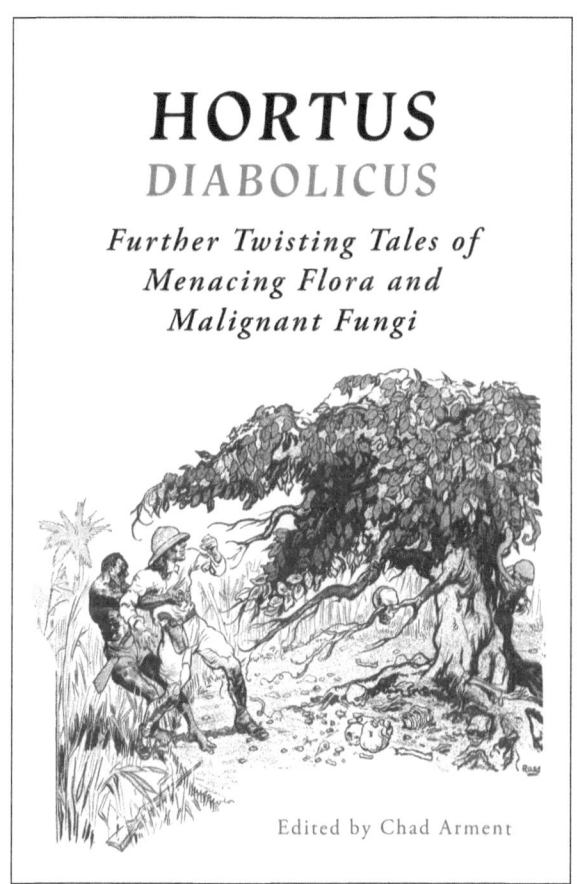

Details at
CoachwhipBooks.com

Available from your favorite online retailers

Mrs. Searwood's
Secret Weapon

The highly amusing story
of an indestructible lady who
had an unusual guardian angel

by LEONARD WIBBERLEY

Details at
CoachwhipBooks.com

Available from your favorite online retailers

www.ingramcontent.com/pod-product-compliance
Lightning Source LLC
Chambersburg PA
CBHW032033240626
47154CB00003B/887